MW01386135

"M. Christian speaks with a totally unique and truly fascinating voice. There are a lot of writers out there who'd better protect their markets — M. Christian has arrived!"
— *Mike Resnick, Hugo and Nebula award–winning author*

"M. Christian is an exotic, erotic chameleon of an author — there isn't a gender he can't inhabit, a sense he can't excite, or a sexual moment he can't imagine. His stories, queer in all the best ways, shimmer with a vivid versatility . . . "
— *Richard Labonte, series editor, Best Gay Erotica*

"These tales undercut and mutate the old verities concerning memory, desire and loyalty. Truly a book for our post-everything 21st century."
— *Paul Di Filippo*

"*Filthy* is an incredibly tasty collection of Christian's best gay smut: each and every story is an intelligent, boner-popping, wild ride!"
— *Greg Wharton, author of* Johnny Was and Other Tall Tales

"No other writer I know can slip into any gender, any sexual orientation, any bio- or cyber- or mythopoetical body on any planet, and let it pursue any desire to the hottest explosion since the Big Bang."
— *Ian Philips, author of* See Dick Deconstruct

"Hard-boiled, sharp-edged, funny and fierce, these tales brim with unbridled imagination and pitch-perfect satire. And oh yeah, there's loads of hot sex."
— *Jim Gladstone, author of* The Big Book of Misunderstanding

"M. Christian is today's premiere erotic shapeshifter . . . Reading these tales is like climbing on for a sexual magic carpet ride through different times and places, diverse bodies, and infinite possibilities."
— *Carol Queen, author of* The Leatherdaddy and the Femme

"M. Christian is a sick fuck: the best reason I still read erotica."
— *Shar Rednour, author of* The Femme's Guide to the Universe

Other Works by M. Christian

NOVELS:
Running Dry
Very Bloody Marys

COLLECTIONS:
Dirty Words: Provocative Erotica
Speaking Parts: Provocative Lesbian Erotica
The Bachelor Machine: Erotic Science Fiction

EDITED WORKS:
Amazons (with Sage Vivant)
Confessions (with Sage Vivant)
Garden of Perverse (with Sage Vivant)
The Wildest Ones: Hot Biker Tales
Blood Lust: Gay Vampire Stories (with Todd Gregory)
Leather, Lace and Lust: Putting It On to Get Off (with Sage Vivant)
Transgender Erotica: Trans Figures
Bisexual Erotica: The Best of Both Worlds (with Sage Vivant)
Best S/M Erotica 2: More Extreme Stories of Extreme Sex
Love Under Foot: An Erotic Celebration of Feet (with Greg Wharton)
Bad Boys: Steamy Stories from Bathhouses, Backroom Bars, and Sex Clubs
    (with Paul J. Willis)
The Mammoth Book of Tales of the Road (with Maxim Jakubowski)
The Mammoth Book of Future Cops (with Maxim Jakubowski)
Best S/M Erotica: Extreme Stories of Extreme Sex
The Burning Pen: Sex Writers on Sex Writing
Roughed Up: More Tales of Gay Men, Sex and Power (with Simon Sheppard)
Guilty Pleasures: True Tales of Erotic Indulgence
Rough Stuff: Tales of Gay Men, Sex and Power (with Simon Sheppard)
Midsummer Night's Dreams: One Story, Many Tales
Eros Ex Machina: Eroticizing the Mechanical

FOR MORE INFORMATION SEE WWW.MCHRISTIAN.COM

HY

FIL

INTRODUCTION BY FELICE PICANO

OUTRAGEOUS
GAY
EROTICA

M. CHRISTIAN

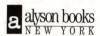
alyson books
NEW YORK

© 2006 BY M. CHRISTIAN.
INTRODUCTION © 2006 BY FELICE PICANO.
ALL RIGHTS RESERVED.

MANUFACTURED IN THE UNITED STATES OF AMERICA.

THIS TRADE PAPERBACK ORIGINAL IS PUBLISHED BY ALYSON BOOKS,
P.O. BOX 1253, OLD CHELSEA STATION, NEW YORK, NEW YORK 10113-1251.
DISTRIBUTION IN THE UNITED KINGDOM BY TURNAROUND PUBLISHER SERVICES
LTD., UNIT 3, OLYMPIA TRADING ESTATE, COBURG ROAD, WOOD GREEN, LONDON
N22 6TZ ENGLAND.

FIRST EDITION: JUNE 2006

06 07 08 09 00 **a** 10 9 8 7 6 5 4 3 2 1

ISBN 1-55583-951-7
ISBN-13 978-1-55583-951-2

LIBRARY OF CONGRESS CATALOGING-IN-PUBLICATION DATA IS ON FILE.

COVER PHOTOGRAPH COURTESY OF MENMACHINE.COM
COVER DESIGN BY VICTOR MINGOVITS

Contents

By Way of a Preface

THE MINOR-LEAGUE, DYING performer finally hit a zinger. On his deathbed he was asked if dying was hard. "Dying is easy," he shot back. "Comedy is hard."

He also might have replied, "Short-story writing is hard." It is hard. It requires the talents of a novelist, and of a dramatist, and of a screenwriter, and of an advertising copywriter, all rolled into one. To write a good short story, you need to establish the time and place instantly. You also need to establish a "voice" instantly, meaning the voice of whomever is telling the story. And since that voice usually belongs to a person, you need to establish that character and her/his relationship to the time and place, and to other characters—also fairly instantly.

After that, you've merely got the usual problems of any fiction writer in any other medium: developing an original idea or significantly well-done twist on a familiar idea, a unique character, a distinct point of view, a particularized perspective on the world, a compelling narrative, and an ending that satisfies.

Oh, and you've only got two to six thousand words to do all that in.

Go on. You try it.

See what I mean? Short-story writing is hard.

M. Christian's new collection of singular and satisfying short stories, *Filthy*, is subtitled *Outrageous Gay Erotica*. Emphasis on "outrageous." Although each of them does deliver a more than adequate erotic charge, Christian is after bigger game here. He's writing short stories. You know, like the ones you had to read in high school: anthologies about suburban Connecticut teens and hardscrabble poor white trash and adventurers desperate to light a fire to stay alive. The ones you had to discuss in class, using terms like "irony" and "thematic development" in those seconds before your forehead hit the top of your desk out of total apathy.

Take heart. Christian's stories are sexy, smart, and a lot more fun.

Several of the tales here are entertaining take-offs of famous movie classics. "Suddenly, Last Thursday" is a sly turn on Tennessee Williams's never-indisputable play, and to my mind it actually plays a lot better than the original. Reader and writer certainly have a more interesting time here, arriving at the questionable ending. I won't spoil it by spilling exactly how Christian bends it.

"Hollywood Blvd." is, of course, the old William Holden–Gloria Swanson flick redone so that she's a he, a former Porn Star Diva. The journalist character is, well, not very distant from the original, if—like me—you never quite believed the writer's "beard" of a girlfriend in the movie. The same moral applies here as in the Billy Wilder film. But I wonder . . . Did you, like me, ever ponder what really went on in that big house after the star went to sleep and the German manservant was still awake—and dressed in leather?

Possibly less familiar, if equally cool, is "That Sweet Smell," based on the lurid 1950s model play and then the movie *The Sweet Smell of Success*. I was pleased to see that I wasn't the only viewer who wondered what the real connection was between the characters played by drop-dead sexy (and recently revealed to be bisexual) Burt Lancaster and the still very cute Tony Curtis. In Christian's clever and very noir update, even the "heavy" cop got me wondering, as well as hot.

If, like me, you like science fiction, but you like it "soft," that is, without too many gizmos and objects (read: weapons that do everything but masturbate you while offing the entire population of a Midwest city) but with a real look at how we may possibly live and interact, then you'll like two of the longest and most realized tales in *Filthy*.

"The Hope of Cinnamon" begins semi-typically as sci fi in that it is set in a postapocalyptic future. What makes it totally untypical is that its setting is an orbiting mini-world of gays known as Stonewall. The intriguing story is about the time-travel "rescue" by this new society of liberated homosexuals persecuted in earlier times. The protagonist, Gen, is concentrating on what historian Richard Plant called "Men of the Pink Triangle," that is, German and other European men oppressed to death because they were homosexual. Christian's story is moving, tender, and questioning, as one after another salvaged man chooses self-destruction rather than life in a "perfect" and free gay society. The author's representative opts for a perilous yet surprising path to understand why.

Another futuristic narrative, "Utter West" takes a fresh look on that much iterated adolescent dystopia combined of suburbia and the family, though the old folks here are mostly absent, if only as a result of their own self-involved excesses. It's a tale of first love and wild nights, and of the first time you realize that who and what you idealized into a dream was too busy getting on with life to live up to your high criteria.

Remember those high school stories with suddenly reversed endings: O. Henry, Bret Harte, etcetera? Christian does that well, too. In "The Greener Grasses," the narrator leaves his humdrum existence in favor of Mr. Lawrence, his leather master, only to receive the shock of his life. In the tightly controlled story "Bitch," a gay man's homophobia assumes a life of its own, with a scorpion's sting.

Then there's the indefinable, "Friday Night at the Calvary Hotel," which I'm tempted to categorize as that rarest of objects: a gay religious story. Not because of the obvious trapping of the tale, but because of the underlying spiritual investigation made by author and reader in tandem.

I could write about how clever and writerly M. Christian is. But if you've read this far you're ready to read the stories. Enjoy.

— FELICE PICANO, AUTHOR OF *Onyx*

The Greener Grasses

WHEN I GOT home, Terry was in the kitchen, working magic in a pan. It was a Thursday, so I knew the steaming mixture was rice, shrimp, tomatoes, onions, and all the rest that went into creating Terry's magical paella. It was wonderful—spicy without being too spicy, full of elegant flavors—and it was always on Thursday.

"Hi, honey, how was your day?" he said as I walked in. Terry's glasses were off, lying on the kitchen counter, so they wouldn't steam up. I could have been bleeding from the eyes and he wouldn't have been able to tell, wouldn't have changed the typicality of walking in the door, Thursday or not.

"Fine," I said, struggling to keep the teeth out of my words. My lover, my husband—or wife, depending on how he, or I, was acting—was working in our kitchen, making me a wonderful dinner. But all I wanted was for him to throw me down on our Spanish tiled floor, undo my belt, zip down my fly, fish out my cock, and suck me, right then and there.

"That's good," he said, adding something sharp and flavorful to the mixture. We'd been together for five years, and I still didn't understand what went into that pan, just that it was good. Always had been good, and always would be good. "Mr. Lawrence behaving himself?"

Mr. Lawrence was my boss. He'd been in Paris for a month, and wouldn't be back for another one. I'd told Terry that at least a dozen times. "He's fine, too."

I got a beer out of the fridge and watched him cook for a minute. *Tell me to suck your cock—order me to suck your cock.*

Fuck me till I bleed. Make me stand naked in the rain. Make me jack off into your mouth. Shave me. Cut me. Mix my come with my blood and drink it down. "That's good. I'm glad," Terry said, never taking his eyes off his pan. "I love you, sweetheart."

"I love you, too," I mumbled, finishing the rest of my beer. Pierce my nipples. *Put your fist up my ass. Carve your initials in my back. Whip me.*

Then he did something nasty. He put the pan aside, wiped his hands on his KISS THE CHEF apron, got his glasses from the counter, and walked over to me. Kissed me. Not deep, not hot, not hard, not viscous—just his soft lips to mine. Then he did something worse: "I'm so glad you're here," he said, when our lips separated.

Restrain me, wrap my cock and balls in fishing line, make my dick hard and blue. Maybe needles, maybe current, voltage, maybe a single, quick touch of a smoldering cigarette—maybe a lot of things, but surprise me, shock me. "I—I am, too," I stammered.

He went back to his cooking. I got another beer. I usually only have one, but he didn't notice. I loved Terry—loved him with all my heart—but I also hated him like I'd never hated anyone before.

"Dinner will be ready in just a sec," he said, stirring, stirring, stirring, his head becoming hazy in the steam from his pan.

"I can't wait," I said, walking away.

xxx

DINNER WAS GOOD—as it always is on Thursday nights. We talked as we ate, saying nothing really important, nothing different. They say that domesticity isn't pretty . . . well, what we had was a serious form of ugly.

"You're seeing Robert tomorrow, right?" Terry said, sipping a glass of red wine.

"Yeah," I said, pushing rice, shrimp, tomatoes, and onions

around on my plate. Robert. Mister Robert—not Master, not Sir, just Mister. Mister Robert had made me scream, cry, bleed, and come too many times to count.

"Give him my best," Terry said, smiling.

"I'll do that," I said, smiling back, my face painful from tension. Terry was a sweetheart, a treasure, and a prize—he understood that sometimes you need more in a relationship than just one person, one way of doing anything. If he didn't, if he'd thrown things and screamed, I'd be much happier.

After dinner, we watched *Buffy*. Terry laughed and smiled the whole way through. I wasn't paying attention. *Cover my eyes. Tie me up, make my wrists and ankles burn when I pull against them. Light a candle; fill my nose with the smell of hot sulfur. One burning dot, then two, then three—wax splashing on my rigid body: making me scream, making me hard . . . so hard.*

After, we went to bed and had Thursday sex. Paella sex: spicy without being too spicy, full of elegant motions—and it was always on Thursday. Good sex. The problem was, I wanted great. I wanted fantastic.

After, Terry faded into sleep. I couldn't though. Wide awake, I looked out our bedroom window at the bright moon shining on our carefully manicured garden, the silhouette of distant trees waving gently back and forth. I'd done it before, for a long time— but that night, that Thursday paella night, I balled my hands into fists until my palms throbbed.

XXX

IN THE AFTERNOON, Saturday afternoon, I took Terry out to Valentino's. It was unexpected, different. Saturday afternoon meals were usually something grabbed in the kitchen, or snacked on as we did whatever we had to do that day. Valentino's was special, but also—that day—unexpected. Even though he was smiling as I drove us across the city, we both felt the tension in the air.

After we ordered our meals and small talked, I felt like screaming. I felt like crying. Then Terry said the one thing he never should have said: "What's the matter?"

I want out I want out I want Mister Robert. I want Mister Robert all the time. I don't want a happy home, I want to be property, 24/7. I want to feel what I feel with him all the time. "I . . . this isn't working," I finally croaked out.

"What do you mean?"

"I think I need to leave, Terry. I want out. I'm sorry."

He was quiet for a long time. "Can you at least tell me why?"

"I'm not too sure," I said, looking down at my meatless lunch. *I want to be thrown down and fucked. I want a knife at my throat. I want to wake up in ropes. I don't want just to be loved; I want to be owned.*

"We've been together for five years. I think you owe me at least that."

Whip me, beat me, cut me, tie me up. Tell me what I am; show me what I am. I don't want to love, then hate, then love—I don't want complexity, compromise. I want to be an object. That's safe— this isn't. "It's complicated."

"Life's complicated. I didn't hear you complaining before."

Mister Robert isn't complicated. There the world is just me, a possession, and he, my owner. "I just want out, okay—don't make this harder than it has to be."

"Five years together doesn't make this easier," he swirled whatever was on his plate, becoming hypnotized for a minute by the colors. "I think I know what this is all about."

Anger tensed my spine, flushed my face. "What?" I knew he didn't understand, that he never could—that he thought he did made me angry, cheapened what I was feeling.

"It's Robert, isn't it?" He watched my face, blue eyes staring through me. "It's better with him—easier." He saw something, and added: "I thought so. I was worried about that. What we have is special—don't tell me otherwise—but that's scary, isn't it? I love you, you love—or loved—me. But it's not like being a plaything, is it? It's not easy . . . "

"Go on, Terry, tell me what I'm feeling. You've got it all figured out."

His hand reached out toward mine, but I pulled back—and when I did his face darkened. "Go on, play your games with 'Mister' Robert. With him you don't have to pay the bills, do the laundry, listen when he talks about his day, hurt when he hurts. Go on. I'm sure it's better for you—and that's sad, that's really fucking sad."

I didn't say anything. Terry never swore. I knew he was angry, knew that he was hurt, but that one word shocked me. I was about to say I was sorry—and meant it.

"Fine, we'll break up. If that's what you want. I'm going to miss you, but I certainly don't want you around if you're not going to be happy."

"Okay," I managed to squeeze out. We sat and stared at each other for a long time, until the check came.

Paying (because it was my turn), I wanted to say something, anything, to either make it better between us or to let out the fury that was churning my stomach, but I didn't say anything. We drove back in silence, to coldly work on the logistics of turning two into a pair of ones.

xxx

HAND ON THE doorknob, I took a deep breath. I resisted checking my watch again, not wanting to show, even just to myself, how nervous I was. Rules formed the world, framed it, and defined it. The door would only be unlocked from 1:15 to 1:25 p.m. After that the bolt would be thrown, and I'd have to come back next week—to a frightening punishment for being late.

I turned the knob. Open. I stepped in and closed the door

carefully. Japanese. I felt Japanese—or at least what I imagined being Japanese might be like—a member of a rigid world, where punishment for transgression was certain and terrifying. But I knew one thing for certain: I belonged to Mister Robert.

Down the hall, through the door at the end. The playroom. The room where I lived, where I existed: black carpeting on the floor and walls—even over the door. Bare wooden ceiling of rough, exposed beams flaked with original white paint. Track light with three high-intensity pots. One wall had a board bolted to it, on the board a line of cheap coat hooks. On the hooks, the dark leather of the toys. Another board on the opposite wall, this one with two big eyebolts. In one corner, the sawhorse. This is the room I wish I never had to leave.

I got undressed, carefully folding my clothes in a corner. I waited. Ten minutes, exactly. Then the door opened.

I didn't turn. To turn would break a rule. I was property; I belonged to Mister Robert. As Property I wasn't a man, with desires. Nevertheless, I was happy.

Eyes straight forward, Mister Robert walked into view—and I momentarily held my breath. Every time I saw him I tried to absorb more details, for afterward. He was tall and broad, strong and smooth—not a hair on his body, his head, or his face. He was skin and muscle, and skill—that was Mister Robert. Bald and chiseled. Voice like breaking rocks. Mister Robert.

"Are you ready, Property?" he said, eyeing me like a connoisseur. Pride made me tilt my head back. "Yes, Mister Robert." I felt my cock stir.

"Good. Today you'll need to be ready." He walked over to the row of toys, ran his fingers through the hanging leather, feeling one, then another—weighing them for some unknown and terrifying quality. He hesitated over one, carefully unhooked it. I looked but couldn't see what it was, which made my fear and excitement even greater. "The sawhorse," he said, not even bothering to gesture. I knew what to do.

The sawhorse. Wood, nails, and a piece of thick leather. Mister Robert. Muscles, skin, bone, and will. I felt like crying as I walked over to the horse, bent over it, exposing my bare ass to my owner.

A tough hand ran over my ass cheeks, examining my skin for some elusive quality, and finding it: "You are breaking in nicely, Property. Very nicely indeed."

I felt a tear well and fall. "Thank you," I said, very softly.

Not softly enough. Property doesn't speak unless spoken to. Pain splashed against my ass, shot through me, made a short, sharp sound explode through my clenched teeth—which gave Mister Robert no other choice but to swing what I then knew to be the whip again. This time I kept my teeth together, capturing the offensive sound deep in my throat.

"You learn well, Property," Mister Robert said, caressing my ass with the strands of leather. "It is always a pleasure to use you."

That was my world, the world I wanted to be in all the time. Property, the cherished Property of Mister Robert. His favorite plaything. There was nothing better.

The whip fell, a beginning stroke—no punishment, but an introduction followed by many others. Quickly, the individual falls blended together, becoming nothing but waves and waves of something not like pain, not like empty pleasure. Then it grew in frequency and modulation, as did my breaths, and the thumping of my heart. I tried not to make a sound, tried to keep it in—to please he who owned me—but some escaped, a deep bass sound that bounced off the floor in front of my face, a human accompaniment to the sound of the whip on my bare skin.

Then it broke—not the toy, not my ass, but the feeling deep inside, and I made a sound, a roar from down below my soul.

The whip stopped and I felt tears again. I feared that I had broken a rule, feared that I hadn't but he was going to stop anyway. But he did stop, saying, "On your feet, Property. Face me."

I did. Despite the reflections on my cheeks, and the water in my knees, I was still the property of Mister Robert, and my cock was hard.

He put his big hand around my cock, close up, so his fingers wrapped around my balls as well. His grip was steel, iron, unbreakable—and I didn't want to break it. "Handsome Property," he said. "You may speak."

"Thank you, Mister Robert."

"Now you may not speak. One word, one sound and I stop, you get dressed, and you leave."

I had been ordered not to speak, so I didn't. Not even to say I understood—after all, if I had spoken I wouldn't have been worthy of being his property.

He smiled, sly and quick—which told me that he also understood. Then, still smiling, Mister Robert started to squeeze.

At first it was just a firm handshake around my cock and balls, but then it grew with force and intensity until my breathing became quick and ragged. It felt like my cock and balls were being slowly, inexorably squeezed in a flesh and bone vice. The tissue of my dick didn't hurt—at least not that much compared to the deep, throbbing ache of my balls. Despite my will and training, I felt myself start to curl against the groaning tug of his hand around me. I straightened, even though it meant even more pain, my stomach muscles pulling against the crushing of my balls. I was breathing so fast that I started to whistle, sharp and high.

He didn't stop, he didn't even hesitate. He kept squeezing, squeezing, and squeezing even more. Suddenly I felt fear—that he would never, ever stop, that he would crush me, crack my eggs, destroy my cock. But I didn't say anything, didn't open my mouth except to wheeze and softly, deeply moan, because I was his property and would do anything, even offer up my cock and balls to the will of Mister Robert. In pain, I was never happier.

Then—nothing. He stopped, pulled his hand away from the agony of my cock and balls . . . and I screamed, bellowed as blood rushed into the empty veins and arteries. Despite my training, I doubled over, my face pressing into his smooth skin, my breath mixing with the rutting, heavy masculine smell of him.

"You're hard," he said, in a tone of voice I had never heard before, almost tender, almost proud—and I pulled away, a *thank you* unspoken on my lips, to see that he was right. My cock was hard, very, very hard.

He extended a hand, palm up, just under the bobbing head. "Come in my hand. Now."

My cock was slick with sweat, a bead of pearl at the tip. One stroke, two—my rhythm matching my owner's with the whip until I felt the come start to tug, to push its way out of me—and then I did it, my come spurting, jetting out into the open hand of my owner.

Then he said it, and all was right with the world: "Thank you, Property. You did good. Now clean yourself up and get dressed, but do not leave—not yet."

I did as he ordered, underwear, socks, shirt, pants, shoes—all of it. But I wasn't aware of anything except my owner's voice, my owner's praise. This . . . this was where I belonged. Here and nowhere else. This was what I wanted: to be the Property of Mister Robert. I had just finished tying my shoes when he walked back in. "Come with me into the kitchen for a minute. I need to talk to you."

I didn't know what to say, or do, but being Property took over and I did as I was told. In the years I had been Mister Robert's, I had never been anywhere except for the hall and the playroom. I didn't want to go anywhere else—but he was Mister Robert.

It was a simple kitchen, smelling faintly of gas and cat food. An antique '50s table, Formica decorated with sickly yellow flowers. Rough wooden shelves. Rows and rows of spices.

"Sit down . . . please." He'd also gotten dressed. Simple jeans and a white T-shirt. Work boots. He didn't look like Mister Roberts; he just looked like someone you'd pass on the street. I tried not to look at him, at what he was wearing, and instead just tried to look at his face.

"We've had a wonderful time all these years, haven't we? Lots of great sessions. Lots of great afternoons. But I have to tell you something . . . this is going to be our last time together."

I couldn't say anything. Even if I had known what to say, I was still Property—and Property didn't speak, didn't question, didn't argue.

"It's nothing you've done, or even something you haven't done. I . . . I've just reached a point in my life where I need to have something else in a relationship. This is great, what we have, but I need something deeper, more meaningful." For the first time he actually looked uncomfortable. "I need to be in love with someone, I guess. Someone to pay the bills with, to really understand. It's a hard decision, but one I need to make to be really happy."

I hung my head. The world—the only world that mattered— had fallen apart. Yeah, Property shouldn't speak, but suddenly I wasn't Property—would never again be the Property of Mister Robert—and I still didn't know what to say.

"I hope you'll understand," was the last thing he said to me, before shaking my hand and leading me outside.

Hollywood Blvd.

THIS ISN'T ONE of those nice Hollywood stories. You know the kind, where the hero—usually the guy with top billing—rides off into the sunset. Not this time. Not this story.

I guess you could say it had a happy ending, if you look at it the right way. All I ever wanted was a nice place, like one of those great big houses on the 10000 block of Hollywood Boulevard. A place with a nice big hot tub.

Well, I got it. But not the way I wanted it, of course.

xxx

THERE'S JUST BEEN a murder in one of those big Hollywood houses. The homicide squad's on its way there now, sirens wailing down that famous street. A guy's been killed: two bullets in his back, one in his stomach, his body left soaking in one of those room-size tubs.

You should hear this story from someone who knows firsthand, before those big Hollywood columnists get their hands on it, turn it into something cheap and sleazy.

Look at me, bobbing there, blood staining the expensively treated water. Poor dope, all I wanted was a hot tub. Unfortunately the price was just a little too high.

xxx

I WAS ONE of those journalists you don't hear about. You know the kind, the one whose name always seems to escape being tied to a headline. Definitely not one of those columnists who get to turn tawdry into sleazy. I'd had a couple of good scores. Remember that big piece a couple of years ago, about that old heartthrob who people almost forgot all about until he got linked to that cute little high school jock? No, I didn't get the scoop, but I proofed it for the guy who did. I was that kind of journalist.

The only thing I had to my name was the cheap furniture in my cheap apartment, an ancient laptop, and my car. It wasn't much, but it was my life. The problem was that things were tough: My money was almost gone. I'd had to hock whatever I could, and it still wasn't enough. My landlord was a nice old queen who I knew I could stall for at least another two months—but my car was another matter. The finance company was getting more and more nasty. If I didn't pay, they'd come and drive it away.

Can you imagine being in LA without a car? It was a cruddy car, but it got me around. I was driving it that Thursday afternoon, going from one paper to another, trying to get someone to give me something on spec—anything, I needed anything, to keep the repo man away, when the thing sputtered and died. I managed to pull into an alley off Hollywood Boulevard, down where those big old houses haven't been torn down to make way for cheap apartments like mine. The place was really overgrown, tangled weeds and vines covering the front gates and the tall brick walls all around it, but you could see that at one time it had been fantastic, all deco and style. Once it had been grand, but now it was just dirt, dust, and weeds.

I noticed that the huge iron gates were ajar. I don't know why I went in; maybe part of me was curious. It was part of old Hollywood, from the era of roller disco and platform shoes. I wanted to see what was left.

Inside the gates, the place was big—really big. There was a pool, empty of water but full of leaves. There was a big Cadillac in the drive, once pink but now deep red with rust, sitting on four flat tires. I was just starting to walk up to the big front door when it opened.

"You're late," he said. "He expected you hours ago."

When you're older, drag usually doesn't work. It's just a man's cross to bear, I guess; put on a wig and you're suddenly five years older. Sometimes it's pathetic, other times it's just tragic. But he . . . or she . . . was old, maybe in his mid-fifties, and yet somehow on him it worked. He wasn't Cher, but he could almost have been Bette Davis. He wore curls as red as that rusting Cadillac, a simple white dress, and just enough makeup, so he didn't look like he'd been hit by an explosion at Max Factor. His incongruous voice was a deep rumbling bass, with a hint of a German or Hungarian accent and no attempt at femme tones.

I went in. White shag, pink leather sofas, mirrors everywhere. A disco ball in the living room. A huge television on one wall, and on the other, movie posters: *Backroom Boys*, *Disco Dynamite*, *Roller Leather*, and the like.

"This way," Bette said, leading me toward a brass and marble staircase winding upstairs.

"Excuse me," I started to say, "but I just came to . . . "

Then someone from upstairs called: "Maxine! Maxine! Is that him? Bring him upstairs this instant." Bette turned, looking down at me from the first step, and said, "He is waiting for you. This way."

So I went up those stairs, following behind Maxine, noticing as I walked that the brass was green and the marble deeply cracked.

XXX

HE MUST HAVE been a special hamster, maybe related to some famous hamster, though I couldn't think of any. He was lying on a velvet pillow, his little feet stiff in the air.

It took a few minutes to get it straightened out. No, I hadn't come from the vet; no I hadn't come to take the little creature away. I was just in the neighborhood when my car broke down, and I just wanted to use the phone.

I answered his questions, trying not to stare. I knew him from somewhere. The moment Maxine brought me upstairs, opening the door to the big master suite and ushering me in with a gravelly "He's here," I realized that something about him was familiar . . . but from where?

He was handsome. There was no denying that. Standing by the huge round bed surrounded by gold-veined mirrors and floodlights, his beauty struck me instantly. It had faded, certainly. Skin that had once been clean and smooth was now rugged and deeply tanned; a body that had once been strong and broad-shouldered was now stooped and softer. "Well, what are you doing here then if you're not going to take little Manuel away?"

His voice was marvelous, deep and rich with a purr that reached down and tugged at me. It was another piece of the puzzle, another clue to who this man was, but my mind was still not putting it together.

"I was just in the neighborhood. My car broke down. I just came to use the phone."

"The phone?" he cried, that powerful voice slipping into a glass-breaking screech that made me wince. "You came into *my* house, disturbed me, over the *phone*?" Without waiting for my response, he turned and bellowed to Maxine, who was standing in the doorway. "Show this gentleman out."

Then it hit me. As Maxine reached for my arm, I turned and blurted it straight out, without a clue in the world where it was going to lead me, what was going to become of it: "You're Norman Desmond. You used to be in porno. You used to be big."

"I *am* big," he said, his voice ringing with injured pride, thundering with a vigor that defied the stooped shoulders. "It's *porno* that got small."

XXX

EVENTUALLY IT CAME out that I was a writer, and that changed everything. Blue eyes sparkling like new rhinestones, he took me by the hand and pulled me past a sneering Maxine and into the hall. "Ah, a writer! Just the kind of man I need to see. Just the man . . ."

The hall was more white shag, more gold-veined mirrors, and rows of tiny white lights where mirrors met shag. He took my hand in a firm grip and pulled me along, our reflection an endlessly duplicated couple, striding into infinity.

Norman Desmond . . . there was a name that took me back. One of the greats, if not the greatest. Before Norman Desmond, queer porn was all greasy-mustached plumbers or pot-bellied sailors. Loops long on cock-sucking but short on plot. Sure they would get you off, but they didn't stick in the mind beyond the mechanics that happened between the plumbers and the plumbing. Then came Norman Desmond: handsome, strong, virile—but more than that, a presence. Norman Desmond filled the screen with attitude, with charisma. You didn't look for one of his flicks to see where his impressive cock would go, what he did with it, or who he did with it, because of who he was.

Now I remembered those films—*Backroom Boys, Disco Dynamite, Roller Leather*—the movies those posters downstairs belonged to. They were some of his greatest. The best of the best. I was in shock; I was in awe.

But more than that, I was hopeful. Norman Desmond, *the* Norman Desmond—alive and well and living in that great big house full of memories and stories, right off Hollywood Boulevard. It was just what I needed. It was a story—possibly a kick-ass story— and he wanted to tell it to me.

XXX

THE BACK ROOM looked like a set, something straight from *Hollywood Hustlers* or *I Love the Hot Life*: crystal chandeliers, a big leather sofa, mirrors, mirrors and more mirrors, and—a hot tub. Not just any hot tub, mind you, but rather, *the* hot tub. Sure, some may call *Hot Water* derivative; I mean, how could you not, considering the plot was stolen from an old '40s film. But for me it was pure Norman Desmond. I stood and stared at it, running the flick over in my mind. The bubbling, steaming water where Norman took Roger Biggies from behind, his muscular ass driving Biggies till he screamed, his come mixing with the churning water in simple cinematographic genius. The water where he splashed with Tumescent Dan, taking his impressive tool down his throat in one awe-inspiring swallow. Looking at the water I felt my own cock stirring, aching for a touch, any touch.

"Here," Norman said, retrieving a thick manuscript from a table next to the sofa. Five, six hundred pages at least. It felt like a phone book. "Salome: The Norman Desmond Story," it said. I looked up at him. "You're a writer," he said. "You'll be able to help. I'm not really so good with . . . words. Now the pictures— that I'm good at. But this . . . this is something I could use some help with. I want to tell my story, to remind everyone of who Norman Desmond was. Yes, yes, to show them all that Norman Desmond is still here, just waiting for the right chance to get back up there on top where he belongs."

I held the manuscript in my hands. "You want to make a comeback?" I asked, my voice catching somewhere between throat and lips.

"No. I hate that word. No, I'm going to return—that's the word, *return*—to the thousands of people who have never forgiven me for deserting the screen."

I didn't say anything. I just stood there, weighing the heavy book in my hands. Though older, there was still a power about him—something beyond the crow's feet, thinning hair, and gentle potbelly—something remaining of the legendary Norman Desmond. I also weighed my tiny apartment, and my even tinier life.

I said something, probably "Yes" or "I'll do it," but to be honest I don't remember. All I remember is his hand on mine, piercing blue eyes looking straight into me, filling me with some of his boundless determination, looping me into his dream of returning to the movies, and tugging at my memories of the great Norman Desmond.

So that's how it happened, the very first step. I had no idea at the time where it would lead me, or just how far it would go.

xxx

AT FIRST I only visited the grand old place on Hollywood Boulevard a couple of times a week, but quickly I realized how empty my apartment was compared to the grandeur of Norman's house. My old laptop and knock-off furniture just couldn't compare to the glamour of hundreds of films and thousands of fan letters. Being back at my place reminded me how small I was, how pathetic. One day I was sitting at a huge steel coffee table in Norman's living room while he was upstairs watching and rewatching his films in the tub room. Maxine was puttering around, dusting the furniture and polishing the mirrors. Looking over Norman's manuscript, I muttered something to myself about his fantastic life as one of the true legends of the porno screen. Maxine must have overheard, because he stopped polishing and walked over to me. "He was the greatest of them all," he said. "In one week he received 17,000 fan letters. Men bribed his hairdresser to get a lock of his hair. There was a prince who came all the way from England to get one of his jocks, and later the prince strangled himself with it! You are privileged to be here, privileged to be allowed to work on his return to the screen."

Eventually I was living in a tiny room above the garage,

spending most of my days going over the book. At first occasionally, then frequently, Norman came by to check on my progress.

It wasn't all work, at least not on Desmond's part. Not by a long shot. The fragile ego that was Norman Desmond required constant feeding. First there were the fan letters that arrived every day, brought to Norman by Maxine on a silver salver, opened and gushed over with great enthusiasm. "Wonderful," he would warble in his melodic voice (the very same voice that had demanded, "Suck my cock" in *Alley Tails* and "I'm going to fuck you long and hard" in *Beachfront Property*) as he opened them.

Then there were the movie nights. He'd escort me upstairs to the tub room and we'd sit and watch movie after movie. The steam from the water formed clouds that caught random fragments of light from the old projector. I'd seen a lot of them before, of course, but having Norman there was like a personal tour through the heyday of Hollywood queer smut. I heard all about the stars, the directors, the gossip, and the dirt. It was fascinating, and I began to look forward to those nights more and more.

Then everything changed.

I'd been working on the book, finally starting to realize what a mess it was. The heart was there, the passion that was Norman Desmond the legend, but it was lost, polluted by bitterness, delusion, and outright fiction. I had to be careful—very careful—about what I cut. Editing was starting to be a problem, with Norman screeching in a piercing falsetto—over any suggested change.

When Norman walked in that day, I readied myself for what I expected to be the usual fight over the book. He shocked me by putting a hand on my shoulder and saying in his purr of firm masculinity, "You look tense. Why don't you come up and soak in the tub for awhile?"

The tub. To be honest, I'd never really thought of Norman as someone who'd have any interest in me. Not that I'm a troll—I never had to look hard to find a date on a Saturday night—but

I was simply not in his league. I worked out just enough, I took care of myself just enough, but I definitely could have done more. And yet here he was, the legend of 8mm loops, of *Backdoor Romeo*, inviting me up for a soak.

I felt like I was walking into a loop myself, standing in front of that famous hot tub. I realized it was just like the one I'd always wanted because I'd seen it, this very tub, in one of his movies.

Norman stripped quickly and efficiently, as if performing some kind of magic trick they taught in porno movie school. It was as if he was in one of his old loops, clothes simply vanishing from one scene to another. I sat on the edge of the tub, dimly aware that the bubbling, steaming water was soaking my pants and shirt, but I couldn't continue. Norman Desmond was a very handsome man. Very. Age had come on him slowly. He had all the evidence—wrinkles, sags, that little belly, the thinning hair, a few liver spots on his arms, a few rose marks on his chest. But these insults were restrained, at least for a while, by his overwhelming determination to remain an idol, to freeze himself at the height of his career.

My cock was instantly hard, and Norman was instantly aware of it. He still projected in the flesh what he'd delivered so many times on the screen: a tremendous sexual presence. Part of the arousal, too, was that I was getting naked for the man who had been part of my sexual dreams for so long. Wrinkles couldn't take that away; in fact, I doubted anything could.

Naked, hard, I stood in front of him, bubbling waters of the tub behind me, adding to the heat that rose and kept rising in my body. I was sweating, gleaming, but only partially from the steam.

He reached out and wrapped his hand around my hard cock. He held me that way for a good long time, never once looking at anything except my eyes. Locked on me, rigid, he slowly smiled as he looked deep into me. Then, never taking his hand from my cock, he led me into the hot, churning water.

It was good, better than I thought it would be. But there was something else, something that skated over the surface of my mind, refusing to come together until much later, when I'd cooled down. He took my cock in his mouth and brought me close to tears. I touched him, amazed by the noises he made, the way he played his body like a fine instrument. He stroked me, working my cock like a master—which he was. I felt self-conscious returning the favor, but he seemed to truly enjoy himself, and when his come followed mine into the steaming water, I smiled at his deep, rumbling growls of pleasure.

We spent a long time in the water. The heat of the tub added more and more steam to our play. My fingers wrinkled, and my head started to swim from too many bouts of near overheating, but we kept at it. I remember details of it, captured crystal clear as if on one of Norman's old reels. The pebbled texture on the bottom of the pool. The white, almost translucent plastic. The moment when Norman playfully took a deep breath, vanishing into the wildly boiling water to take my cock in his mouth. Catching myself and Norman reflected back and forth in the mirrors, which seemed to superimpose us like actors in one of his films.

Finally he started to tire and we climbed out, toweling off. I worked back into my clothes as he slipped on a big terrycloth robe held out for him by Maxine.

As I walked the long, mirrored hallway back to my room— the intimacy of actually sleeping with Norman Desmond never occurring to me—he called my name. I turned, seeing him at the far end of the corridor, silhouetted against the wavering light from the hot tub room. "You see," he said, his voice breaking slightly, "you see, I can still do it! I still have it! Soon it'll be just me, the cameras, and those wonderful people out there in the dark!"

Suddenly chilled, I gave him my best smile and returned to my little room over the garage.

XXX

WE QUICKLY SETTLED into a nice little routine. I continued to work on the book, and Maxine continued to dust and clean and deliver, every day, a new stack of fan mail for Norman. At night, it would be me and Norman in the tub—me in awe of the great porno star, he needing my fresh, new admiration. It was good—at times very good—but there was also something else there: a vague feeling that hovered, like something you can just barely see out of the corner of your eye, but can't name.

Sometimes as Norman was sucking my cock in the burbling water I'd look down to catch him gazing off into the distance, playing for the cameras, the audience that wasn't there anymore. At other times he'd prance a bit too much, or work too hard at sucking or stroking me, acting for the director in his mind.

His "return" began to obsess him more and more. The world could have burst into flame and shrunk down into ashes, and he'd have cared only whether there were enough fans left to send him mail. Cloistered in the old house, I started to stand in front of the window, stare out at those high walls and their dead creepers, and wonder about the world. Sure, it hadn't been a great world—at least not to me—but it was real. It was a world that revolved around the sun, and not Norman Desmond.

I started sneaking out at night rather than returning to my little room over the garage. Exhausted from Norman's tongue, lips, and hands night after night, I tried to walk as far as possible just to prove to myself that the world hadn't ceased to exist.

One night, Maxine was waiting for me at the door. The Master was asleep, but he was waiting for me all the same. At first I was ashamed of leaving the all-encompassing light that was the great Norman Desmond, but then I felt a stab of anger. "What is it, Maxine? His Highness miss my adoring presence for ten minutes?"

He glowered at me through his thick black lashes, hands clenched. "You are not worthy of him. He is Norman Desmond and you . . . you are just a distraction. He is great, one of the greatest that ever lived."

"Take it easy, Maxine," I said, seriously wondering for a moment if the old drag queen was going to have a stroke. "I just needed a breath of fresh air. No harm done."

"You do not realize how important he is. How carefully I have maintained him for the moment when he returns to his rightful place on the screen. I will not have you ruin him before that great time when he is accepted back as the legend that he is."

I was getting very tired of the Worship Norman game. I had taken my walk, and I had seen evidence that, even at night in the dark, there is more in the sky that the Great Norman Desmond. "He's a big boy, Maxine. He can take care of himself."

"Do you really think so?" he answered. He stepped back and started to close the door, leaving me to tramp around to the side entrance. "Then I suggest you check the handwriting on those fan letters."

xxx

THE NEXT NIGHT, the feeling that had been lurking at the edges of my mind was right there in my face, obvious and more than slightly grotesque. It happened after a worshipful showing of *The Plumber Rings Once*, after Maxine floated through the flickering lights of the tiny 8mm projector to hand us our martinis. Norman stood with a flourish, saying, "Maxine, you may go. We want to be alone."

There we were: me, Norman, the hot tub, and the precious myth of the famous porn star—a myth that was more important, and more real, to Norman than anything else.

We got into the famous tub. Norman was in fine form, and for a long time the suspicion and depression were in abeyance. It was just Norman and me. He kissed me, something he hadn't done before. Standing in the hot water, bubbles nibbling against my balls and my quickly hardening cock, he gently bent forward to touch his lips to mine. His lips were soft, something I knew very well from having them attached so often to the head of my cock, but with that kiss I realized they were almost too soft to feel. Cautiously, his tongue touched mine and time seemed to stop. We stood there, water teasing our hard cocks, and just kissed. It was good. It was just very, very good.

Soon we really started to heat up, and only partially because of the steaming tub. As we kissed I gradually became aware of his cock touching mine, an unconscious dick duel in the gurgling water. Then he broke the kiss and smiled at me. Norman. Not Norman Desmond, just Norman. I thought, I wanted, really and truly, to believe.

Then he pushed me back against the edge of the tub. Before I could say or do, anything, his lips were on my cock, the water smoking and boiling around his tanned shoulders. Good before, fantastic now. I knew he was older, that he had his share of wrinkles and gray hairs, but none of that mattered. Yes, he was fantastic.

He worked me for what felt like hours, maybe even days. Finally when I was ready to explode, he released me, a thread of saliva vanishing into the steam. He stood, facing me. Then he said it, and it all fell apart. "Jerk off for me."

It took a few minutes for the words to reach the part of my mind that was actually capable of thought. It was an uphill battle, struggling through all that lust, long minutes with my hand wrapped around my cock, stroking myself slowly, then faster, the water like a thousand hot little tongues on my shaft and head. I was close, so close, when those words hit me. It wasn't just the words, because I'd heard those words before, but rather the way he said them, the way he was standing, the look that went past me—looking for the camera again. *The Plumber Rings Once.* Action for action, word for word, a performance. On stage, always on stage. I had been wrong. Norman wasn't there, probably had never been there. It was all Norman Desmond, the great, the legendary, Norman Desmond.

Cold water. Not hot. No, not hot at all. Cold. Ice cold. I stopped, with a pearl of pre-come just forming at the head of my cock, which slowly dropped into the hot water. I stood stock-still. Anger flared through me, my body rock-hard with fury and tension. I climbed out. He might have said something, standing there looking lost and alone in the bubbling water, but I didn't hear it.

"Darling, come back, darling!" I finally realized he was imploring me as I furiously thrust on my discarded clothes.

"No," I finally said. "No, Norman, I'm going. I have to get out of here. I have to get out of this damned museum. I have to breathe real air, not this dusty celebration of who you used to be."

"No!" he screeched. "You can't leave me! I'm Norman Desmond. You have to love me, just as all my fans love me."

I stopped, looked at him. I was angry, but seeing him—careful hair mussed by lust and hot water, face scarlet with emotion—I was also sad for him. I was sad for the lies he spun around himself, the fantasies that had become more important that reality. "Do yourself a favor, Norman. Look at the handwriting on all those letters, and talk to Maxine about it." Then, and I really did mean it, I said, "I'm sorry, Norman. I really am."

"I'll kill myself," he said, those perfect blue eyes unhinged with fury. "I will, you watch! You watch!" He walked over to a small table and opened a drawer. The pistol was small, like a toy in his big hands. I knew what it was and what it could do, but seeing it in his hands only reinforced the sadness of how far down someone so talented, so hot, had gone.

"No, Norman, you won't. Wake up. There wouldn't be anyone to appreciate the gesture. It's just you and Maxine in this empty house."

"This isn't over," he said, his voice slipping back into the thunderous command of those long-ago loops. "I'll be back, you'll see. I'll be back up there on the screen where I belong. I'll be back. I swear it! I'm Norman Desmond!"

"No," I said. "You used to be Norman Desmond."

Then it happened: Three shots. Two in the back, one in the stomach. There wasn't a lot of pain, which surprised me. The bullets hit and spun me around, slamming me face down into that famous hot tub, maroon blood unfurling in the bubbling water.

xxx

THIS IS WHERE we came in, at that famous tub, the one I always wanted. It's morning now, and everyone's here: police, photographers, and those trash-talking columnists, too. But don't believe them—believe me, I was there.

Like I said: not exactly a happy ending. I got my hot tub—but not in any way I could really enjoy it.

Norman? Norman put on quite the show as they led him away in handcuffs while the flashbulbs popped and the hacks called for statements. He may have gotten the best deal of all—walking out into infamous celebrity, the star of tabloids for years to come. It may have been his last close up—but he was more than ready for it.

Flyboy

IT'S HARD NOT to think of him. It's hard not to be reminded of that summer five years ago. Other boyfriends come and go all the time—random flashes of memory, hit-and-run recollections—when I see a pair of snakeskin boots, smell gnocchi with smoked mozzarella, hear a John Lee Hooker tune. But he's special, and all I have to do to remember him is to look up at the sky.

×××

EVER SPEND A winter in New York City? If you have then you know why I packed up my life, wrapped myself in down, waded out in the slush, scraped off my windshield, and drove as fast as I could to Arizona. Never been there before, but all it took was standing under a furnace sun, sweat pearling on my face, heat mirages hazing the distance, and realizing it was January for me to never, ever, go back.

Still, ice can work its way into the strangest places. So, to completely, totally, utterly remove the chill from my bones, I bought some clay, built a kiln, and did what I'd loved doing in college.

I never thought I'd be able to make a living at it. Didn't even try. Not really. I just put brick on top of brick, wrestled with hose and propane tank, and beat the crap out of mounds of clay. I was warm, and that was all that mattered.

But even being warm can get dull, so I stopped slapping my wet earth and actually tried to make something out of it—and of myself. Soon I could look at what I made and not wince. A little after that I could look at my cups and saucers, plates and bowls, jars and platters, and smile. Before you know it, I'd cleaned up my little house, printed up invitations, and hoped that someone, anyone, would pay for a lump of fired, glazed clay.

The turnout was sparse but sincere, mostly friends I'd made at the art supply store plus a few I'd brought home from the only queer bar in town.

"How much?" Not tall (which is good, as I hate to be looked down on), but not short (I hate stooping to kiss). Hair short but not buzzed, shoulders straight and true, like he used a level along with barbells. I wish I could say I wanted to know him better, but to be honest I wanted to see him naked in the worst way.

He had to repeat himself, smile beaming even and very white teeth, holding out a turquoise and jet glazed lump. I was instantly embarrassed by it. He deserved better. I just wondered, suddenly ashamed, if I could ever make anything good enough.

I guess I must have sputtered a price because the smile only increased, bringing lines to his face that made the day even hotter, my heartbeat all that quicker. Looking at him, right then, I felt like I could never, ever be cold again.

"That's too cheap. Way too cheap," he said, holding that ugly thing in his smooth hands. Not a worker, I thought quickly, or maybe he is but he just doesn't work with his hands.

He handed me a pair of bills, way too much. "I can't take that."

"Sure you can. Simple hand-eye coordination. You make stuff like this, you can certainly handle taking this money from me."

"That? For this? Come on, it's not worth that much. Believe me, I made it."

"Maybe," he said, turning it in those smooth hands. "But the potter's worth a lot more."

That's how it started—something soft and malleable made hard and firm. Both me and my pot. His name was Scott, I quickly learned as I took the money and shook his hand. The afternoon waned, faded, the furnace of the sun dropping behind distant saw-toothed mountains—and we didn't stop talking.

Until, that is, I looked up from my third glass of wine-from-a-box to see the most perfect pair of hazel eyes looking into mine. Then I stopped talking. Then he stopped talking, and we kissed for the first time.

A little later, after the crickets started to make their nightly cries for companionship and the moon began to crawl across a desert sky sprayed with too-bright stars, we stopped kissing and went on to other things.

It wasn't the best I've ever had, but it was good. Very good. The best kind of good, the kind where you know—just know—that it was only going to get better.

Salt in my mouth, pubic hairs between my teeth, I sprawled on my Navaho rug bedspread and looked up at his long body, the monument of his chest, the white crescent of his own happiness, and thought *oh crap*.

Oh crap was right. In the morning I made him breakfast—just English muffins and coffee, but, hell, I'd never made anything for anyone before—and we just stared wordlessly at each other. It wasn't that we had nothing to say to each other. We did; we just weren't saying it out loud. My finger slowly circled the palm of his hand, playing with life and happiness lines while he stroked my forearm. We didn't need to say anything else; we both felt it. That, nasty little word you aren't supposed to say, definitely not the first time and never, ever the morning after.

But I was in it, and so was he, and it did get better, each and every time.

Sort of. He'd come over, usually on the weekends, rarely during the week, and we'd have a little red ordinary from a box in the fridge, laugh and giggle for a while, and soon his hand would be on my shoulder and his eyes would be bigger and brighter than the sun I came all that way to pursue, and then our lips would touch and . . . and we'd go somewhere wonderful together.

Now, of course, I wonder why I didn't see it. I've never been a big pot smoker. A toke now and again to relax, to try and understand *Twin Peaks*, that kind of thing, and I do like it before a good fuck. But the first time I pulled out my little brass pipe, on maybe our third or fourth date, he froze, waved his hand in the air even though I hadn't yet flicked my Bic. "No way," he said, words clear, tone unmistakable. I put it away and never brought it out again.

He'd go quiet. We'd be sitting outside, watching the sun set, or the moon rise—when we weren't inside, that is, his cock in my mouth, mine in his. We'd sit outside, maybe staring up at the stars, watching them blink back at us. I'd usually be saying something stupid, recounting some run-in with a bitchy queen, or other queer drama, when I'd look—really look—at him and see that he wasn't there. Oh, he was sitting there all right, relaxed in my crappy lawn chair, but he also wasn't. Head back, eyes wide, he was looking up and out, lost in the higher atmosphere, far away from me.

He didn't like to be under me. Always on top, that was him. Normally I'd be twitchy about that, looking sideways for oncoming sexual weirdness, but with him it was just the way he was. I can't say what we did, because it would just sound like a fuck-and-suck shopping list. You had to be there, or maybe only he and I needed to be there.

Not just on top, but standing. Always standing tall. Like he wanted to be as high as possible. He'd stand there, at the foot of his bed, cock out straight and true. Not above me, because there was just the two of us, but his head was somewhere else, up in the clouds.

I'd snake along the bed, put lips to that dick, suck him hard and fast, or slow and wet, and he would smile, peering down at me. Not too tall, not too short, but he was still above me. His was a good cock, I have to say. One I think of a lot. Big, but not too big. Just right for sucking—and when he came, and he came well and often, his come salty, sweet, and damned good.

His was a damned good cock for fucking, as well. After we came together—he in my mouth, me in my hand as I sucked at him—I'd turn and give him my ass. Still standing, he'd touch his tip to my ring and then, carefully, because he wasn't an impatient bull, he'd push his way inside.

We'd fuck like that for eons, or maybe just half an hour, I never could tell. Maybe he'd come and sink down beside me, hard prod of his cock sticky against my back, or maybe he'd want something else, give me a chance to be inside.

We wouldn't just switch. Instead, I'd roll over on my back, cock up like a flagpole, and he'd crawl up onto the bed, squat over my dick, ease me inside. Then he'd fuck me, and I'd fuck him, our hips in a natural rolling rhythm for maybe a millennia, or just an hour. Again, I never checked.

See? A shopping list. A little from column A, something from column B—no heart, no soul. Maybe that sounds hot to you, but that's because I use dirty words, talk about two men sucking and fucking, but it was more than that with us. Hallmark cards fucking, champagne-and-roses sucking. Love-of-my-life fucking and sucking.

How did I miss it? He was just . . . Scott. Just "Scott." No last name, no job, no family, no stories. Still, you don't fuck, or get fucked, by someone and not know a bit about him, but in his case I knew only one thing for certain—that I loved him more than I'd ever loved anyone else—but that was all.

Cop? I thought, but I couldn't see him wearing a badge. *Fireman?* Nah, that didn't light my fire. I even debated FBI but he didn't fit the profile.

It didn't matter at first, but as we spent more time together, and he got to know me better, I started to realize that I didn't know anything about him at all.

As with anything that was just too right, too perfect, too

much fun, when anything starts to even hint at going wrong, it becomes the End of the World. In this case, lipstick on his collar. No lipstick, and certainly no collar, but I became sure there was someone else, someone he was hiding from me.

Finally, one night after a long and ecstatic ballet of cock and mouth, asshole and cock, and many, many marzipan kisses, I looked at him and saw him somewhere else.

"Who is it?" I finally growled.

"Heh?" he lazily responded, eyes dropping from the ceiling to my face. He smiled. "I'm sorry, what did you say?"

"Come on, fess up. There's someone else, isn't there? I can tell. You're not always here. Not that I'm complaining about when you are here . . . " I circled one hair-ringed nipple with my tongue.

He lifted my chin, kissed me. I tasted come. "You're perceptive. Just one more thing I adore about you."

"Don't try and change the subject. Something's on your mind. In my worldly experience that means someone else. Who is it?"

Rolling over onto his back he let out a steady, slow breath. "You wouldn't understand."

"Fuck that. We did the three-little-words thing, remember? That might mean fuck to you but it means a lot to me. You can tell me. Just . . . if you have to break my heart, make it quick. Like pulling off a bandage."

"That's not it. It's just . . . it's risky."

"What is he, a bruiser? He's going to break my thumbs or something?"

"Not like that. Risky for me."

"I'll protect you. We're in this together, aren't we? Three little words, remember?"

Silence. Lead-lined quiet. Finally he turned, looked me in the eyes. "Okay. But not here. On Monday, okay? I'll show you what I mean. On Monday."

A few days later, day not night. Outside, not inside. Hot— damned hot—not a hint of shade. He told me where to go, jotted it down for me and everything. The road to drive on, where to park, how far to walk, and when exactly to be there. There would be a bunch of boulders on top of a low rise, surrounded by tumbleweeds, populated by jackrabbits (which I saw) and probably rattlesnakes (which I hoped I wouldn't).

So I sat there, waiting for what, I didn't know. In the middle of nowhere—a hot, dry nowhere. It was hotter than even the desert should be, but I stayed. The old me, the frozen, icicle-dripping New Yorker would have yelled *Fuck it!* and hoofed it past the bunnies and serpents and simply have chalked it all up to life, a good fuck, and saying those stupid three words when I should have kept my yap shut.

But I didn't. Scott had asked me to come, and so I had. I wanted in, wanted to be with him like I'd never wanted to be with anyone else, ever. And if that meant sunstroke, I'd do it. If it meant dying of thirst in the kiln of the wide-open desert, then I'd do it—because I'd meant those three little words. Meant them with all of my heart.

What was that? Something, a flash, a gleam, something reflecting off the horizon. No, not on it, but just above it.

Then it was there, right over me, coming with an explosion of broken sound before I could even blink. Then it was gone, roaring past and up into the pure blue sky, climbing impossibly fast, twin furnaces staring back at me. A jet. A damned fast jet.

And I knew, then and there, who the other in his life was. An other I could never compete with. Still, I smiled, shading my eyes with one hand, watching twin trails of white streak higher and higher into the sky.

Compete? No, never. But he'd shown me, exposed himself in a way I knew he'd never done before. The sky was his true lover but that didn't mean I couldn't be there for him when he was on the ground.

xxx

IT WAS DIFFERENT after that. He looked down more often than up, but the pure blue sky and a plane to take him there was always behind his eyes. To be straight with you, a lot of it went (vroom) over my head as fast as his jet had. But I let him talk, absorbing rather than digesting what he said. One of the strangest things he told me was that people called him "Sir"—and I had to bite my lip to keep from asking to call him that myself. He was a pilot, but not just any. He was elite. Not an angel but a bat out of hell, a fighter jock.

He'd talk and I'd listen, but I'd also watch. Acronyms and terminology that I couldn't begin to understand, but when he talked about flying, about being out there in the sky all by himself, nothing but the atmosphere and a machine whose body and guts he knew better than he'd ever know mine, his eyes would glaze, lose focus, and I'd know that he was back up there, embracing the atmosphere—flying.

It was even better after that. I quickly realized that though I'd fucked and sucked Scott, I hadn't known the man, the pilot. Knowing him, having him open up to me, share himself more than just sexually, made those three little words just three little words. Because after that day on that high rock, they were just that. I didn't have words, three or three million, to say how I felt.

I think he felt it, too. No, I *know* he was right along there with me. I could see it in the way he moved, the way he spoke. He could share. For the first time, he could say what he wanted to say, about him and me, about how we felt, but also about how he felt . . . up there. You could say he came out to me.

Which makes what happened so much worse.

Damn, you'd think I'd be over him by now. Deep breath. Okay. Anyway, it was good, better, best after that. Before, he was reserved, hidden, tucked away. Grounded, you could say. After, he flew with me: laughing and not just smiling at my jokes, holding my hand when we sat in the yard, kissing me on the forehead after he came in my mouth—romantic stuff like that, or as romantic as he could be.

Then, yeah, that one time. We were in town, sitting down to a red-and-white-checked tablecloth dinner of burgers and chili. The waitress was cracking gum, and cracking wise as she streamed coffee into our mugs. Scott was looking out the window, watching another jet cut across his sky; a white streak against painfully cerulean blue.

"Jealous?" I said, slurping my malt, winking at him with one eye.

His smile was wide and true. "Strange, isn't it?"

"Not really," I said. "I think I know the way you feel."

"Do you?" Not suspicion—interest. "Come on, spill your beans."

"Here? Now? With all these people watching?"

"Stop kidding around."

I took a breath, said what I'd been thinking: "I think the same thing, looking up there. Jealous—because it got to you first. I wish I . . . could be first in your life."

"That's not it at all."

"Shush. Let me say something. And don't worry, it's not going to be heavy. It's just that, you know, not being first isn't all that bad, especially since I'm up against flying a multimillion-dollar piece of state-of-the-art engineering through the sound barrier. Second place doesn't seem that bad."

He'd said it before, but when he said it this time, hand on the red-and-white checked table, it meant so much more. "You're not second place. Not ever. I love you."

"And I, you," I said, and put my hand on his. That's when he did it. No, that's when I made him do it. I leaned forward, offered my forehead.

He kissed me, light and quick. His lips were hot on my skin. It was one of the best moments of my life.

And the worst. I expected him to say something, do something.

But he didn't. After a too-long moment, I lifted my head, opened my eyes, and saw him looking beyond me, at the front of the diner. Following his gaze, I turned and saw double doors swinging shut, and a man in an air force uniform walking out.

XXX

HE CALLED ME —from the base, I guess—almost a week later. He sounded fine. Too fine, too relaxed. Kept saying that things were going to be okay, that I didn't need to worry. Naturally, I didn't do anything but.

He asked me about my pots. He had never asked me about my pots before. "What's going on?" I asked. "Can't you tell me?"

"No," he said, one word saying more than just one word. Like the sniff before tears. Then, he said it again. "Don't worry." I could tell he wanted to say something, like three little words, but couldn't. Maybe someone was watching. I don't know.

I saw it on the news that night, a special report. An accident out in the deep desert. Fighter plane from the base, cause unknown.

I went out to the boulders in the desert the next day, got very drunk—angry drunk, screaming drunk, sad drunk, lonely drunk. I screamed, I cried. I missed him so much.

Then I laid out on my back and looked up at the sky, under the shadow of a gray cloud. I thought it was going to rain, but, like me, the sky just couldn't cry. We were both too sad.

XXX

I STILL THINK about him. A lot. My Scott, my flyer. The man I loved, the man who loved me—and who loved the sky. I don't feel jealous of the clouds, the pure blue high above, when I look up. I know we felt the same way about him, we shared him; when he was on the ground, and when he was flying through. We both miss him.

Oroborous

"**WHAT DO YOU** mean 'the wrong one?' You said 'snake,' man. You didn't say what fucking snake. I gave you a snake, 'kay?"

"I didn't want *that* one, I wanted *this* one. That's what I pointed at. Why the hell didn't you ask me if it was the right one?"

"Why the hell didn't you make sure I was looking where the fuck you were pointing? Besides, it's a snake, man, a pretty damned cool snake."

"It's not the snake I wanted."

"But it's the snake you got, man. You can get it taken off, but it's gonna cost ya. Hurt too. It's your skin. But I still say it's a fucking cool snake."

xxx

HAND ON THE door, pushing. Traffic noise rolling in. Cool outside air mixing with warm inside. Ass, face burning. Glancing back, expecting a smirk, seeing only a shaggy head dipped down, earnestly concentrating on wrinkled green sheaves in the cash register drawer.

Tracking back toward the door, the street, and out, eyes gliding over cardboard covered in plastic. Cheesecake girls winking at the world, tigers bearing feral grins, Chinese symbols with English meanings underneath, MOM with hearts and arrows, tribal blacks and boldness, coils of barbed wire, flaming skulls, leaping cobalt dolphins, bleeding crosses, Madonnas, periodic tables of symbols and icons, flaming lips, phrases in German, horned type—and snakes. The one he'd pointed to, a cobra pulled back to strike, and the rest: coiled vicious threats, fangs dripping brilliant venom, DON'T TREAD ON ME, heads with slit eyes and flickering forked tongues, and then—his face grew redder, his back hotter—*that one*.

Fat and coiled, ringed like a puckering asshole, tail slipped wet and bulbous into mouth, sucking itself. A photo of that snake, brightly tattooed onto a perfectly toned, gleamingly shaved, perfectly smooth ass.

That snake, the one he hadn't wanted. The one he'd got.

Shamed pink, he bolted out, sure the entire world was laughing at him.

XXX

"**IT'S NOT TOO** bad."

"Yes it is. It's bad. I didn't want this one. I wanted the other one."

"It looks good on you. Kind of suits you."

"No it doesn't. How can you say that?"

"Well *I* like it. Makes your ass look . . . cute."

Hand on waistband, preparing to pull his pants back up. Then her hands on his, stopping him.

"I know what'll cheer you up," she said, kneeling.

Fished out of his shorts, warm in her mouth, he tried to smile. Good? Yes, always. Both of them liked what she did, which made it fun for both of them.

But . . . not the snake he'd wanted, not the pissed off cobra, with a flared hood and the quotes of fangs, the coiled muscle of a cold-blooded reptile.

Not his snake, but the wrong one. Thick and pale, veined and glossy. Alabaster. Gleaming, moist and turgid. Around and around, from behind to front. Fat tail in the mouth, down the throat.

The photo of it showed a ring emblazoned on the cheek of an ass, on a tight, buffed cheek. A mark, a badge, a label.

She sucked, but all he could think about was the snake. After a long time she gave up, stood up. "Is it something I'm doing?" she said in a wounded voice.

"No," was all he could say, pulling up his pants. "It's not you."

xxx

"SO, CAN YOU take it off, doc?"

"Haven't seen one of these in quite a while. Takes me back. San Francisco in the seventies. Bathhouse days."

"Don't touch it."

"Have to—if you want me to remove it. Yeah, that's a trip down memory lane. Knew this guy, real hot—anyway, so you want it off? Can't see why. Damned good work, if I do say so myself. Looks good on you."

"No it doesn't. Can you get rid of it or not?"

"Well, yeah, I can. But it's going to be expensive—and painful. Sure you're up for it?"

"Yeah, I am. Do you have to touch it like that?"

"Like I said, got to know what I'm going to be working with. Still it's really quite a remarkable piece of work. Just look at this detail. Sure you won't reconsider?"

"I don't want it. It's not me."

"Not to contradict, but it sure as hell is. At least from where I'm looking, of course."

xxx

"SO, WHAT DID the doctor say?"

"He'll do it, but I can't afford it."

"I'd like to help, but . . . you know."

"Yeah . . . I know. Guess I'm stuck with it."

"It's not so bad. I still think it looks good on you."

"I hate it."

"Guess you're just going to have to live with it."

"I don't want to. I want it to just go away. I don't like being . . . marked this way."

"I'd try to make you feel better, but that hasn't been working for us, has it?"

"Sorry, got a lot on my mind I guess."

"You're not the only one. Look, I need to go out, get some air or something. Why don't you call me when you want my company, okay?"

xxx

"NOW THAT'S SOMETHING to look at."

"Huh, what did you say?"

"Well, if I was a rude jerk I'd say 'your ass,' but I was really looking at your tat. Nice work. Who did it?"

Jerking up his gym shorts. "Some guy."

"Well, 'some guy' does some nice work. Grade A, in fact. Been thinking of getting that done myself. Little something to put me outside the herd. You recommend this guy?"

Closing his locker with an echoing bang. "Not really."

"Well you should. Damned fine work—for what I saw of it. Classic design, too. Simple without being dull, all kinds of interesting connotations. You could do a lot worse."

"I guess so. I try not to think about it."

"But you should! Just think about it; you're a little gallery, carrying something wonderful around with you wherever you go—with you forever. Cool, that. You should be putting it out, not hiding it away."

Was that a smile? "Thanks, but I wouldn't call it a good frame."

"I would—a damned fine gallery, not to be too fawning or

anything. Tell ya the truth, though I mentioned your artwork, that wasn't the first thing I noticed about you."

It *was* a smile. It stayed. "Thanks, I guess."

"No need to thank me, you're the one with the eye candy — artwork and frame both. Made my day, matter of fact."

"You're something else."

Stepping up close. "That makes two of us."

The kiss was unexpected. Not there one moment, there the next: lips to lips, locker room getting hotter.

Hand on waistband, preparing to pull them down. Then a pause. "Okay?"

"I . . . I don't know."

Grinning, bending close for a continuation of the kiss, but before that, "I'll take that as a 'maybe.'"

Hand back on waistband, pulling the shorts down. His cock, which he realized was never so hard, came out. It pointed, bobbing gently, at the other man's mouth.

"Nice," was all the other man said before opening wider, moving to wrap smooth lips around the head of his cock.

"Oh," was all he said as the other man opened wider, wrapping smooth lips around the head of his cock.

Both of them really, honestly liked what he was doing, which made it really, honestly fun for both of them.

Lips he knew; mouth he knew; throat he knew; teeth he knew; tongue he knew; hands on his balls he knew; hands snaking around to circle his clenching, unclenching, clenching, unclenching asshole, he knew. Or he thought he did. Good before, wonderful now. The smells, sensations, views were different, new, fresh . . . right.

The sharp bite of salt in the air; the wet, hot tube swallowing his cock; glancing down to see the man's head bobbing, amazed by his hydraulic actions. The smells, sensations, views were more than different, new, fresh, or right — they were wonderful.

He began to make noises, soft mews of delight. He began to

move, sharp pelvic fucks to push his cock even harder, faster into the other man's mouth.

Then, he felt it. The body rush, the tension and the hot liquid gush from deep in his body, his balls, and out. His come was overwhelming, taking out his knees and making his heart race— two beats doubling then tripling in excitement. Stumbling back, hand flopping toward a cold steel locker door, he braced himself, breathing deep until four beats became two and he could breathe without whistling.

"Well, that was fun," the other man said, climbing up off his knees and wiping come-gleaming lips with the back of a smooth hand. "Up for something else?"

He didn't know what to say, and even if he did, he couldn't say it. Lungs burning, chest heaving, he could only smile and nod.

"Put your hand here," the other man said, taking a right in his left and pulling him to his waist. "Feel that? See what you've done?"

A hard cock, nothing but thin gym shorts between their skin. A day for *many* firsts.

The shorts came down, the other man pulling them off with a quick gesture. A hard cock, not even thin gym shorts between their skin. Then he reached down and wrapped a nervous hand around the other man's cock.

Without being asked, he started to stroke. Slowly, carefully, not knowing exactly what to do but doing what he knew he'd like to have done to him. A smooth, steady rhythm, circumcised head, down the muscled shaft to the tangle of short hairs at the back, then repeat.

It was like a circle, one cock beginning where one ended, one mouth leading back around to another. Two men becoming one man, round and round, round and round. The other man's dick might as well have as been his own—it felt the same, smelled the same, and the sounds the other man made were the noises he suspected he made when he stroked himself.

In his hand it was thick and pale, veined and glossy. Alabaster. Gleaming, moist, and turgid. Stiffening, jerking. The noises the other man was making changed, new tempo, new volume, higher frequency.

"Turn around," the other said, and he did—without thinking or questioning, without fear. How could he, after all, be frightened of himself?

He did, and felt the sticky warmth of come on his ass. Even though he didn't see it, he knew where it had landed: in the middle of a ring emblazoned on the cheek of his ass, on a tight, buffed cheek. A mark, a badge, a label—of what he was. Forever.

Then, in the midst of the warm, wet feeling, a pair of lips. A kiss to his ass, to the snake. "Now that's a pretty picture," the man said.

XXX

"HAPPY?"
   "Very."
   "That's good. That's real good. What a perfect day to go to the beach."
   "Every day is pretty perfect with you."
   "You're just trying to get into my pants."
   "Been there, done that. Want to again."
   "Even after—what? Six months?"
   "I guess so. I haven't been keeping count."
   "And they say the only thing you can get in a gym is buff . . . Hey, that's your cue to say something witty. You know, like 'I sure got something buff.'"
   "Oh, sorry—I just saw someone I know. Here she comes."
   Across the sand, hesitant steps. "Hi," she said, arm tight around the bicep of a bronze and broad man. "I thought that was you."
   "Hi, how are you doing?"
   "Better. Thanks for asking. You?"

He wrapped his own arm around his own bronze and broad companion. "Much better. Thanks for asking."

"Well, we have to get going. Nice running into you."

"You too. Take care."

Watching them walk away, his boyfriend turned. "Well, you never know," he said, in a playful voice.

"Seems like ages ago. Don't worry, I know where I want to be."

"I'm so glad. Really." Turning, he watched the other couple walk away. His eyes scanned the man. "Hey, look at the tat on him."

He looked as well, seeing a pissed off cobra with a flared hood and the quotes of fangs, the coiled muscle of a cold-blooded reptile on a tanned back.

"Nice," he said, hugging his lover closer, "but I love the one I have."

2+1

OKAY, IT'S A bit freaky—I admit that. Some people got their whips and their chains, putting needles through their dicks, clothespins on their nipples, or dressing in Mommy's old dresses, but me—I get hard from dish soap.

Not just hard, mind you, but rock and steel erect. Same for seeing a roll of paper towels, or a pair of rubber gloves—not latex, that would be obviously kinky, but rather just a pair of yellow scrubbing gloves. Walking through the cleaning supplies aisle at the Piggly Wiggly can get real interesting, especially having to hide a throbbing dick from the bag boy.

You see, those guys with the pins through their tits, the welts on their asses, they've got their dungeons and playrooms. Dan and I, we've got the kitchen. Mostly the kitchen sink.

Can't really say how it happened, not really. I mean, I know the first time was—what?—six months or so ago. There I was, playing wife and doing the dishes, when Dan decided that the view of me bent over the sink, ass out in a pair of old gym shorts, was just too much to bear. It was good. It was damned good. Dan's always been a really great fuck, but that day he was possessed or something. A fuck like you'd find in a porno flick or something—though I doubt Jeff Stryker would have done someone with his face buried in the sink, breathing lemon-scented soap that softens your hands while you do the dishes.

I don't know what was into Dan that day—not that I'm complaining—but I know what kept me bent, open, smiling, and happy. His name is Oshi, and he lives next door.

He wasn't involved the first time Dan grabbed my shorts, jerked them down, and gave my asshole a good, wet kiss. He wasn't there when one of Dan's fingers, then two, then three, then four went deep in me, feeling where his dick wanted to go, loosening my tight muscles. No Oshi when Dan's dick finally did find my mark, pushing steadily, strongly, till his pubic hairs tickled my ass crack and his balls gently tapped against my cheeks.

In fact, no Oshi that first time at all. But the next time—ah, that was different. Great different. Fantastic different. Tremendous different.

It must have been about a week later, and I was being the Ms. again. There's something kind of sensual about doing the dishes—water splashing on the china and shimmering on the cutlery, the soap making everything slippery, the water steaming. I guess Dan agrees—or agreed—with me, because sure enough, right when I was between soaping and rinsing, but before drying, I felt him walk into the room.

Dan . . . what can I say about Dan? I love him. No duh, right? I mean not only is he fucking me, but I'm doing his dishes—and I'm not into that "slave, do the damned dishes" thing. We're lucky, I guess, not that we found each other but that our domesticity hasn't gotten ugly yet. After five years I guess that's quite an accomplishment.

We fuck in the living room. We fuck in the den. We fuck on the front lawn (okay, it was 3:00 A.M., but we still did it). We fuck with me on top, with Dan on top, and with both of us lying side-by-side—and, yeah, we've even done it a couple of times in the bedroom. We can sit and giggle at *Sex in the City* and fuck like we're trying out for an Olympic event. We've got it, whatever the hell it is, and I'm damned glad.

The living room, the den, the front lawn, even the bedroom—but almost every Saturday afternoon, while I'm doing the lunch dishes, we fuck in the kitchen—and I love it.

It's good—it's fucking good—when Dan pulls my shorts or

pants down, lubes me up (another great use of dish soap), and sticks his very handsome, very big cock up my ass. But it's even better when Oshi is there.

Oshi lives next door. He moved in about six or so months ago. Nice guy. Smiles a lot, you know? I've never really been into Japanese guys, but there's something about him. Sexy. Very, very sexy. Big, but not like he graduated from the Muscle Academy— just the right amount of nice muscles in all the right places. Bald, too—smooth round head, polished like the marble bust of a samurai.

The way he moves, too, like he's on well-oiled bearings. Smooth. Watching him walk out on Sunday morning to get the paper, in just a simple kimono-like robe, you can tell—just tell—that he fucks like an artist: steady, inspired strokes. His mouth, too—plush lips, strong jaw. Just the right amount of suck, a perfect degree of tongue, maybe even a hint of teeth. The blow job of an artist.

The first time with Oshi was damned good. My hands were slippery and warm, face flushed from the hot steam, Dan's hands suddenly on my ass. My shorts around my ankles, Dan's cock pressing against my pucker, then—hard, steady, pushes—inside me. Good, damned good.

Then Oshi joined us. Damn, two was good, but three was incredible. I just wish Oshi and Dan knew they were both there, too.

Maybe they don't believe in curtains in Japan. Maybe he just couldn't find the right chintz for his bedroom. Whatever, there was just bare glass between my kitchen window and his bedroom— the bedroom where he slept, the bedroom where he worked out, the bedroom where he slept and worked out in the buff.

When I saw him, all stretched out on his futon, defined and strong, I was in lust. Dizzying, distracting, heart (and dick) thumping lust. Okay, the fact that Dan's cock was sliding in and out of my tight little asshole might have had something to do with it, but I don't think it was the only thing. Two good, three better.

Looking at Oshi sprawled out on his bed, body so well-defined, helmet of a half-hard cock peering slyly out of a dense tangle of—I could guess—scratchy hairs, I was lost.

Dan's dick on one end, conducting his metronomic fuck, his zen fuck, while on the other I saw Oshi get up from his bed and smile wryly. The expression on his face transmitting an obvious *You think that's good, you just wait.* As he walked toward me, his muscles doing their wonderful dance, his semihard cock swayed back and forth, with each back and each forth getting harder and harder until, when he finally walked up to me, he was gloriously hard, spectacularly hard.

He stood there in front of me. He was still bobbing, but only because of Dan's dick sliding in and out of me. My breath came in harsh rasps, a kind of near-come waved back and forth through me. Sometimes I even broke out in chills—a wash of goosebumps, almost like a kind of fear of how good this all was.

I wanted to grab my dick. I needed to grab my dick—but I didn't. I knew if I'd touch it I'd come, shotgun blast hard and that'd be it. My asshole would seize, my legs would go, and the stars would come out behind my eyes—so I didn't. I hung on, trying not to pay attention to the throbbing, pulse-pounding demands of my cock. Instead, I focused on the three of us: Dan's big cock in my ass and Oshi's handsome member bobbing right in front of my eyes.

Two are good, three is religious. In one end and lingering, hauntingly, teasingly, in front of my face. Cocks are so damned pretty, you know, just look at one: pale pink shaft, tickling hairs where it connects to its owner, soft yet hard bulb at the end, that little vertical slit where the good stuff comes out—nice, damned nice to look at.

But even better, to be fucked by one, as I was by Dan's. Filling then emptying, filling then emptying, filling then emptying—from feeling that it might be a whole damned fist in you, to really

needing to shit. In and out. One of the best damned things ever—
and Dan was really, really good at it.

But beyond better, is best: to have one sliding in and out of
your ass and another one, a lovely, hard one, bobbing in front of
your face, lingering, teasing. At the tip a pale drop of salty come,
the shaft starting to get that "really, really hard" shine to it.

That's where I was, in the best of places, between two cocks
in the hard place (sorry). Then it got better, if that was possible.
Oshi took a single, small step forward and his cock, that wonderful
hard cock, touched my lips. If cocks look great, they taste even
better, and Oshi's was just right—skin, sweat, salt, come, funk,
and a bit of soap.

I've never been one to do anything halfway—all the way or
nothing, that's me. A kiss would just not do, so I licked him—
watching his cock lift then drop when my tongue left his head—
then wrapped my lips around the head and rolled all of my mouth
around and around him.

Oshi didn't make a sound, but his eyes—what I could see of
them, looking down at me from on high—glazed over, and I knew
that I'd gotten to him. So I sucked, as I was fucked, and—lord—it
was good.

Time vanished, and I was just a tube for cocks, just a mouth
and an asshole for these two lovely, hard men. Three is a magic
number. Three is the best number there can be.

Finally, the pressure built too high and I had to, just had to.
Tie my hands down and I would have given anyone anything to
get them free and on my cock—my ATM code? Yours! My credit
cards? Take them! Everything I own? Cart it off!

But I wasn't tied (thank god), so my hand did fall down to my
own hard cock. Hand around myself I was shocked by exactly
how hard, how hot I was. It felt like someone else's cock, a fourth
person in our little trio—and the thought of that, yet another
person, is what pushed me right over the side.

Heaven, bliss, damned hot—that and more. Sex is supposed

to be good, right? Well, this wasn't good—it was great.

Or at least it was in my mind. Seeing Oshi sprawled out on his futon, oblivious to me, to Dan's dick in my ass—then and whenever he was in view . . . well, I have my imagination, right? All I have to do is close my eyes and Oshi's right there with us, adding his dick to our fun.

I've thought about talking to Dan about this, maybe having Oshi over some night to see if he'd be game to join us. You can't tell me that Dan hasn't thought about it. He has eyes as well as a cock, after all.

But I think I know why he wouldn't, and it isn't because dish soap gets his rocks off. In our minds, as he fucks me and I get fucked, it's all perfect—ideal. No leg cramps, hurt feelings, or drama. There it's always wonderful, never disappointing.

Maybe we'll have Oshi over someday—or maybe we never will. But in the meantime I'm really getting off getting fucked while I suck him off, the three of us in cock, mouth, and asshole ecstasy, with me bent over the kitchen sink with lemon-scented soap tingling my nose.

Happy Feet

BAM! *DOOR* *SHUT* behind, harsh sunlight grouchy from squeezing through dark clouds, hard on the eyes but it's still a good morning. Step down, tap, step down, tap-tap-tippy-tap—a little impromptu shuffle—then back up, step, tap, step, tap, tap-tap-tippy-tap GOOD MORNING WORLD. Feet awake and frisky, toes merry little piggies, ankles loose and fflleexxiibblle, legs tight and strong, the rest—oh, who cares about the rest? Tippy-tap-tap up the top of the stairs, nice little turn, tush up on the polished banister and a joyous slide down to the sidewalk, drop to knees, arms wide outstretched, GOOD MORNING WORLD. Oh, yes; oh, certainly; oh, positively; oh, fantastically—no clouds, no cold winds, no bustle and hustle. No, siree. It's a great morning, a grand morning, a morning to kick up the heels and dance!

xxx

THE OLD MAN opened his front door, slowly, careful not to pull too hard—if such a thing were even possible. It'd been a long time since he'd been able to do anything too hard. His hands wrapped meticulously around the knob, turn, turn, turn, until the bolt was withdrawn. Then, one hand still on the knob, other on the scuffed cheap pine, he pulled. The door was silent. A stronger pull, and it made a noise like a deep, old ache. Then it was free. His heart hammered, fear flushing his face, but the door just opened. It didn't fly toward him, didn't hit him in the arm, the chest, or the face. The success made him smile, but then he didn't, compressing the grin down with thinly pressed lips.

He swung the door gradually open. The air beyond was cool, almost cold, the sun missing behind an overcast sky. He stood and looked out for a long, slow minute, then turned to the umbrella stand by the closet door and withdrew an elegant black umbrella with a curled bamboo handle. Classic. He needed a cane; an umbrella would do. Sometimes it just works out.

A few steps and he was outside, the cold brass sucking at his fingers. He turned—always slowly, always carefully—with the umbrella hooked over his thickly coated arm. Hand on the knob. Cold. He had a sudden thought of frost needles, of parchment skin sticking to metal. He pulled, reversing a minute before. The door shut, locking with mechanical certainty. Next, the stairs. He wondered what other people were scared of: bombs, fires, earthquakes, or mean young men with muscles and bones that didn't break.

His arm tight around the chipped banister, he put his right foot down. The smoothed marble felt secure, not too slippery. Left foot down. Good, he stood and balanced. The stairs were long, like a tunnel dropped down to a still sea of cement, wave crests of ancient gum and drink stains. One thing at a time. A memory struck him right then: tenement steps, his mom's wallpaper-paste dumplings boiling in the kitchen, steaming up the windows. The old man across the alley, mumbling for every step down, every step up. It was a long time before he finally realized that each step was a line of the Lord's Prayer. Years later, and he was saying his own prayer, one step at a time. Modern times, he thought with a sly grin, are all about streamlining. His own trial was simpler: five steps.

He slipped his hand down the rail, got another grip. One thing at a time. One step at a time. No rush. The ground's not going anywhere. No, it's waiting, like a concrete lion—gravity, if anything, is patient. It has nothing better to do than wait for a misstep, a bit of hurry, a lapse.

One step down, another step down. Balance. His hand slid along the rough wooden railing. The Lord is My Shepherd. One thing at a time. Suddenly he heard a sharp sound and felt the narrow tip of his umbrella skid across the smooth stone steps. His heart thumped at it, seeing it too clearly: losing his balance, his hand tearing away from the banister, his legs collapsing, arm outstretched, snapping bones.

Then he's there, at the bottom of the stairs, standing on the sidewalk. He smiles, true and wide. Everest descended. One thing at a time. Amen. Then the smile slides away, as before, into stern resolve and a bitter taste. It's come to this: a great accomplishment is walking down the stairs.

xxx

COME ON SWEETHEART, *you know the steps, you know the drill—you feel them like a song in your bones. It's instinct. You know that left follows right, which chases left again. One, two, three, one, two, three. Artist's got paint, writer's got words, music man's got notes, a dancer's got his feet, and you're a Picasso of the soft shoe, a Hemingway of the step, a Mozart of the tap-tap-tap. From the hard, cold down to the prancing, dancing up: on your knees, right arm wrapped around steel pole, feet up, walk around the pole, climb that pole, round and round until you're standing, hanging. Kelly in* Singing in the Rain, *on a* NO PARKING *signpost here, a lamp post back then. Kelly with a hundred-and-three-degree fever, me with just dancing fever. What did the Man say that day—handsome, handsome, handsome Kelly with that twinkle in his eyes and genius toes—just you and a dozen or so hoofers on a cold Hollywood studio floor. "Know the steps, but more importantly feel the steps." Yes, Mr. Kelly. Certainly, Mr. Kelly. Take your shoes off, Mr. Kelly, so I can see those pretty pink toes, those strong toes, those sweet feet that dance the true magic, the wonderful magic. Take them off, Mr. Kelly, and share*

the magic with the rest of us club-footed, tone-deaf just-goods and
not GREATS.

xxx

WAS THAT A drop of rain? He stood, an erratic breeze tugging at his coat. He put his hand out as if begging for change, really begging that it wasn't a drop, wasn't rain. Rain meant back up the stairs, back inside with the dark stuffiness.

He waited a long minute—as long as only a minute can be to the old. But no drop. No rain. He sighed, slow and easy, and turned his gray eyes down the sidewalk. The grade was apparently gentle, but nothing was gentle anymore. Cats had claws, dogs bit, even plain foods would stab him in the guts.

Deep breath. One step at a time. Walk, never run. Those days are over. Set yourself a realistic goal. That NO PARKING sign, for instance. A simple distance, easily reachable. One step, two. Keep focused on the task. From there, maybe, to the next sign, or perhaps the corner itself. It was a Tuesday afternoon, thank goodness. He would never try a walk to the corner, down the street, to the market, on any other day: too many bodies, too much hustle, too much bustle. Too easy to get stepped on, knocked over. To the boys, the men, the Castro was life and lively. To him it was the terror of "Excuse me" or "Sorry, I didn't see you there" or "Move it, you old fart." He should move, take his slow submergence somewhere else, but packing, dealing with heavy boxes, finding somewhere else to stay were even more frightening. One step at a time. One small goal at a time. Not evil, but the lesser of two terrors was what surrounded him.

Cold metal. Very cold metal. But he held on, took slow, deep breaths, feeling throughout his papier-mâché body for aches, pains, surges where they shouldn't be, or surges where there should be but weren't. All was . . . not right, but what it was. Not the way he wanted it to be, but at least not any worse.

XXX

GET THOSE TOOTSIES *in gear, girls! Oh, Gene, oh, Mr. Kelly—so butch and strong, so nimble. A cat, a gazelle, a real dancing man. The dancing man, oh yes—he's standing there in the line, watching him swing, tap, swing, tap, the room cold but him hot. Sweat shining, shirt clinging, every muscle doing its own special dance, watching those feet move, turn, point, stamp down with force, drama, strength. He's hanging around backstage, where he shouldn't be, just watching, watching, he peers, straining to catch a look, a glimpse of the toes, the arch, the tendons. They say dancer's have the ugliest feet, bruised and battered, hammered and warped by step, pivot, step, point, step, but no, no, no never, not for Mr. Kelly, not then, not ever. Artist's got his brush, writer's got his pen, music man's got his instrument, a dancer's got his feet—and Mr. Kelly's were all of that and much more. He danced brilliance, stepped genius. He turns, catches you looking, young man, dancer on the way, where you shouldn't, but instead of a bite or a bark, a smile. White, white teeth, magic man sharing the love of the step, turn, tap, sweep:* "Hey, kid, you did great today." *The tears wanted to come, the tears almost did come. The saint of the shuffle, the king of the dance, god of the step saying that the magic may live in your own bunions, cramps, stumbling, and trips.* "Thank you, Mr. Kelly." *But the bad boy inside you didn't just want the magic, no kid, he wanted to get down there and kiss the feet of the wizard, take their smells and calluses into his hot hungry mouth and suck, suck, suck. Tongue wrapping around* Summer Stock, The Pirate, Words and Music—*a kiss of love, a kiss like sucking a cock, a kiss to draw in the magic. But, no, he stayed on his feet, didn't miss a step:* "Thank you, Mr. Kelly" *and that was all, that was it, and it wasn't everything but it was enough:* "Thank you, Mr. Kelly."

XXX

HE STOPPED IN front of Twin Peaks. The place was quiet. A few men inside, sipping and talking. He wished he had the strength of spontaneity. Drop in for a drink, see what was up, shoot the shit, share lives, look into another man's eyes, kiss— but instead he just stopped in front of Twin Peaks. Already his legs were hurting, much earlier, much closer than the last time. Suddenly he wanted to cry. His eyes burned and he had to blink and blink again to hold them back. One step at a time. No time for tears. Got to keep moving. The bus bench was a goal. A few dozen steps. One foot in front of the other. He tried to remember what running was like, what . . . other things with his legs, his feet had been like, but then pushed the memories away. Stay focused. That was then and now—now he just had to walk a dozen or so steps to the bus bench. A dozen or so steps to the bus bench so he can rest. One step, two steps, more steps. Hand outstretched, reaching for the edge. So dirty, but not much of a choice. Then a touch, old hand to dirty public metal again. Get a good grip, pull as you walk a bit more. Letting go, rounding the corner, traffic so close—steel tigers waiting for just one slip, one step in the wrong direction—then a sight of the bench. Good, small miracles—no one sitting there, no smelly, foul, frightening bums on the seats. Just those uncomfortable and frightening-in-their-own-way spinning seats. Scary, but we could still rest. Another step followed by another and then he was there. Turn and ease down, slowly sit. His weight came off his legs, feet, back with the skittering of the metal umbrella tip on the sidewalk, the tension release almost as painful as the aches, the throbs, the shootings. Almost, though, and that was important. After a time—a few slow breaths, a few struggling beats—the pain faded, eased, dropped into the background, and he really was able to rest.

XXX

STEP, TURN, AND turn and step, step, step—what a wonderful day to prance, what a great day to swing, what a fantastic day to dance! Mr. Kelly again, and he wanted a smart, clean, pressed sailor suit and bellow, sing, proclaim the love of steps, the love of the city. Not "New York, New York" but rather the city that was his stage, the town that was his home . . . "San Francisco." No sailor suit, no "The Bronx is up, the Battery's down" no "Steamboats ride through a hole in the ground." No, this 'down' was the Castro, the Haight, the Park—a smart city, a grand dame city. Tap and turn, tap and turn and stop, look down the crest of the hill, at the slope to the city, the towers beyond, the men hand in hand, the smiles, and no, not Mr. Kelly, not Singing in the Rain—no, now in elegant tux, classic cuffs, smart bow tie. The music wasn't joy, wasn't sprite, didn't reach down and lift you up, put you down on your feet. No singing, no. Instead: "Let's stop the music and dance." No Ginger, just Fred . . . Mr. Astaire—maybe looking for another Fred, but did Fred need a Ginger or even a Fred when he swept around that boat cabin in Royal Wedding? Oh, Fred, lovely, pretty, Fred. Beautiful Mr. Astaire. He was roses, Fred was ballrooms and balconies, Mr. Astaire was orchestras and embassies. Cool, calm, precise. Mr. Astaire was smiles and sophistication. Mr. Astaire was smiling, showing the steps: "turn step, step, turn, turn step." Mr. Astaire showing the young dancer the way, the correct way to do it. Mr. Astaire sitting on the stage, naked feet dangling into the orchestra pit. Mr. Astaire's fine instruments, powdered and perfect, smooth and sleek, champagne glass feet, crystal feet, beautiful feet. Mr. Astaire's smile, the way to woo a prince or princess, a man who heard the music, who danced with every step, every gesture. A polished man. Seeing him there, that day, he wanted it bad, so bad. Not the handsome, the earthly, but the divine and the saintly. To kneel at those feet, to put a hand under their perfect, strong arches and lift them, gaze at their ivory perfection and, sinner to saint, gently, reverently, put lips to skin, to touch, to kiss the purity, the refinement, the elegance. No, instead nothing. Not a smile, not a word of encouragement. Nothing of the sort. But in a more special way it had been good to simply look at those feet and not see the ivory, the gold, the crystal, the orchestra. Instead he saw that Mr. Astaire had five toes, fine little nails, an ankle, tendons, and all the rest, and when he went home that night to a tiny bungalow in Hollywood he took off his own shoes and saw, he saw, he saw, he saw nothing ugly, nothing wrong, nothing ugly but just . . . five toes, five nails, ankles, tendons. Feet. Feet on the small-time hoofer. Magic all around, magic between them—something special and wonderful in common: the beauty of the step, the joy of the dance. Feet.

xxx

THE OLD MAN'S breath was ragged, like it'd been crudely torn off. He felt like there was something abraded, broken deep in his lungs, his chest. One step at a time, he thought, trying to keep his breath steady and easy, like each breath was a step down, a step up.

After a time—several rasping inhales and exhales, a few laboring thuds of his heart—it all started to ease. First it was relief, and he was pounds lighter and years younger, but then he realized that he was blocks from home, and almost an equal number of blocks from his destination. Relief, but there was a decision to make: blocks home, or blocks to the market, a few light groceries, and then back. He didn't have much left, just a few essentials in his fridge, some sprouting veggies, stale cereal. He could call someone—he had before—but while it meant he could eat better there was something about the smiling, cheerful mobility of the kids who brought it all that made him feel . . . empty. Better eating, but better eating for a hollow, dried up old man.

A dried up old man. He didn't like that. Not at all. But sometimes you need to look at the world clearly. He might be old, fragile, brittle, but at least he could still walk. Looking down at his feet, his sturdy old-man's loafers, he thought, Get me home? The answer was silent but assured: Get us home.

XXX

AH, YES, OH, yes, the language of the dancer, the phrase and flow of step, turn, step, turn, turn, step; of tap-tap-tippy-tap; of "just like this," from the choreographer. Still Mr. Astaire, still flowing water, grace and lithe and lively. By the handsome boys, the rowdy boys: the cowboys, the sailors, the roughnecks, the leathermen, the poster boys, the sweater boys, the drag boys . . . the boys. "Just stop the music and dance." Do you want to dance, handsome? Here, here, it's not so hard, just stop thinking and start feeling with your body, your muscles, your bones, your feet. Let them lead you, show you the way—step, turn, step, turn, turn, step; tap-tap-tippy-tap. That's it, that's it. Live free and dance, dance and be free. All those days, all those nights: step, turn, step, turn, turn, step; tap-tap-tippy-tap. A cheap Hollywood bungalow, nights on polished wood, days on polished wood. Calluses on calluses, but his feet knew the songs, knew the steps. He walked the streets, the avenues, the boulevards (Sunset and Hollywood and so many others) with the other limber young men. Cheap dinners, cheap dives, cheap booze, cheap tickets. "There I am!" Cheering and screaming at the Bijou when one of them was on the screen, in the chorus. Back at the cheap dives, his cheap bungalow, dicks in asses, dicks in mouths, hands on dicks, but no matter the dick or the ass or the mouth or the hand they sat or stood or walked around his cheap little bungalow without shoes and without socks because they knew and he knew that they were not just dicks, asses, mouths, hands, they were the poets of the floorboards, the maestros of movement—the disciples of dance. Bare feet, handsome feet, pretty feet—they were what was cherished, rubbed, fucked, licked, tickled, bound, wrapped, tapped, nibbled, and more and more. He was good on the boards, even great on the boards—"Thank you, Mr. Kelly" and others—but in

*the cheap bungalow, in the cheap dive he was Gene, he was Fred,
he was Hermes Pan—lithe and lively and perfect. Lithe and lively
and perfect . . . lithe and lively and perfect.*

xxx

THE UMBRELLA WAS not a good cane, but it worked well
enough. Bending forward he scritched the metal tip until it
wedged, neat and tight, in a crack. Carefully, he leaned on it,
pushing down on it as hard as he could. His legs shook, hinting
at a paralyzing cramp, but then he was moving, rising up. Then a
rumble, overcast and cold, thunder. Rain?

No, anything but rain: wet streets, people running, knocking
old men out of the way. The rumble, the thunder then rolled up,
blocking the sun. A bus. A city bus. The old man relaxed, then
tensed when the door opened and the passengers flowed out. The
men, the boys. He wanted to smile but those days were way gone.
Instead, he gripped his umbrella and tried to keep his balance as
they flowed around him: tight jeans and wife-beater shirts, leather
pants and vests, feather boas and eyeliner, pretty, handsome,
rutting bulls and pretty satyrs. Pretty, handsome, rutting bulls and
pretty satyrs once, now just an avalanche, a tidal wave. Then just
a few, then none.

The thunder left, heading up Castro toward Geary, and the
street was quiet again. One step at a time. Left, then right, holding
onto his umbrella, hanging onto the bus kiosk. One step at a time.
One foot in front of the other, up the slight hill, heading back
toward the corner, Twin Peaks. Back toward home. Pretty boys—
all of them—long gone.

xxx

WHAT A LOVELY *morning. Ah, not memory, ah, not anything
to keep the magic from the toes, the music that floats through the*

air. *Dance with me, handsome. Dance with me. Swing those hips, tinkle those toes, and kick up your heels. For lithe and lovely you have Mr. Astaire, for handsome and strong you have Mr. Kelly, but for the dance of love, the dance of sex, the dance of decadence you have to put on your glove, put on your tights, put on your bowler hat, cock your hips, and snap, snap, snap. Hollywood long behind, back behind the floodlights of Broadway. Floorboards during the day, floorboards at night. When it's not snap, shuffle, snap, shuffle, then it's bathhouses and the Village. But that wasn't the sex of that time, those days and nights, those years. No sir, no way, no how. Sure suck cock, sure fuck ass, sure lick dick, sure jerk off—sure, sure, sure but only because it wasn't days on the floorboards, nights on the floorboards, wasn't Bobby. Oh, Bobby, how I wished it was your smile, your hands, your cock, any and all of that but also mainly, especially, your toes your nails your ankle your feet those years.* Pippin, Sweet Charity, Cabaret. *Watching, in love and loving with each step. It didn't matter that it wasn't to be—a touch a kiss a suck a lick a fondle—because when Bobby Fosse was there, demanding, ordering, pushing, pushing, and pushing some more, he knew it more than he ever had that there was the sex of dicks and ass, cocks and lips, and there was the best there was, the best there ever would be, the sex of the dance. He moved, he jumped, he strutted, he snapped and snapped and snapped again and it was good so good and always better. He danced like Bobby asked him to and more. His feet had wings, his feet were cocks, his feet took him away like the Little Prince. His feet did everything, and he did everything he could for them. So there you see, stranger, that you might suck, you might lick, you might rub, but it's your feet—those pink little magic carpets—that will really take you from here to there. From here to there . . . from here to there and so many other places. Yes! All is fine, all is love, all is sex and* DANCING . . . *until (sigh) until (sob) until (tears) until what has taken you to so many wonderful places decides to leave you behind, leave you for wrinkles and brittle bones, aches that never leave, weakness and big veins.*

Until they are gone . . . and then they are gone . . . gone and will never, ever come back.

x x x

THE OLD MAN climbed his stairs. One step at a time. His prayer in reverse, and ending with one, the top step. Umbrella tip down on the slick marble, then a push and a step. It was always hard going down, but it was always hard coming back up. The fear down was in looking down that long, cold, hard flight of stairs, while the fear up was in slipping and slamming down—hard—into unforgiving marble. Going out, there was at least some energy, but back up, there was also exhaustion—tired and weak muscles, distracted mind, too easy to be already in when there was just one more vicious step left.

The fear of a fall was constant, even more than regular breathing, a steady beating of the heart. But not this time: his hand was on the knob. He pushed, the reverse of leaving. Not too hard, it might cause it to suddenly open and spill him into the hall. Then it was open. Ease in, eagerness just an infant accident, turn and close the door. Home. Umbrella back where it belonged, and into the living room. Still risky, but now the territory was familiar.

He sank into his chair, the faded cloth and sprung springs welcoming him with support and tenderness. He closed his eyes for a moment, feeling his body relax, unwind. His heart was beating regularly, his breathing was ragged but steady. He was home.

After a bit he bent down, bones dully cracking and creaking, and pulled off his socks, his shoes. Bare feet, cool in the room.

Thank you, old friends, he thought. *Thank you for taking me where I needed to go. Thank you for being there, as always.*

Love

"YOU COULD HAVE stayed with me," he'd said the first time I went to Seattle to see him but stayed in a motel. I hadn't even thought of it, and so the disappointment in his eyes.

I never went back. After he got promoted there wasn't any point.

You could have stayed with me evolves into a fantasy in which those four days play out differently: an invitation made earlier, my discomfort of staying in someone else's house miraculously absent. Fresh off the plane, strap digging into my shoulder (I always overpack), out of the cab and up a quick twist of marble steps to his front door. A knock, or a buzz, and it opens.

A quick dance of mutual embarrassment as I maneuver in with my luggage, both of us saying the stupid things we all say when we arrive somewhere we've never been before. Him: "How was your flight?" Me: "What a great place."

A son of a decorator, I always furnish and accessorize my fantasies. I imagine his to be a simple one-bedroom. Messy, but a good mess. A mind's room, full of toppling books, squares of bright white paper. Over the fireplace (cold, never lit) a print, something classical like a Greek torso, the fine line topography of Michelangelo's *David*. A few pieces of plaster, three-dimensional anatomical bric-a-brac on the mantel. A cheap wooden table in the window, bistro candle, and DON'T FUCK WITH THE QUEEN in ornate script on a chipped coffee cup.

Will we have dinner? No, my flight arrived late. Coffee? More comfortable and gets to the point quicker. We chat. I ask him about his life: Is everything okay? He replies that he's busy, but otherwise fine. We chat some more. I say that it's a pleasure to work with him. He replies with the same.

I compliment him, amplifying what I've already said, and he blushes. He returns it, and then some, making me smile. My eyes start to burn, my vision blurs, tears threatening. I sniffle and stand up.

He does as well, and we hug. Hold there. Hold there. Hold there. Then, break—but still close together. Lips close together. The kiss happens. Light, just a grazing of lips. I can tell he wants more, but I'm uncomfortable and break it, but not so uncomfortable that I can't kiss his cheeks. Right, then left, then right again.

But his head turns and we're kissing, lips to lips again. Does he open his first or do I? Sometimes I imagine his, sometimes mine. But they are open and we are kissing, lips and tongue, together. Hot, wet, hard.

But not on my part. Wet, definitely—in my mind it's a good kiss. A generous and loving kiss. Hot, absolutely, but only in a matter of degrees as his temperature rises and mine does in basic body response.

Not hard on my part, but I am aware of his. Between us, like a finger shoved through a hole in his pocket, something solid and muscular below his waist.

Does he say something? "I want you," "Please touch me," "I'm sorry," are candidates. I've tried them all out, one time or another, to add different flavors, essences, spices to that evening. "I want you," for basic primal sex. "Please touch me," for polite request, respect, and sympathy. "I'm sorry," for wanting something he knows I don't.

"It's okay," I say to all of them, and it is. Not just words. Understanding, sympathy, generosity. All of them, glowing in my mind. It really is okay.

I'm a pornographer, dammit. I should be able to go on with the next part of this story without feeling like . . . I'm laughing right now, not that you can tell. An ironic chuckle: a pornographer unable to write about sex. Not that I can't write about myself, not that making who I am—really—the center of the action is uncomfortable, because I've certainly done that before. I've exposed myself on the page so many other times. What makes this one so different?

Just do it. Put the words down and debate them later. After all, that's what we're here for, aren't we? You want to hear what I dream he and I do together. You want to look over my mental shoulder at two men in that tiny apartment in Seattle.

I'm a writer; it's what I do, and more important, what I am. So we sit on the couch, he in the corner and me in the middle. His hand is on my leg. My back is tight, my thighs are corded. Doubt shades his face so I put my own hand on his own, equally tight, thigh. I repeat what I said before, meaning it: "It's okay."

We kiss again. A friend's kiss, a two-people-who-like-each-other kiss. His hands touch my chest, feeling me through the thin cloth of turtleneck. I pull the fabric out of my pants with a few quick tugs, allowing bare hands to touch bare chest. He likes it, grinning up at me. I send my own grin, trying to relax.

His hand strokes me though my jeans, and eventually I do get hard. His smile becomes deeper, more sincere, lit by his excitement. It's one thing to say it, quite another for your body to say it. Flesh doesn't lie, and I might have when I gave permission. My cock getting hard, though, is obvious tissue and blood sincerity.

"That's nice," "Can I take it out?" "I hope you're alright with this." Basic primal sex, a polite request including respect and sympathy, and the words for wanting something he knows I don't—any one of them added more depth to this dream.

My cock is out and, because he's excited or simply doesn't want the moment and my body to possibly get away, he is sucking me. Was that so hard to say? It's just sex. Just the mechanics of arousal, the engineering of erotica. Cock A in mouth B. I've written it hundreds of times. But there's that difference again, like by writing it, putting it down on paper (or a computer screen) has turned diamond into glass, mahogany into plywood.

Cheapened. That's the word. But to repeat: I am a writer. It's what I do. All the time. Even about love—especially about this kind of love.

He sucks my cock. Not like that, not that, not the way you're thinking: not porno sucking, not erotica sucking. This is connection, he to I. The speech of sex, blowjob as vocabulary.

I stay hard. What does this mean? It puzzles me, even in the fantasy. I have no doubts about my sexuality. I am straight. I write everything else, but I am a straight boy. I like girls. Men do not turn me on.

Yet, in my mind in that little apartment, I am hard. Not "like a rock," not "as steel," not "as a telephone pole," but hard enough while his mouth, lips, and tongue—an echoing hard, wet and hard—work on me.

The answer is clear and sharp, because if I couldn't get hard and stay hard then he'd be hurt and the scene would shadow, chill, and things would be weighted between us. That's not the point of this dream, why I think about it.

So, on to sex. Nothing great or grand, nothing from every section of the menu. A simple action between two men who care about each other: he sucks my cock. He enjoys it and I love him enough to let him. That's all we do, because it's enough.

He sucks me for long minutes, making sweet sounds, and I feel like crying. He puts his hand down his own pants, puts a hand around his own cock. For a moment I think about asking him if he wants help, for me to put my hand around him, help him jerk off. But I don't. Not because I don't want to, or because I'm disgusted, but because he seems to be enjoying himself so much, so delighted in the act of sucking me, that I don't want to break the spell, turn that couch back into a pumpkin.

He comes, a deep groan around my cock, humming me into near-giggles. He stops sucking as he gasps and sighs with release, looking up at me with wet-painted lips, eyes out of focus. I bend down and kiss him, not tasting anything but warm water.

I love him. I wanted to thank him. I hope, within this dream, I have. The night that didn't happen but could have.

For me, writing is just about everything: the joy of right word following right word all the way to the end. The ecstasy of elegant plot, the pleasure of flowing dialogue, the loveliness of perfect description. Sex is good, sex is wonderful, but story is fireworks in my brain. The reason I live. The greatest pleasure in my life.

And he has given me that, with nearly flowing letters on an agreement between his company and me, between his faith in my ability and myself. He looked at me, exposed on the page of a book, in the chapter of a novel, in the lines of a short story, and didn't laugh, didn't dismiss or reject. He read, nodded, smiled, and agreed to publish.

Sex cannot measure up to that. Bodies are bodies, but he has given me a pleasure beyond anything I'd felt: applause, and a chance to do much, much more with words, with stories.

He doesn't have a name, this man in my fantasy. There have been a lot of them over the years, and will be a lot more in the future, no doubt. Gay men who have touched me in ways no one has ever touched me before, by making love with my soul through their support of my writing. Each time they have, this fantasy has emerged from the back of my mind, a need to give them the gift they have given me: passion and kindness, support and caring, and pure affection.

I worry about this. I worry that they won't understand, take this secret dream of mine as being patronizing, diminishing them to nothing but a being with a cock who craved more cock. I've confessed a few times, telling a select few how I feel about them, how I wish I could do for them what they have done for me, to be able to put aside my heterosexuality for just an evening, an afternoon, and share total affection together.

Luckily, or maybe there really isn't anything to worry about, the ones I've told smile, hold my hand, kiss my cheek, say the right thing, and to this day, even right now, make me cry: "I wish we could too, but I understand. I love you too."

Am I bi? I know I'm physically not—I simply don't get aroused by men—but that doesn't mean I don't adore men: the ones I care about, the men who have touched my soul through their support and affection for my stories and writing, I wish I could change. More than anything I wish I could give them some of what what they've given me.

With a cock or a pen, with a story or hours of wonderful sex, it all comes down to one thing: love.

Six Inches of Separation

WILLIAM SWARTZ WAS determinedly fucking Todd Brewster on the big, thick-legged table in the main room of the Men's Club. His thick cock slid in and out of Todd Brewster's greased asshole like the cylinder on some thunderous, powerful locomotive: chug, chug, chug, chug, in, out, in, out.

Thick drops of grease plopped down onto the raw cement floor with every pull back, a slithering, smacking, suction echoed through the tiled bathhouse with every thrust in.

William Swartz's body was doing the determined fucking, but his mind was back at the office, still burning, still blistered from Old Man McAllister's chewing him out. His boss's face, slack jowls and eyes like thumbs pressed into fresh dough, hung in from of him. He wished it was his saggy face he was hammering his iron dick into. It wasn't his fault, after all, that their shipment of medium-sized, inlayed Japanese puzzle boxes was late. The rest were coming in, for Christ's sake—maybe not in time for the scheduled delivery to Pier 1, but it wasn't like they were going to lose them as clients or anything. Hell, they'd accepted partial orders before without bitching.

It was just like McAllister to notice that one fucking glitch in Bill's otherwise well-run department, and to use it as an excuse to question his entire job performance. One little fucking problem and twelve years of good work out the fucking window.

It made him feel small, like a boy, to be treated like that. He didn't like that. Didn't like it at all. It had taken him forty years of hard work to become a man, and a man he wanted to stay for the rest of his life. He worked out to build up manly muscles, he fucked and didn't get fucked, he got sucked but never sucked, he ate steak, he never cried—even when he wanted to, when he ached to. Sure, he wanted to punch McAllister in the face, but he also wanted to reach out, his big hands on his loose, flabby face; lift his head; stare into his eyes. Why can't I ever be good enough for you? he wanted to say. Crying, he wanted to say it.

William Swartz's orgasm came around his blind side, his rage and frustration like static on the channel of his fucking, the slick and tight grip of Todd Brewster's asshole around his cock. When Bill came, it was a dull jolt of pleasure—more a thudding kick to his balls than a voltage scream of joy. Rather than screaming, he simply grunted out the thick cream of come into Brewster's ass. As he came he felt good, but as he came he knew it could have felt even better—but for a man like himself, that was as good as it was going to get.

xxx

TODD BREWSTER WAS being energetically fucked by William Swartz on the big, thick-legged table in the main room of the Men's Club. As the stranger's dick plopped and slurped into his asshole, Todd sucked the cock of Steven Reineer. Todd was sucking exactly the way he loved to suck, as if his whole being was doing the sucking, not just lips and tongue, but rather a soul suck, a deep self suck. Sucking like this, Todd's mind faded, skipped somewhere close to a dream. Impressions and images danced through him as he worked Steven's big cock: half thoughts, wildly associated memories.

Standing on the street corner. Standing on the street corner near the Castro. Sunlight, like a big, warm hand cradling his face. A good day. A day of birdsong and smiles, of sweet words and held hands. A day for picnics. A day for barefoot walks through the grass.

A day to look at the world, to admire it. To see the everyday beauty that so often gets pushed aside in the rush from point A to point B.

A day to fall in love. Just like that—with the snap of fingers. Standing on the street corner, waiting for love to come, he saw the young man: tight jeans, black boots, tight white T-shirt. He fell in love. He fell immediately in love, absolutely in love. He wanted to kiss this young man. He wanted to hold his hand. He wanted to take barefoot walks with him. He wanted to suck his sock. He wanted to bake a cake for him.

But then his beloved turned, looked at Todd looking at him and said: "What you looking at, faggot?" The young man made fists, moved toward Todd with intent. Todd had turned, ran off— all the way down the street, away from the Castro, back to his apartment. His cold, dark little basement in the Mission.

Being fucked by William Swartz on the big, thick-legged table in the main room of the Men's Club, sucking Steven Reineer's dick, Todd just wanted someone to look at him, smile, and take his hand.

xxx

AS TODD BREWSTER was being rhythmically fucked by William Swartz, Todd sucked the cock of Steven Reineer. Steven was into the suck, as deep and soulfully into a suck as a man could get, in fact. It was a great suck, a spiritual suck—more so for Steven than perhaps for any other man in the main room of the Men's Club that night. It was a suck, and a night, he'd waited just about his whole life for.

He was getting his dick sucked in a room full of men getting their dicks sucked. The air smelled of sweat, of come, of wet leather; of steaming piss; the earthy musk of shit; the metal tweaking smell of poppers; the sticky, sweet smell of pot; the vacation smell of hot rubber, of latex partially melted, of friction heat; it even smelled of pennies, of spilled blood somewhere. It smelled the way he'd always hoped it would smell, and much more—a thousand olfactory surprises, presents of new aromas with every fresh, deep breath.

And the sights—the sights were images he'd take with him the rest of his life: getting sucked by an alabaster young man, who, in turn, was being determinedly, energetically, rhythmically fucked by a great hulking, muscular brute of a man—a flesh and bone fucking engine. In one corner, a bald boy—a punk with polished skin and too many silver rings in his ears to count, was kneeling, sucking an elegant silver-haired black man. In the other, a couple were holding each other, an exhausted pietà, no marble but shimmering sweat making them looked carved from smooth stone. Others, too many to see except for quick takes, were half-impressions—sections of a mosaic of a Saturday night at the baths, put together all around him to make a beautiful, wonderful, picture.

"May I?" Toby Jillian said, reaching around from behind Steven Reineer, thumbs and forefingers rubbing inches in front of Steven's tight nipples.

"You may," Steven Reineer said to Toby Jillian—and so Toby Jillian started to play with Steven Reineer's nipples as he was cosmically sucked by Todd Brewster, who, in turn, was being determinedly, energetically, rhythmically fucked by William Swartz.

This night, this place. Ever since he looked at his first boy and hoped—by the looking and the thoughts that came along with the looking, as well as the hard-on that came with the thoughts and the looking—that these kind of places existed: a place of men, of naked men, of hard men, of hard men being hard together. A place of men and men sex.

Getting older, doing more than just looking at other boys, he read, he asked, he looked and found out that they did exist, these places where men, naked men, were hard together. With that confirmation his home of cornfields and tractors, of fertilizer and of the seasons as gods, became so much smaller.

It had taken him years of corn fields and tractors, of fertilizer and worshipping the gods of winter, summer, spring, and fall before he'd had enough to escape. Years before he'd left it all behind to hitch a ride with a truck driver heading west—all the way west.

Years before, he'd come with that one truck driver to this town, to this place, this night—the night when he could finally walk in and be a part of a room full of naked men, doing naked things together.

That other place was where Steven Reineer had been born, where he went to school, where he kissed his first boy, but the instant he walked into the Men's Club, he knew that in this place, and doing these things, he was finally home.

XXX

PLAYING WITH STEVEN Reineer's nipples as Steven Reineer was being cosmically sucked by Todd Brewster, who, in turn, was being determinedly, energetically, rhythmically fucked by William Swartz, Toby Jillian smiled sweetly to himself. This was good, this was very good. This was just about as good as it could get. He was playing with a handsome little guy's nipples.

Not that he was gay or anything. He just liked nipples. Guy nipples. He really didn't know where it had started. But it was there, nonetheless. Some men cruised for tits, others for asses, still others for legs—but Toby looked for a good flat chest, a plane of tight muscles. Flat was too busty for him. He liked toughness, muscles and bones, not soft skin.

Not that he was gay—he just liked them firm, hard, tough, strong.

Women came close . . . sometimes, but it was never enough. And so Toby went out, hunting down the best nipples and chests he could. He went to places like the Men's Club, where he'd ask—politely, mind you—to touch, to fondle, to kiss, to lick, to nibble. Like tonight, standing behind Steven Reineer while he was getting sucked by Todd Brewster, who was then being fucked by William Swartz.

Nipples, any nipples, in his hands were great. Nipples like these, right then, were even better. Down below, he could feel his cock swell and strain, push against his briefs, tenting the fabric with his good time. It felt good, it felt damned good. The nipples between his thumb and forefinger were tight, hard, with just the right ring of fine hairs around the areola. Twirling them, tugging at the nipples was like a cord, a rope between fingers and nipples and his hardening cock. Each pull, each tug, each caress of the rubbery flesh was like a stroke of his dick. The connection was base, primal, and powerful.

If he stopped to think about it, which he only did when his cock was full and hard and beaded with a pearl of liquid, salty, bitter excitement, he may have been able to trace it out: beginning to today, then, playing with Steven Reineer tight, rubbery nipples. The feeling of a warm sun on his bare shoulders. A Saturday kind of day—which is what it was—a summer Saturday when the only thing anyone, anywhere was supposed to do was go swimming. So, there at the huge public swimming pool, old enough to have feelings, too young to know just what those feelings were, he watched the young lifeguard walk down the rough concrete edge of the pool, chest a solid geometry of muscles, and there—aggressive, tempting, strong, certain—were his nipples: The nipples to end all nipples, the nipples that were the start of his pursuit, the founders of his quest. But he really wasn't thinking about those two nipples today. No, he was too much into Steven Reineer's nipples, and the thudding, hammering horniness they conjured up.

Despite himself, Toby groaned, deep and operatic as his cock swelled and pushed away from himself, like an arrow pulled by the bow, straining to launch itself out, away, toward anything and anyone, but more importantly in the direction of a wonderful, definitive, thudding orgasm. Then something deep inside himself, something coiled around his balls, snaking all the way up his spine into the dim parts of his hidden mind, let go of the bow, and with a shake, a quake, a shudder, and a small scream he did, right then, in his shorts, come—and it was good, so good, so damned good.

Not that he was gay or anything.

XXX

WATCHING TOBY JILLIAN play with Steven Reineer's nipples as Steven Reineer was being profoundly sucked by Todd Brewster, who, in turn, was being relentlessly screwed by William Swartz, Jack Sawtell had one, just one, thought: Here I go again. He was in love.

To be honest, Jack fell in love quite easily. Checking out boys, cab drivers, salesmen, strangers on the street, inappropriate relatives, total strangers without even the barest of social contexts, Jack looked, and fell fast and hard.

Standing just off to the side of the groaning, heaving, working, sweating, steaming tableau of queer bliss, he looked at Toby Jillian and felt himself fall down the long, slippery slope. Looking at Toby, he wanted to kiss him—to touch lip to lip, dance tongues, breath each others' breaths—and he wanted to touch him—to slide his hands down his taut chest and have the other man do the same to him—and he wanted to fuck him—to slide his cock deep, in and out, in and out—and he wanted to be fucked by him—to have him fuck his own asshole until he cried and begged and screamed for him to stop, but always hoped he wouldn't.

Jack was in love, and it felt good. He watched Toby Jillian play with Steven Reineer's nipples as Steven Reineer was being wonderfully sucked by Todd Brewster, who, in turn, was being dynamically screwed by William Swartz, and Jack felt the same way he always felt when he fell in love—that all was right with the world and it would all work out well.

But then, as always happened when Jack Sawtell fell in love, he woke up. He was in another bathhouse, watching other men have all the fun, while he stood there with his cock in his hand. As with every time he fell in love, he remembered the beauty and perfection of his first boyfriend, who had left him—long ago and far away. It had been more than good, it had been wonderful, but then it had ended. It wasn't the ending so much, but what had been spoken, a curse that shadowed Jack Sawtell every day, because every day he fell in love.

Walking out, leaving, his boyfriend had turned and said, "Yeah, you might fall for someone else, but you'll always think of me—because I'm your first."

Standing there, sadness laying heavy on him, wilting dick in his hand, Jack Sawtell watched Toby Jillian play with Steven Reineer's nipples as Steven Reineer was being gloriously sucked by Todd Brewster, who, in turn, was being poundingly fucked by William Swartz, and Jack felt the same way he always felt when he realized that no matter how much, how often, he fell in love, he'd always think of the beautiful bastard who walked away, and said those cruel words that still haunted him.

XXX

PETER LOWELL STOOD by the door, watching Jack Sawtell look longingly at Toby Jillian playing with Steven Reineer's nipples as Steven Reineer was being miraculously sucked by Todd Brewster, who, in turn, was being beautifully fucked by William Swartz.

Peter watched Jack. There was something beautiful in the way Jack Sawtell stood there, watching Toby Jillian tweak Steven Reineer's nipples as Steve Reineer was, in turn, blown by Todd Brewster, who, in turn, was being fucked by William Swartz.

In the whole room, in the whole of the Men's Club, there was nothing quite so lovely as that handsome young man standing there, watching, entranced.

There was something about him. Something in the way he stood, in the exact way he watched the men suck, fuck, and all the rest. He was excited, his semi-hard cock was proof of that—and what a handsome cock it was too—but there was something else. Something lost, like a little boy who was the last to get picked for playing ball, like the kid who never got a valentine. He was standing right there in the room, but he also seemed to be miles away.

Looking at Jack Sawtell, Peter Lowell remembered another young man, standing lost and alone in a place like this one. He remembered the way he wanted to join in, wanted to just step up and become one with the group, but for some reason felt lost and alone—too much old baggage dragging him back, holding him in place. He remembered how someone, completely out of the blue, had walked up to him, took him by the hand and brought him in, made him feel welcome. The memory was as fresh as yesterday morning: the heat but also the chill at standing outside of it all, the way the older man had walked up, put his rough hand on his, and said five brief words. After that Peter had been inside, part of it all. He owed that older man a lot, a debt he was still repaying. Taking a slow, deep breath he walked across the floor toward where Jack Sawtell gazed at Toby Jillian playing with Steven Reineer's nipples as Steven Reineer was being elegantly blown by Todd Brewster, who, in turn, was being bestially fucked by William Swartz.

He didn't know what exactly he'd say to the slightly sad young man, but he knew it would be very similar to what he'd been asked so long ago. If he was lucky then they'd have a good time—and if they were very lucky, who knows where it could lead?

Love, Peter Lowell, had discovered, can be found in all kinds of places.

XXX

INTO THE REST of the night and into the very late morning they all played: Peter Lowell, Jack Sawtell, Toby Jillian, Steven Reineer, Todd Brewster, William Swartz, and many others. Some of them had good times, some of them had great times, some of them had okay times, some of them had bad times—as many kinds of times as there were men in the club that night.

In more than one way they were connected. With cock, mouth, hand, asshole, fist, and all the rest to be sure, but in other ways as well: a structure of happenstance and coincidence, luck and synchronicity—a web as complex as the men in the club that night.

The older man who had helped Peter Lowell become part of the party rather than just a spectator was the same lover who had hurt Jack Sawtell so long ago, who'd also been a lifeguard back in the small town where Toby Jillian had grown up, who'd given Steven Reineer a ride to the big city, who'd made a clumsy pass at the little skinhead creep who'd insulted Todd Brewster, and who'd been late delivering William Swartz's delivery.

Six men in the club that night, joined in bliss in many ways.

Moby

YESSIR, THE GOOD folks around these here parts are particularly struck by the telling of a good tale. Some like to say that it's 'cause we've not—how shall I say—"misplaced" how to sit a feller down and spin out a damned good yarn. Others though, they like to gesture toward those there damned high and awfully wooded peaks and say that it's got more to do with the fact we all got shit-poor TV reception.

Like any collection of folks—that is, folks who knows how to put the right collection of words together to spin out a handsome yarn, or got more than snow on the local tube—we've got a few we like to tell a bit more than others. Like the one about how Old Uncle Conti done helped Miss Oleander birth her seven little young ones in the middle of that awful thunder-and-lightning show we had back in '60. Or that time Crazy Jeb got too big a taste of the shine and went on his rather reckless excursion with Huge Henry, Mr. Larkin's bulldozer. Or even when Crazy Jeb at the Dry Goods found himself at the business end of a shotgun in the hands of that no-good eldest Barnaby boy, and how he done turned the tails on that no-account without being able to see his wrinkled old hand in front of his dead-blind eyes.

But there's no one we like to chew the fat about more than that Beast of the Highway, our Monster of the Road, the Legendary Creature of the Blacktop.

Yeah, that's him, that's the man—if "man" could be quite the word to describe him. It'd be more accurate to call him a force of nature, or like a tiger someone done educated enough to stand up on his hind legs, a cyclone wearing size-sixteen boots, a motorcycle-riding fiend from the deepest, darkest depths of your wildest nightmares. That's Moby.

Moby, we like to say, ain't just big, 'cause that makes anyone who'd never had . . . funny, but I was just about to say "the honor to see him," but you know that sure is not right, 'cause anyone who done see Moby sure as shit did not call it anything like an "honor." No sir. But anyone who has laid eyes on him would have to say that "big" just ain't the right word. Three little letters just ain't enough to describe the heights of the man. They say—and I can neither agree with such nor deny, for I've never seen such a thing myself—that Moby ducks his head so as not to hit the sun hanging low on its way to setting. And that he's able to reach up and tie a peaceful-looking cloud into a righteous twister with just the twirling of his finger. Yeah, I know, that's tall for even a tall tale, but I'll tell you, friend, I have seen Moby myself and I cannot only say that it was not any honor, but that he's taller than even the tallest tale I or anyone else could ever tell.

Another thing that people who meet the Hog Rider from Hell say about him is—well, how could I say this, being we are in polite company? Let me put it this way, the man has a "presence" that announces his imminent arrival even before the ground starts to do its shake and shimmy from his size-sixteens crushing down on the hardest packed asphalt, crushing good cement to powder, cracking stones like walnuts. Moby—and to be right straight with you there really ain't no way to say this and retain civility—has a hellish fragrance. Wherever he rides, he leaves a rooster tail of reek, a hurricane of stink, a billowing cloud of stench. I've heard it described in all kinds of ways, from the sweat off a bull's balls— and I did say there was no polite way to say it—to May Tilly's septic tank on a hot Saturday afternoon in the middle of summer. And if you know the kind of seasons we have in these here parts, and if you know May Tilly, you would know that Moby's truly a hideous proposition in regards to fiendish aromas.

The only thing said to be more potent than Moby's emissions is the strength that courses through the big-ass muscles that you can see knotting and cording around his mountainous biceps and hydraulic thighs. Some say that he's strong enough to bend quarters twice, making two bits into four bits, just between thumb and forefinger. Others like to point out how he parks that roaring hog of his: no backing and forwarding for Moby, no sir. Instead, the biggest of the big and strongest of the strong finds himself the perfect old spot to put his chrome and grease-dripping machine, and he just lifts it up in one brawny hand and drops it down right where he wants it—and what with the power of those arms and that stink, it's just about anywhere he reckons to.

Now Moby, he's quite a lot of other things—more even than his size, his aroma, or his brawn—but those are what you might call other kinds of observances, less on the great list that is tales that folks like to tell about the biker. But there's another thing about Moby that's right there up on the top, even greater than his cloud-rippling height, his eye-watering stink, or his ground-shaking muscles. But for that one I've got to give you a little bit more than some homespun metaphors and back-porch similes. For that I've got to sit you right down—you comfy now?—and spin you a downright special tale, the one I like to tell more than any other about that leather monster, that motorbike hurricane, that beast on two tires.

For that I've got to tell of the time Moby came barreling down to our sleepy little town, needle tapping out a high-octane, fuel-injected rhythm against the top of his speedometer, rumbling engine like the four-stroke from hell. Fast? He was way more than fast, friend. You could even say he'd just left *fast* way behind, past blasting through *quick*, leaving *breakneck* in his dust.

That day is the one I'm talking about. The day he come through—and the day a certain officer of this here municipality decided that he'd had quite enough of this hog-riding, quarter-folding, reeking tower of a man. That, you see, was the day he decided to give Moby a speeding ticket.

Who knows why he done it? When we get just a smelliest bit tired of telling tales about Moby, someone or other will bring up that day, ponder over some shine and a smoke, just what did possess that certain Officer Langtry to take it into his head to bang his own motorcycle to life and take off in pursuit of the demon. Jeb over at the old Wicker place likes to say that the sun that day must have cooked his brains into something that may very well have resembled grits, while Miss Barlow is more akin to the theory that the only thing that could explain the whys and wherefores of that pursuit of Moby is that Langtry's family tree must have had some very shallow roots.

They say what they say, friend, but I can tell you for a fact that no one, least of all that officer of the law, knows quite why he did it. But he did it—he sure as hell did it.

Right up there with the whys and wherefores of Officer Langtry's darned earnest pursuit has to be another important element to this tale of his meeting with the Moby—in other words, why in the heavens above and hell below did that Harley Davidson maelstrom look behind, clearly see the flashings and the wailings of the law behind him, pull over, and—puzzle of mysteries, strangeness of weirdness—*stop*?

But he did. He did. Right over there, in fact, at the fork where the main thoroughfare curls off toward River Road, by that very same gnarled old pine. That's just where Moby glided that chrome-and-grease machine to the side of the road.

Who could say what Officer Langtry thought when that happened? More than likely a sense of some kind of professional satisfaction that it was his lights and his siren that did what no one else had done. That his own bike, his own authority, had reached out to the bad craziness that was Moby and reined in that wild biker bull. But just as there was a smile on his handsome young face, you have got to know that riding right along with him was more than a bit of the old stomach-clenching, jaw-tightening thing you and me and everyone on this whole darned world call *fear*.

But Langtry was *Officer* Langtry, more than he was young and handsome, and for him that was enough to relax that jaw, calm that stomach, and steady his racing heart. He had his badge, the authority invested to him by his good little town, this right honorable state, and this glorious nation—and he wasn't going to let no legend, no big, smelly, or even strong biker blast through his quiet little world without paying the price for his reckless disregard for those laws of town, state, and country.

And with that authority in him like a good belt of something smoky and well aged, but with a kick like a mule who woke up on the wrong side of the barn, he glided his own two wheels up next to the biker, killed the engine with a quick twist of the wrist, and dismounted.

It would be honest to say that, at that moment in his young life on this planet Earth spinning through space, that officer of this here town, state, and good ol' wonderful country, and even with the badge and nifty uniform, and let's not forget that pearl-handled, brushed chrome Smith and Wesson dangling there at his hip, Officer Langtry couldn't have been more terrified. This was Moby, people, and don't you forget it. His rough-hewn brows parted the clouds all up on high, tufts of them vanishing like the steam over the old sawmill the day they shut it down. His hellacious aroma curled every single nose hair in the vicinity and caused more than a few pigeons to drop from that summer sky in shock as he climbed off of his grease-glimmering motorcycle. It is said by more than just me, your humble storyteller, that there is nothing more important to Moby—not putting the fear of hideous death in the minds of the citizens of this region, not the destruction of road and all wildlife foolish enough to attempt to cross it, not . . . other even more fiendish activities I will not even dare to mention for there are ladies here at present—than that motorcycle. And so to put it aside from even the most casual of damage—heaven help anyone who would do such a thing—he demonstrated another of his Moby attributes and lifted it up off the ground with one mighty flex of an arm and put it down as neatly as a mother putting her youngest to bed.

Fear or no fear, terror or no terror, dread or no dread, Officer Langtry of the Town Constabulary was invested with all the powers of the previously mentioned town, state, and wonderful country, and as such he had a duty to perform, a higher order if you will, a task that no one in the history of this town, this state, or even this here country had even managed to accomplish: He had to give the dreaded hog-driving Beast of the End Times a ticket, and that's what he was going to do.

And doing such, there was, shall we say, "rituals" that were necessary to accomplish the giving of a Motorvehicular Citation for Excessive Velocity on a Municipal Thoroughfare, payable to the officer himself or via the local courthouse, and Officer Langtry wasn't about to simply shake in his boots (even though he was) and twitch his hands (even though they were) and just, simply, only hand the huge, smelly, strong biker a traffic ticket.

And so, even through his shaking and twitching, hoping the fear he felt did not leak out through his manner of speaking, Officer Langtry walked forward, stuck his thumbs in the belt loops of his uniform pants, and said in his best law-enforcement parlance, "Do you have any idea of how fast you were going?" I should mention to all of you that to complete the aforementioned ritual correctly, there is the insertion of a word at the end of that there sentence to fully convey to the perpetrator to whom a law-enforcement officer is speaking, and that they are truly in the presence of a formidable authority figure. But while Officer Langtry had those many levels of authority—and I will not try your patience by reciting town, state, and country once again—he was still in the looming, mountainous, aromatic, Herculean, and smelly presence of Moby and so, possibly wisely, did not conclude his statement of "Do you have any idea of how fast you were going?" with the word "boy."

To this, and to the absence of the word so often used by members of the law-enforcement community, Moby replied with stony silence.

"Well, I'll tell you how fast you were going," Officer Langtry continued. "You were in excess of the posted limit by more than fifteen miles per hour. That's breaking the law, and there are penalties for the breaking of our laws. Harsh penalties, some might say."

To this additional commentary from Officer Langtry, Moby also did not reply.

"I say that no penalty is too damned harsh that'll keep the streets of our fair city safe from reckless no-goods like yourself who seem to think that every road is their road, or that stop signs are just a suggestion."

Again, there was only tall, strong, stinky quiet from Moby.

"That's right, you heard what I said. I opened this here mouth and called you a 'no-good,' and by the Lord above and the laws of this fine town, noble state, and great country, I stand by that statement, because, Mister, I can tell just by laying eyes on you that I may in fact have been more than necessarily polite in my description."

Moby only repeated his silence, eyes showing nothing but a steely glimmer.

Now my more perceptive listeners might be thinking that our Officer Langtry might be more than slightly putting his size-twelve official shoes over the line between what a law-enforcement officer should be saying and what any person who knows of the biker called Moby would say. In this I would have to say that those who are thinking such thoughts are completely right in wondering such, for even Officer Langtry himself was no doubt engaged in the back of his brain wondering just such. But the words were there, coming out before he could even stop himself, one after another like bubbles coming up from a glass of cool beer, and just like you can't put your finger through the foam and stop them from coming up to the top, neither could Officer Langtry stop himself from saying the things he had wanted to say, and probably many folks have wanted to say to that monster of the motorbike, for a good many years.

"Just look at yourself, son. Take a damned long, hard look at yourself. You call yourself a man? A beast, more like. Big, sure as shit you're big. Strong—that too. Muscles all rippling and moving under that tight denim vest, calves like tree trunks under those jeans, chest like mom's old washboard, hands the size of one of Old Mrs. Gator's prize sows. And the stink—Lordy, don't get me started on your foul emissions. That's the worst of all, I say; the bottom of the barrel. Get rid of the reek—and once again I can only think of one of Old Mrs. Gator's hogs—and you might, and I do say 'might,' come out the other end of such scrubbing and cleanliness to be a halfway respectable sample of . . . masculinity."

Moby stayed quiet as an owl flying across a deep night sky, but while he did not say anything, his face spoke through the raising of one eyebrow.

"It's not too late, son. You're still not on the other side of that hill. You could be something, do something with your life aside from pissing people off and scaring the local inhabitants. Clean yourself up some, get yourself some kind of respectable form of transportation, settle down with some . . . girl, I guess. Do you really want to go on down the road you've been driving, end up in jail for the rest of your years or maybe dead on the side of the road somewhere, like some stinking skunk too slow or dumb to get out of the way of two pair of radials?"

Nothing again from the biker, nothing but stone silence. But his hands, great monster mitts with fingers the size of extra large sausages made from the best of Old Mrs. Gator's prize pigs, dropped down to his waist.

"Hold it right there, son—you just hold it right there. No sudden movements now. You keep your hands right where I can see them or you're going to find out, right personally, just how fast I can draw this here gun and put a .38 slug right in your well-defined chest."

But Moby did not stop, not at all, and all the time he did not speak as he did not stop. Hands to his waist, thick, beefy fingers forward, a twist of the thumb to push aside a narrow strip of road-filthy denim, then a pinch of zipper and down.

Down, as they say, and out.

"Smelly," it has been said—by myself as well as many others who like to talk about the biker known as Moby—is the stink that follows, making even the foulest smelling of creatures run for cover. "Strong," it has been stated, like a bear, like a bull, like a four-by-four truck, a locomotive, and any other thing that might come to mind when you think about things that can lift, push, or pull really heavy things. "Big" has also been mentioned: that when he walked, birds and light aircraft have known to move out of the way of his towering immensity, that his shadow has been known to fall across county after county stretching far out yonder.

But I have yet to hear anyone else talk about Moby's . . . "manliness."

There's no other way to say it, ladies and gentlemen, and so I have to beg your humble apologies for having to be so blunt about such matters, but there really is no way to continue to tell this tale of Moby and Officer Langtry without using words that will no doubt offend some of you with their coarseness. I shall put my all into trying to use some terminology that will, shall I say, singe rather than burn the ears of some of my more sensitive listeners. To remove the shock of such words long before they happen to appear in the telling of this tale, I am going to put them out into the air right this very moment. You all ready now? Prepared and cautioned enough for this? Well, then, here you go:

in regards to the part of Moby that hangs well below his knees, I shall call it his . . . *privates* (because that part of a man is just that), *willy* (because I had a pal by that name), *old friend* (because I dare you to find a man who doesn't feel at least that fondly for that part of himself), *dick* (because I had another pal with that name), *manliness* (as I said before), and *penis* (because that's what it is).

And there it was, right in front of Officer Langtry on that warm summer day. In all its . . . well, now, I was about to use the word "glory," but that's not exactly an accurate description of that there biker's privates.

Because, good listener, this intimate part of Moby's anatomy reflects much of what we've all learned about the man, and none of that anyone, least of all myself, would call by that churchlike word, "glorious."

See, upon the opening of those greasy, torn-up jeans a powerful reek of oil, sweat, farts, and other rank body emissions wafted forth, befouling the otherwise ordinary scent of that day. Like an animal in rut he was, with that kind of aroma flowing out of his pants and up into the atmosphere.

Then there was that other aspect of the man—the muscles and lifting, the sinews and strength, the brawn and potency, that were reflected in that awesome willy. Men know that sometimes the spirit may be ready to perform its duties but the flesh may be more than occasionally drunk and weak, but not for that biker, and definitely not that day.

Now, if I were a coarse gentleman, not one of a refined disposition and the like, I would stroll off into perhaps a bit overly long description of the biker's manhood, going into some too-exact details such as how the veins along the length of it pulsed and quivered with primal juices of pure animal lust, or how the end was as big and hard as the ball on top of the flagpole in front of our beloved town hall, or how the entire flashy assemblage seemed to be as long and as steely hard as that very same flagpole. Or maybe I'd mention, casual like, how from the tip of that mighty manliness a gleaming bead of anticipatory emissions had started to form. But, like I said and continue to defend, I am not a coarse or rude man so I won't be saying any such thing.

Then there was the fact that, like the man himself, Moby's . . . extension was just such a thing. Big, you see, doesn't touch on the immensity of the organ that emerged from the man's fly. If you think of such things, kind of ponder how big something like that could get, I can bet you dollars to donuts that you will not even come close to the prodigious measurements of that man. After all, he is not called "Moby" for just the whale of his size, but rather the whale size of the last part of his particular moniker, the word that follows Moby. I speak, of course, of "Dick."

Now as to what the long arm of the law thought about the appearance of that certain part of Moby's body . . . well, you could guess and would guess right that the man was rightfully shocked by the accusing arm of the biker's privates, jutting out at him from his fly. So, to the appearance and the appurtenance's owner, Officer Langtry—an arm himself of the law, which he hoped then and there was bigger than the penis of the dreaded Moby—coughed quickly and managed to sputter out, "You p-put that thing away right now, son, or I'll have your ass rotting in jail before you can say fucking 'Jack Robinson.'"

To this Moby maintained nothing but stony silence, though he did move, just a bit, to wrap one of those Mrs. Gator ham-sized fists around the thick length of his dick.

Officer Langtry still managed to say, "Now you stop right there. I'm only going to tell you once, put that damned big . . . hard . . . thing away. You do it right now or you're going to be spending more than just one night in my less-than-comfortable can . . . I mean jail."

Quiet again, no words—not a lone one—from Moby, but the beast did move his fist up and down the length of his old friend, a bright gleam in his nasty eyes.

"I'm telling ya, you put that thing . . . that thing . . . away or

I won't be accountable for what might happen again," Officer Langtry said, licking his suddenly dry lips.

Still not a word from the huge biker, who was still lazily committing the sin of Onan standing out there in broad daylight on the main road.

"Yeah, might not . . . know . . . what could happen," Officer Langtry said, words getting all soft and sensitive-like. Then it happened, folks, the thing that shocked him just as you're going to be shocked by my telling of it. You see, Officer Langtry was one of those fellers who thought he was right with himself, comfortable in the house of his life, you know? He knew just where everything was, and why it was there. His ma and pa, his work, what he liked to do on Saturday nights, his favorite sit-down meal, his favorite stand-up eating, the movies he liked, the tunes he listened to, the books he liked to read—of that, but that sunny summer day, the day he pulled over the biker called Moby, he came to realize that while he knew what went where in the house of his mind, he also came to know, with shock, that there was a whole other room in his house he didn't know existed.

In that room there were two folks, Officer Langtry and Moby. Moby was just as he was there on the road, standing with his dick out, hand around it, but here is the shock—the thing that made that room so much more different than any other room in Officer Langtry's mind. In that room Officer Langtry was on his knees with Moby's penis in his mouth.

Now don't say I didn't warn you—don't you dare say I didn't prepare you for what I definitely said would be a shock. Don't you go opening your eyes all wide or putting on some swoon or other. But I do understand just how much of a remarkable thing this is to hear, and so I'll give you all a bit of time to sort yourselves into a state where you can actually understand what I'm going to be telling next.

Ready? You sure now? Well, then I shall continue.

So there they were, the biker and the cop, the biker with his dick out and all aroused-like, and the cop who wanted nothing more in this big old world than to drop down to his knees and start sucking at that pole of manhood like a calf working his mamma's teat.

Now things would have been great, for the cop that is, for Officer Langtry, if that's what would have happened. Now I'm not one to say what one does for pleasure and all that. I'm what you'd call a churchgoing fellow, but I don't think the Lord above would fault one person for doing something mutual and fun, for the lack of a better word, between himself and even another himself. God is Love, am I right? And love can mean lots of different things to different people. So I'm not saying that what Officer Langtry wanted to do to that big, smelly, strong biker that day was a bad thing. No, sir, I am not saying that. Because I know for a fact, as one man can know anything, that sucking on that man's penis was the only thing in this wide world that Officer Langtry wanted to do at that moment in time and that his desire was good and true and free of any kind of game or cruelty. Officer Langtry, you see, looked into that room he didn't know he'd had in the house of his soul, and he realized that it was a room he wanted to spend a lot more time in, a room of love—even if it was a room of man-with-man love. It was still love.

But what happened next was not love, no sir. In no way. What happened next was the height of cruelty to man, an act of pure mean. This is something else a lot of folks know about the biker called Moby, a thing right up there with his towering height, his awesome strength, and his offensive aroma. You see, beyond all that, Moby is one thing and one thing even more powerful than his muscles, greater than his height, even more overwhelming than his stink.

Moby, you see, is pure mean.

How mean is he? Well, I could go on for hours at a stretch telling you the various and sundry acts of cruelty this man has enacted upon his fellow beings on this globe, but none would say it as well as telling you all what the biker did to Officer Langtry that day, a single action that would hurt that man most of all, rub him down deep in the ground and harm him in ways that no physical injury could ever go.

For, dear listeners, what Moby did that day was to smile his most vile of grins, fold away his hard and pearl-beaded manliness, get on his bike, kick it to life, and thunder off down the highway — leaving Officer Langtry there alone on the side of the road, mouth hanging open for the dick he'd never have, in an act so mean, so cruel, so vile that it was as if someone had taken a righteous bowel movement in the room he'd just that moment discovered within himself.

That's my story, people. That's everything that happened that day between the two of those men, the peace officer and the biker. The honest man who discovered something new about himself, and the biker who was meaner than them most rabid of dogs. I wish I could say that things ended well, but to be honest with you, I can't say such. Officer Langtry, it's true, did discover a new way to spend his Saturday nights, a new kind of physical affection to share with his fellow man, but that day of rejection and humiliation by the side of the road still burns in his soul.

How do I know this? Well, friend, I am pleased to make your pleasant acquaintance. Langtry's the name, Officer of the Local Constabulary. Who, after all, would know such details of that day other than the man himself who was involved?

And Moby? Well, to this day you can see his head towering over the tallest of trees, feel the thunder of his hog as he roars by, smell his deep beastly stink as he passes, and hear his bellowing laugh as he continues on his journey from one cruel and heartless act to another.

Big, strong, reeking, but most of all purely, absolutely, horribly mean, is that biker Moby.

Heart in Your Hand

WHY HIM? WAS what Stan's friends said—or wanted to say—Why, of all people, did he have to start seeing Clint?

Sure, they thought—and mumbled to each other when Stan wasn't around—Clint did have a kind of rugged charm, a hairy mountain-man muscularity that could reach down and pluck your cock and balls like a tight E-string. But there were lots of boys, and men, who did the same or better.

Clint was . . . well, he was more than rough. With a stone-cut chest, a bristle-brush haircut, and a tight, sneering mouth, Clint skirted the edge of being a mean bastard. He was macho, a hard-edged top who never walked off stage. He was tough in the boardroom, in the bedroom, on the street, at the movies, and everywhere in between. Clint wasn't one to buy you flowers—he definitely was one who was more than willing to beat you silly . . . if that was what you were into.

Someone kind, gentle, fun—full of laughter and hot tongue kisses—was who his friends could see Stan with. Not tough-as-nails, ready-with-a-whip Clint.

But, they had to admit, there was something there between them. Sitting in some noisy club, all chat washed away by a thumping top-ten beat, Stan's friends could see, yeah, that there was something connecting the rough-and-tumble Clint and their angelic buddy.

What they didn't see, couldn't see, was what really connected the angel to the leatherman, something that brought equal smiles to such unequal lovers.

XXX

SOMETIMES IT WAS in Stan's little Castro apartment, full of Japanese furniture and black-and-white prints. Sometimes it was in Clint's SoMa loft, full of hard-edged industrial crap and lots of cabinets with lots of toys.

It really didn't matter—especially not to Clint and Stan. But wherever they were, the scene was always the same: it was perfect.

Big, strong, hairy, muscular Clint was on his back, legs like furry tree-trunks spread wide. His asshole, a dull pink pucker, stared out at Stan. Beyond, over the gentle rise of his strong chest, Clint's piercing blue eyes watched.

Stan smiled and ran a finger around Clint's asshole, felt the tight muscles, and smiled even more at the gentle invitation that came when he pressed just-so-slightly downward—the invitation of Clint's asshole opening just a little.

Stan was a traditionalist: stick shortening was at the ready. His hands were small, the fingers elegantly tapering, almost hairless, nails cut very short. Lathering them with a big scoop of the pale greasy stuff, he rubbed a good amount on Clint's gently pulsing sphincter. Pushing some carefully inside with a slow finger, he also rubbed the strong contours of his ass, and even gave a long, strong stroke of Clint's big cock.

The first finger went in easily, like taking a breath—one long finger slowly easing into Clint's ass, feeling around, getting reacquainted with the old territory. Two was also easy, sliding past the tight grip of Clint's asshole to feel the silken contours of his anus. Three was the same, Clint's pucker opening wider and wider to take in Stan's fingers. Foam started to form around the dark opening, and that sweet music of handballing—that slick, slick, slick noise had started to play.

Four was the real start of the dance. At four Clint's tight asshole really started to relax, really started to bloom under

Stan's careful caresses. At four, Clint's dark, muscular hole really opened up and started to admit Stan's fingers in earnest. Not for the first time—because this was far from the first time—Stan was amazed at both the velvet-smoothness of Clint's anus as well as its determined strength. It felt like a hot, heavy, soft weight wrapped around his slowly churning fingers. As always, Stan was aware of how fucking hard he was—but, as always, he was too busy to do anything about it.

In front of him, a flagpole with only a creamy drop of pre-come at it's tip, Clint's stick bobbed back and forth with each new unconscious spasm around Stan's hand. Then, before it seemed either of them knew it, Stan was up to five. He was in. He was in. He was in.

Stan's fist was iron wrapped in a velvet-asshole glove. He could feel the sweet softness of Clint's asshole expand outward, swallowing his fist and allowing him in deeper, deeper, deeper. Absently, lost in the methodical, slow fucking action of his hand and wrist in Clint's asshole, Stan didn't realize that the fine hairs on his arm were tickling at the edges of Clint's frothing asshole.

His cock was more than throbbing, it was pounding with his heartbeat—a tempo echoed by Clint's right in front of his face. Playfully, Stan smiled, leaned forward, and swallowed Clint's thick meat, tickling his own smooth-shaved face with Clint's thick forest of pubic hairs. For a second, for just one of their mutual heartbeats, Stan sucked—just enough to tease, not enough to let him come. That was for later.

For now, it was better than just dick-fucking. Five fingers, his wrist, a good part of his arm—Stan was deep inside Clint, deep inside his hot, muscular, silken body. He was fucking him with his hand, his arm, his whole being. He was deep—deeper than any cock had ever gone. He was so deep—and then—he was that deep.

The sound of their moans mixed, combined in a two-part harmony of fucking excitement: Clint moaned because Stan's fist was churning in and out, in and out of his asshole, fucking him like a piston, like a five-fingered cock; and Stan because he was deep—so deep—in Clint's asshole, feeling the tight slickness of it wrapped around his arm.

Stan knew how his friends felt about him and Clint—how they were confused by his love for this rough and tough leatherman. Thinking of them, he smiled as he reached far, farther, farthest into Clint's body, feeling his asshole slide ever more along his arm.

After all, how can anyone not love someone with all their being when their arm has been so far up inside them that their pulse, the beating of their tender heart, can seem so very close?

For a long time, they fucked—Clint's asshole around Stan's arm, Stan deep in Clint's body. Mixing themselves more than fucking ever could, they touched pulse and heartbeat, pulse and heartbeat—smiling all the while.

The Hope of Cinnamon

THE RESCUED HAD a smell about them. Even after daily cleansing, a week of rest, hours of medical attention, clean sheets, and plenty of food, the smell—the bitter taint—still lingered. It was subtle, almost an afterthought. The Medicos said they couldn't smell it, though the Helpers discounted them because they were too focused on the more physical needs of the Rescued—too busy making sure their muscle mass reformed correctly, their bones absorbed new calcium at a good rate, to notice that they smelled.

Most of the Helpers said they smelled of the past—a dusty aroma of years. Gen, though, knew exactly what Bissou smelled of. Sitting on a shape-couch across from Bissou, who was obviously uncomfortable with the intelligent polymer intimacy of the furniture, he noticed that the small man had that soft aroma. Gen didn't think it was age. He thought it was cyanide: the smell of death's wings.

"You seem to be improving."

Bissou smiled, moved his hands in a gentle ballet: "It's a great place to be," he said. His German, native and not injected from synthesized RNA like Gen's, was wise and piping, musical—his inflections precise and orchestrated.

Still, Gen caught the hesitation, the phlegmatic pause. Helpers were trained to detect such subtlety, the difference between words meaning one thing in *language* and relaying whole books in the *speaking*.

Gen was an intuitive. He couldn't begin to explain the intricacies of the comm plates, the recycling system, or even the orbital magic that the Stonewall station used to keep from crashing down onto the earth or spinning off into space. His world wasn't material, it was emotional. His universe wasn't filled with matter, it was populated by personalities. He didn't know the details of what had brought Bissou to him, but he did know that a shadow was obscuring the small man, covering his eyes with a heavy weight. It was Gen's job to make sure that weight didn't crush him, reduce him to ash and memories. Gen was there to give him new life and walk him, happily, into his new world.

"I can tell you've had fun playing with the synthesizer," Gen said, smiling as he sat down next to him.

"Have some," Bissou said, passing Gen a plate of misshapen cookies. "It's not an iron oven, but I think it did a pretty good job."

Gen took one, feeling the crumbs skate under his fingers. The sugary bite of the dough was strong in his nose. "I wish we could allow it, but fire is one of those things we don't feel comfortable with."

It was a leading statement, one Bissou was supposed to respond to. He didn't disappoint: "Because of the air, right? Too much something in it?"

Gen smiled and patted Bissou's tiny, almost skeletal hand. "Oxygen. We have a high oxygen content here—that and the corrolis effect makes it harder to control open flame. A fire would be disastrous."

Bissou took his hand away, folded both in his narrow lap. "It's one of those things I'll miss."

Gen sampled the spiced cookie, not because he was uncomfortable, but because his training told him that the young German needed to say something and the act would put him at ease—would show that Gen was there for him, and respected him.

Bissou didn't physically sigh, but his body seemed to radiate the signature all the same: a muscular wave of building and relaxing. His eyes were turned away from Gen, staring down at the plate of ugly cookies.

The silence stretched. Gen put his hand on Bissou's knee, feeling the sharp planes of his bones through the thin material of his coverall. On their second day together, Gen had relented and worn something similar, even though it grated on him more than he was willing to admit. It tickled the backs of his knees, and it pulled much too hard on the back of his neck. Nudity was far better. Nudity was *natural*. But in the name of Acclimation he had started wearing it. Despite his discomfort, seeing the relaxation it brought Bissou had made it worth the irritation—though the instant he left the Therapy Suite the coverall would end up down the nearest recycling chute.

He wished Bissou would relax—drop some of the tension from his body and just be with Gen—but there was something brittle and hard in the young man, something that seemed frightened of the freedom and luxury that Gen was holding out to him. On their third day together Gen had offered Bissou sex. His own reaction still puzzled and disturbed Gen: he couldn't recall seeing the young German's eyes, wide and quivering with liquid panic, without feeling an almost physical pain for him. After that he hadn't offered again, but he had moved to touch Bissou as often as possible. Touch was important: without overcoming his fear he could never be able to Acclimate.

"Have you been cruising channels?" Gen asked, absently stroking the irritating fabric covering Bissou's thigh.

"You mean that machine?" he said, indicating the flatscreen with a small tilt of his head. "I spent an hour with it last night. It was interesting but confusing. I didn't know what I was looking at most of the time."

"You will, don't worry. Much of it would probably be familiar to you if you understood the basic concepts. That much hasn't changed."

"I'm sure. But there just seems to be so much . . . sex."

Gen laughed, but not with a scathing, mean edge to it. It was a teacher's laugh when his student makes an observation close to truth. "Ours is a very sexual culture. It always has been. It's how, after all, we define ourselves. I'm sure that's what it was for you."

Bissou picked up a cookie, studied it, took a tentative bite, and frowned. "Not enough cinnamon. Too much sugar. I'll never get it right."

Gen kissed him on the cheek and, despite the shock that visibly rippled through the young man's body, he said: "You will. You will."

xxx

PAISLEY WAS WAITING for him when he got home. The trip from the Rescued's compound to his own apartment near spoke four had been too quick—much too quick: Elevator up spoke two, ten-minutes of uncomfortable zero gravity, down spoke four, then a ten minute walk to his front door. He could have walked the entire way, Gen realized as he climbed the pseudowood steps leading to his door. Walking it would have taken an hour, maybe an hour and a half. It would have given him more time to think, to pinpoint the tension that seemed to ride somewhere just inside his breastbone, next to his heart.

Unfortunately he hadn't, and so he walked in with the ache throbbing deep inside. It would make him tense and irritable, bitchy. Paisley didn't react well when Gen was bitchy.

As the door slid aside, the strong smell of liquid plastics made Gen's nose burn. The coffee table had been stripped and moved to one side. In its place was a giant easel—and on that was a splash of eye-biting color. A diagonal of yellow. A handprint of black. A crimson slash that could have been the letter s, but since Paisley was illiterate Gen knew it couldn't have been intentional.

In front of the painting was Paisley. There, then, looking at his lover-partner of four months, Gen felt the pain in his chest lift, vanish in the power of his appreciation for him. Many people went too far, allowing too much leeway as they tried to top one kind of iconic beauty over another. At least the skilled technician that Paisley had allowed to sculpt him had shown some restraint, a sense of refinement. Paisley wasn't a Tom of Finland god or some deep-African jungle king. He was a slender man, stepping just from boyhood: downy cheeks, golden long hair, a strong chest, and just a hint of babyfat.

"Oh, you're home," Paisley said without an once of emotion, wiping his brushes on a rag that Gen recognized as one of his old T-shirts.

"Trying again?" Gen asked, moving toward the sensormat, hoping that Paisley wouldn't want to talk—would give him a few minutes to breathe, relax, try and diminish the ache he'd brought with him.

"The artistic process isn't an on or off kind of thing," Paisley said as Gen dialed up a mild sophoritic followed by a quick chaser of Dull Satisfaction. "It's an ongoing process of extension and release, of relaxation and endeavor," Paisley continued. "It's not a linear, logical thing—it's an emotional act, a spiritual act. It's something that comes when you least expect it, seizing control of your spirit. When that happens it takes ultimate precedent."

Seeing that Paisley's "precedent" had left their ceiling flecked with minute dots of yellow, red, and black paint, and that a large crimson smear arced across the carpet, Gen reselected a Pure White Light and slapped the two tiny capsules against his upper arm.

"As long as it makes you happy," Gen said, feeling the precise pharmaceuticals start to work. He walked around the couch and sat down with a heavy release of too-tight muscles.

"It's not about happiness. It's about being at the mercy of an unstoppable muse, a divine light that descends on the artist like a form of madness. When it comes you can't do anything but release yourself to its power, to the vision," his lover said, enthusiastically flicking paint across his canvas, splattering Gen's bare legs.

Last week it had been music, and the apartment ringing with Paisley's experiments with . . . not so much notes, chords, and melody as much as the percussive quality of banging away without rhyme or reason on a pair of sound decks.

As the drug started to inflate his mind, warble at his perceptions, Gen wandered through his fragmenting thoughts toward Paisley— the idea of Paisley. He loved him, certainly, but it was an intangible kind of love—glued together with a physical affection. When he looked at him, however, it was like he was seeing an impression, an outline of a person. He made Gen laugh. He was a glowing foxfire sprite in bed—all tongue, kisses, and cock.

Winds, though, blew through Paisley, distorting him. Smoke, tissue, and glass. There was nothing stone or steel in him. Music last week, painting this week, tantra next week.

The drug? Rock dust bit suddenly at Gen's nostrils. He'd lived in Stonewall all his life. He'd never lived or visited anywhere else. He'd never seen rocks. Lunar soil, of course—it filled the planters on the deck outside—but never earthly stone. But, still, he could swear that he could sense its aroma—even feel a rough surface with his tingly hands, the weight of rock against his muscles.

Bissou was shattered, almost broken. Considering what had happened to him—his previous life in dim history summoned into the present, with a chance to live granted at the barest seconds before death—he should have broken, fissured. Instead he was attempting to learn and to live.

But, still—cracks were there. Gen could see with his carefully tailored perceptions: the collapse was working its way through him, one break at a time.

Getting up was difficult—the drug wanted him to be fascinated with the minute pattern of dots on the rug, the walls, the ceiling. Walking to the sensormat was an EVA, a zero-gravity stroll. It seemed to take forever. Carefully, he dialed up Clear Resolution and Sharpened Reasoning and snapped the capsules, again, against his upper arm.

Clarity, like waking suddenly, roared through him. Without looking back Gen moved, each step becoming more and more certain, more and more stable, until he was in the bedroom.

"Aren't you going to watch me be creative?" he heard Paisley say, little wounds in his musical voice.

Gen put on a firm smile. "Be right back. Go ahead and be creative with yourself for a while."

In the small bedroom he stretched out on their unmade bed. The ceiling was spotless, a uniform white expanse. Emptiness. Outside, their sundeck was slowly slipping into shade, what passed for night on Stonewall. *Bissou*. The thought of the little German man brought a new dose of tightness to his chest. He wished, not for the first time, that he could find the right cord to pull, the right words to say, to make him unwind—drop out of his fear and his shock into the life that Gen and the Helpers were offering him. *It's a beautiful place*, he thought to the wry little man, *can't you see that*?

Gen had been a Helper for three years. Three clients in those three years. The first had been an older man named Goer. Uncomfortable and clumsy, the ex-jeweler had accepted his Rescue with hope. Yes, there had been fear—Gen remembered one night in particular when he had collapsed—as if the life had drained out of him in one giant sob. Gen had held him, quaking with his own fear as the big man shook with tears. He remembered their last day together, sitting on the balcony looking out at the wondrous interior of Stonewall. It was a moment of acceptance for Goer, a step into his new existence.

The second had been a young Pole named Markowsi. He had been harder. Much harder. So hard that Gen thought that he himself would crack, break up into tiny pieces along with the rusty-haired farmhand. Nothing was familiar to Markowsi— nothing. Not even the sexuality that had gotten him arrested and sent to the camps. He was a stranger even among the friends who had rescued him.

It had been hard. Terribly. But, still, Gen didn't feel the same way for the Pole as he did for Bissou. He tried to examine his feelings, bring them out of his unconsciousness and into the light of his present mind. He had walked Markowsi not only into the Stonewall "sunlight" but also into a whole new world. Gen had been his first lover, his first love. Gen had taken his hand, put it on his hard cock. "It's okay to want. There is no one here but us. Just the two of us and love." Markowsi had cried as well—but it was a source of deeper tears: nothing was familiar to him. No friends. No home. No earth. No animals (not counting cats and dogs). No crops to pull from the resistant earth.

Still, Gen remembered their last time together—a passionate embrace on the tubeway as Markowsi's train pulled in. The love that had been between them had bonded Markowsi not only to the love of men but also to the new age that was to be his home.

Thinking of him, Gen moved to the flatscreen and called up his old notes. Reading his younger self's words, he felt caught up in the fear, the hope he'd had as he'd tried to Acclimate him. Nothing like Bissou, though. It had been deep, loving and special—but there hadn't been anything else. Markowsi hadn't been a ghost, a transparent boy-man—but he hadn't held something deep and close as Bissou seemed to, something aching and magical. Something that Gen suspected was lurking just under the pale surface of his chest—something he was slowly bringing out to show Gen.

Absently, he called up the current records for Markowsi.

DECEASED flashed the screen. A chill ran through Gen. He read the word again, hoping the drugs hadn't completely left his system. The word stayed. Heart pounding a fistfight in his chest, he read on. A year ago, eight months after kisses and tears on the tubeway. He'd jumped from the roof of his apartment block. Dead instantly.

Why wasn't I told?

Separation was part of Acclimation—he understood that. Put them on their feet and kick them out into the world, make them create their own relationships, their own lovers. But they had been close, they had been lovers—a kind of Helper-Rescued love, but the ache was there nonetheless. There was pain in seeing that word, reading the details. A pounding pain. Markowsi's hands, rough and hard around his cock. Markowsi's lips, full and soft kissing him, gently washing his cock in hot spit. Markowsi's asshole, pink and pretty as it swallowed Gen's cock. Markowsi's eyes, dancing with wonder the morning after—seeing possibilities. Markowsi was dead. Dead.

He called up Goer's file. The fat little jeweler had suffered some kind of breakdown six months ago. A model, a perfect job, he remembered some of the other Helpers telling him with pride. Stonewall offered Goer so much—genetic retailoring to give him the body he'd always wanted, a world free from hate and war. A world full of men who loved men. It was paradise. It was a utopia for Goer.

He'd broken nonetheless—his cracks might not have been visible, gaping, but they'd been there. They'd grown as he'd tried to Acclimate, to live in the strange world he'd found himself in— grown till there wasn't anything holding him together and he'd simply fallen apart.

Bissou. The face of the young German hovered in front of Gen. His beautiful hands. His face planed and elegant, nose long and thin, lips wide and soft. His hair, black as starless space. His eyes, opals—alive with flicking blue. He was thin and narrow and walked like a dancer, with beauty singing from each step, each gesture. Refined and elegant.

Where would he be in six months? What would happen to debonair Bissou and his cinnamon cookies?

Gen took a stuttering deep breath, squeezing his eyes against the hot tears that had already started to slowly roll down his cheeks. Getting himself together, he started calling all the

Helpers he knew.

X X X

"IT'S THE LITTLE things you remember most, isn't it? You don't know much about your part of the world, your life, but you remember the tiny things the best."

It was against the rules to let them talk about their past too much. *That part is gone*, the philosophy went, *it's time to move on.* But Gen didn't stop him, didn't step on the usual course of trying to get Bissou to watch the flatscreen more often, or encourage him to remove his clothing, have sex. He sat next to him, not even touching the slim young man, and listened to his words.

"I had a little place near the train station. Small and dirty, but it was mine. The concierge was a little widow who'd lost her husband in the first war. She had a shrine to him: dusty glass, a fading photograph, and two medals. I always saw it when I paid my rent. He looked like a god, a Yoden, staring down at me from that wall. His eyes were big and glaring, as if his anger at the photographer still beamed out of his eyes at me and anyone else who came into his widow's apartment."

"Did you like living there?" Gen asked, watching Bissou pacing back and forth—from one cream-colored wall to the other. It was week six of his Acclimation and the flatscreen was on all the time: *cultural exposure.* Get them used to their new world. Gen, though, had turned the sound down until it was nothing but a mumbling whisper. Even though the chaotic fragments of Stonewall's media flashed and pulsed with vivid entertainment, Gen's eyes were only on Bissou.

And Bissou's eyes were back in his tiny apartment near the university.

"I hated that place. I hated that portrait. I hated the words that followed me down the street." He stopped his walking and talking and turned to the brilliant pulses coming from the screen.

Gen noted, almost unconsciously, that the screen had stopped on a bout of the Sexual Olympics: bronzed gods with mammoth phalluses wrestling each other to the orgasmic delights of an immense crowd.

Bissou turned away. Gen noticed his eyes were closed tight. "I was beaten twice when I lived there. One time so badly I couldn't see out of my left eye for three days. I was scared of going blind — but more so of going to a doctor."

"It must have been frightening," Gen said, feeling the emotion himself, or at least a personal version.

Bissou became quiet. Turning back to the flatscreen, to the flickering images of giant, oily torsos and dicks like battering clubs, he finally whispered, "You don't have any idea. The place smelled of cinnamon from the bakery next door. It smelled safe, like my mother's kitchen. Warm and safe. When I was in bed at night that smell meant hope that it would be there in the morning, the next day. That I would be there to smell it."

Gen listened, washing himself in Bissou's words. He saw his crossed arms and memory-glazed eyes. *Seventy-percent failure rate*, he also saw, and the eyes of the other Helpers he'd talked to, red-ringed with the surprising and too-hard emotions that'd come from discovering all of their failures. Seventy percent of the Rescued didn't make it. Madness. Stepping into a high fall. No one understood it. Many were frightened. Why, they had no idea.

"I wish I could make you understand," said Bissou. "I don't think you can. It was bad. Everyone I knew was frightened, in pain. But sometimes we found each other, reached out into the night and found a warm body, a smiling face.

"My first kiss," he said, turning back and speaking with surprising volume, "was a model named Heinz. He was so pretty. So pretty. Eyes like the sun — full of light. His skin was gold. Not brown like a farmer's but gold. I sketched him for many weeks, but it was just an excuse to be close to him, to warm myself in his glow.

"One day I noticed him watching me. Staring down at me from the soap box he was posing on. His face didn't change, but I felt it did. I could feel something about him, something that saw into me, beyond the student, or the painter—something deep down. It frightened me . . . to be known that well, that quickly. I guess it also scared me that he accepted it, acknowledged it. I didn't return to that class for days, pretending to be ill in bed.

"He visited me, all warmth and gold. He brought cookies from next door—cinnamon. That first kiss was like the welcoming embrace of my room. Cinnamon. We didn't do anything more. We just kissed and held each other. Sometimes the best heaven is a pause in hell.

"We stayed together, warm bodies on cold mornings. Slowly I noticed others like Heinz and me." He waved his still-thin, still-malnourished arms at the cream-colored walls, the shape-couch, the wallscreen, at Gen. "There was a kind of shame over everything we did, even if it was just talking out of doors. But my heart was exploding every day, bursting when I thought of them all—of Heinz and my friends."

Bissou came and sat down next to Gen. He seemed weightless, almost insubstantial, the light having drained out of him. "It meant something. Everything had a priceless value to it. Our kisses, our bodies—everything was more precious than anything I had ever known. Even when they came and made us wear the triangles, we made it a uniform—a badge among us all. It was stupid and childish, but it was a time when any amount of love, every kiss, was worth more than anything on earth.

"Here everything is cheap, easy. Nothing means anything. Nothing is special. You don't understand. No one here does."

Gen put his arm around him, held him close. For a long time they didn't say anything, then Bissou turned his head and kissed Gen's cheek. The kiss was a distant flock of birds, almost invisible except when they passed between the sun and the earth and the shadows they cast hit the earth. A ghostly kiss. For Gen it felt like a kiss goodbye.

No! a part of Gen screamed, and a surge of anger and passion rushed up his body, making his head swim. Turning fast he grabbed Bissou by the shoulders, tilted his head and kissed him *hard! Passion!* Bissou struggled at first, a kind of shocked retreat, but then he slowly began to melt. Together their tongues rolled and tugged against one another. A fire started somewhere within both of them.

Startled by his own ferocity, Gen dropped his hands away— and his left grazed the tiny man's lap, feeling a strong, hard cock there.

An image swelled in Gen's mind: the thought of Bissou, alone in a place with dazzling beauty and too-common sensuous joy, where nothing has value and everything is too easily acquired. He thought of him fading away, lost against the vacuum he felt all around him.

Again the anger boiled in Gen, again the *No!* was a mad bell in his head. With a powerful tug he parted the thin material of Bissou's coverall. His cock was crimson, brilliant red with strength. It wasn't half-hard, or even just-hard, it was screaming life, lust, and passion.

Putting a hand, hard, around the thin man's cock, Gen hung on. He didn't care if he was holding on too tight, because he was holding on—keeping Bissou there with him, keeping him close.

Pulsing with the beat of his rapid heart, Bissou's cock in Gen's hand felt like steel wrapped in velvet. It was life, it was the present.

Gen was almost shocked at the strength of it—the image of Bissou as a ghost of a man, someone fading off to sometime in the past, slipped a little bit. He felt like he wasn't just hanging onto his cock, he was hanging onto the one thing, the anchor, that would keep the thin little man from falling—falling down and away from him.

Bissou responded by breathing deep and pulling slightly back, eyes wide with pleasant shock, his arms filled with tension, but he didn't move to stop or break Gen's grip.

I might lose you, Gen thought, his mind remarkably clear, *but I have you here, now.*

Gen knelt in front of Bissou. Before his eyes, Bissou's cock was straight and narrow—not as long as many cocks Gen had seen and sampled, but then Gen's age was one where beauty was affordable and genitals were whatever you wanted them to be. Possibly because of that—that Bissou's cock, balls, and body were what he had lived in, dealt with, and enjoyed—he was beautiful to Gen. More beautiful than any store-bought body, more divine than any artistically enhanced cock. He was just flesh, blood, memory, experience, and desire.

Bissou's cock was proud and strong because his life had made it so.

Gently, being the Helper that he was, Gen kissed the satiny-smooth head of Bissou's cock. He tasted the rich flavor of hot skin and the sharp tang of bitter salt from a tiny dollop of pre-come that had gently oozed out. Above him, he was dimly aware that Bissou had leaned back into the shape-couch and was breathing rapidly.

After the kiss, Gen slowly eased Bissou's cock into his mouth, inching it into the blast furnace that Gen felt himself becoming. Breathing around the fat head, Gen bathed Bissou in his own hot air. When he brought his lips around it again he felt much more salt, much more bitter come taste—and Bissou's cock, impossibly, was even harder.

Then Gen started to make love to Bissou with his mouth. Stonewall was proud of its tradition of teaching, of educating young men in the arts of love. Gen always prided himself on his artistic flair regarding sex and sex play. He'd received high marks from every teacher he'd studied with and had even mastered some of the more arcane arts of erotic pleasure. But that afternoon, with the tiny man from the twentieth century, Gen was just a man, his lover, and his lover's cock. The perfect artistry of simplicity.

Rhythmically, Gen lowered and raised his mouth around Bissou's cock, relishing the taste and feel of his member. Dimly, distantly, he was aware that he too was hard—he felt an ache in his crotch against the confining clothing—but he didn't dare even stroke himself because it might take his mind, and mouth, off of Bissou.

Distantly, but not dimly, he was also aware of the sounds deliciously emanating from Bissou. Like a mantra, he moaned "Jesus, God, Jesus, God—" in his native German.

Gen didn't know those words, at least not clearly, but he took it as a good sign and kept on sucking on Bissou's pretty, pretty cock. Gen felt himself becoming nothing but the excitement and joy of what he was doing—it wasn't so much just sex as breathing life into someone who had come so close to death. He was washing away the stink of cyanide from the gas chamber, the smell of death's wings. He was trying his best to obliterate years of pain and suffering, remove with just a blow-job words like *Dachau, Auschwitz, Relocation, Undesirables*.

Bissou's cock was strong, like a grounding rod into the earth. Gen knew he couldn't wipe away the pain of Bissou's life—but he could, at least, hold him here, now, for a little while more.

Sudden salt, shocking wetness. Above and beyond him Bissou moaned, deep and guttural, a feral, primitive burst of joy as he came in Gen's mouth.

Carefully cleaning Bissou with his tongue, Gen stroked and fondled him—worshipping the shape and strength of his cock, the shape and strength of his forged soul.

When he was clean and oh-so-hard again, Gen stood, quickly tossing aside the coverall that he hated. Naked and also achingly hard, he stood in front of Bissou and didn't say anything, though he thought, *This is life, take it.*

Bissou hesitated, then elegantly kissed the head of Gen's

cock. With his lips he learned the shape of the Helper's—felt the softness, the hardness, the silk, the satin, the velvet, the iron. Slowly, methodically—as if he was memorizing Gen's member so he wouldn't ever forget it—Bissou worked his way up and around Gen.

Watching, hypnotized, to Gen it felt like someone unwrapping a precious gift—luxuriating in its beauty. For many minutes this went on—the meticulous adoration of Gen—then, so slowly that Gen wasn't even quite sure that it was happening, Bissou swallowed Gen's cock.

The sensation scared Gen at first—its overwhelming feeling of warmth, wetness, firmness was so perfect, so ideal that the reality that it was being performed by a Rescued shocked him. But soon the sensation won out over his judgment about who was performing it, and Gen was awash in the beauty of Bissou's worship.

Lips, tongue, hint of teeth, roof of mouth, down the throat, Gen was consumed by Bissou, feasted on—he was eaten so that life could flow into Bissou.

When the orgasm came it was a rumbling earthquake, something that Gen didn't, at first, recognize—a shimmering wave of physicality that raced from his thighs and chest up through his neck into his face and brain. His body responded on its own, bucking slightly into Bissou's mouth, his face. Then he exploded—a burst of thrilling sensation that made his knees weak and his breath labored.

Sitting back down on the shape-couch, they held each other for a long time and fell asleep—until the shadow of "night" passed by the window and another great panel of sunlight started to arrive.

Gen had somewhere to go. Carefully, he got up. When Bissou was awake enough he kissed him, took his hands, and stared into his face.

"I'm going away for a little while. For you just a few days. You must promise me you won't do anything. Wait for me."

Bissou looked scared and confused: "Where are you going?"
"I'm going to try and understand."

xxx

THE SHUTTLEPOD DOCKED with a deep shudder of impact.
Gen closed the flatscreen he'd been studying since they'd set
out for the Anomaly. He had been washing himself in details:
customs, history, maps, economics, the dry facts of a long-dead
age. He'd received a new dosage of German, a heavy layering of
the language over his own. Gen would be able to speak it like a
native. The injection had been so large that he had to think twice
before speaking—he'd confused most of the crew on the trip by
speaking the old, dead tongue.

It had taken some persuading, but in the end the Helpers had
all agreed. Seventy percent failure—they had to know why. They
had to understand.

He'd have ten years. He was going to 1930. Ten years of walking
their streets, eating their food, speaking their language, knowing
their life. Gen, too, would know the triangles, the guns, the trains,
the camps, the ovens. He, too, would be Rescued—but hopefully
he might know and understand what he was being Rescued from,
and being brought to.

Wait for me, Gen thought, thinking of Bissou as the hatch
opened and he floated out into the Anomaly, the gateway back
to the past.

*I'll be back—and when I do, maybe I'll know a priceless kiss,
the hopeful smell of cinnamon.*

Heads and Tails

"SUCK IT," **HE** told me, and so I did. Willingly, eagerly—I opened my mouth, pushed out my lips, and took his swollen cock-head in. It would have been nice to say it was a sweet candy cane—but let's be realistic. It tasted like hard cock. A good hard cock, but a cock nonetheless: salt, the bitter bite of pre-come, the shit-tinge you always get down there, the musky reek of hormones, of excitement.

A good taste, a damned fine taste. A cock taste—and I tried to get every inch of it, and him, down my throat. I've sucked my share, some even bigger than this great beast filling my mouth, but for me—then and there—it was the only cock in the world.

I sucked him as he moaned, and not for the first time—or probably the last—I thought, "playing the skin flute." A bad metaphor in its original antique context, but a favorite with my twist: Yes, lips around. Yes, I was sucking and not blowing. But I really was playing him, applying my lips and making lovely music escape from him.

And what beautiful tunes I was making him perform: moans, groans, sighs, hisses—the entire scale of pleasure. I couldn't do my own singing, of course, with his instrument tickling the back of my throat, but I did hum and moan a bit in accompaniment.

Then it was time to stop. I opened my jaws even wider and slowly let his hard cock slide free, the thick head popping up from my throat, glancing off my teeth, past the roughness, past the playfulness of my flickering tongue, and then out. Shimmering, gleaming with a dribble of pre-come and lots of my spit, he came free, tapping against my nose with the iron of his shaft.

"Time to toss it, boy," he says, grinning wide—and wonderfully mean.

xxx

IT DANCED IN the light, twirling around and around, a sparkling bit of silver in the twilight room. Fast—so fast—he reached out and caught it, snatching the coin before it even fell past my eyes. A slap against his burly forearm. A peek under his hand to see the side—but showing me nothing but a wicked grin. "Tails."

I returned the smile, wiping my mouth free of my come-sucking drool. Keeping my eyes on his, relishing the hunger in his gray irises, I reached over and gently took up the bottle of baby oil.

Then I wasn't facing him, but rather a white wall, a small expanse of eggshell. I knew that soon enough I'd be memorizing it, registering every crack, every deformation. I would never be able to look at that small spot of wall without thinking of what would come next.

Ass high, I offered myself to him—no, I gave him my asshole. He had the rest of me—or could have had as much of me as he wanted—but I knew all he wanted right then was my asshole. I'd heard the compliments, so I showed my hole to him with pride. "A pink delicacy," "a fuckable rosebud," "such a pretty fuck-hole," and so much more.

His hand was on my ass—hot, rough, strong. At first he just held me—gripping one of my cheeks. Preparatory, a way he shook hands with the ass he's going to fuck. Then a gentle pressure around that "wondrous asshole"—a slow, steady pressure around my "delicate hole"—and I knew that he was in me. A finger at first, but he was still within me. It felt good—a gentle invasion. Good, but not great—and so I growled, feral and hungry, and demanded something greater, more powerful, more feral.

And he delivered. Up the gradient of sensation, passing the tickling entry of that finger and beyond . . . beyond even my own fingers, my own toys. He was not just big, he was not just huge. He was beyond all of that—and all of that was now beyond the lips of my asshole, deep within me.

And so, he fucked me. God, yes, he fucked me—in and out, a fucking two-stroke engine of cock and legs, balls slapping against my ass. I felt his hot invasion, the piston-stroke hammering deep inside me. I did what I don't do often—hot tears rolling down my cheeks, burning me. But they were not a sad leaking . . . no, they were tears of wonderful pain, wonderful suffering. It was a good kind of hurt, the sexy hurt of being fucked good and hard.

Then it was over, but not with the usual curtain call—no, that time it didn't conclude with his hot come in the hot recesses of me. No, he pulled free long before that, long before the come boils free of his great, big, hairy balls.

xxx

AGAIN, THE SHIMMERING ascent of the coin—a twirling dance in the dim light of my bedroom. For the first time I noticed the denomination, and felt a delightful wave of shame that I was only worth five cents.

He didn't show me the side after he slapped it silly on his arm. Instead, he rolled back onto his wonderfully tight ass, showing me his rock-hard cock—and such a cock it was. I knew where it'd been, my asshole still throbbing from its absence, but that didn't take away my hunger for it.

An echo, a touch of déjà vu: "Suck it."

So I did, taking his thick cock into my hungry mouth. It didn't taste like shit—but then I wasn't in a position to really tell, or care. All that mattered was my mouth around his cock, his head down my throat, his hairy balls tickling my chin. All was right in the world; I was sucking on my Lord's cock.

I was somewhere else, lost in the sensation of his thick shaft sliding in and out of my mouth, fucking my tonsils, screwing my throat. I was lost, hovering beyond it all in a place of pure lust and driving, hammering, love. Distantly I was aware my cock was throbbing, hard, and that my feverish hand was jamming up and down along it. It felt good, that was certain, but his cock down my throat felt even better.

Then—Jesus—he came—my Master, my lover . . . he came. At first I thought it was just part of my sucking, the twitching that flowed up and down his throbbing cock, but then he started to fill my throat with his hot, salty jizz, his steaming come. I swallowed and swallowed and swallowed some more, sucking his sticky come down my throat as I massaged him, squeezed his shaft with my mouth.

Sometime during this I came, too—jetting onto the sheets, my own orgasm quaking my knees—and pulled myself free of his gleaming cock to fall, panting, onto the sheets.

After a while we slept, curled up in my tiny bed, a warm embrace of spent bodies . . . with just the tiny cool spot of a coin, pressed against my chest, to remind me of why we were sleeping.

Suddenly, Last Thursday

EVEN IN THE clearest, coldest water, gardenias are the white of a virginal bride for only a short time, their purity and innocence turning weary yellow, then bitter brown, in days. Days, yes, if you have the patience to watch unblinkingly—but seconds, it always seems, if you turn away and then back: life before, nothing but dead petals after.

Looking at her, faded crinoline in the hard light of morning, I felt shame that I had faulted in my patience. If I hadn't continued on my rounds, hadn't allowed routine to take me away from this gardenia in the asylum sunroom, then perhaps she would have stayed full rather than continue to drain.

The day was warm, threatening hot, but the threat was prescient in that room: the glass magnified the sun, and I would have said something, anything, to keep her in a better environment—a cool bowl of water rather than a hothouse—but I indulged her. There was something about the heat, about the dancing waves that lured perspiration out of every corner of the body, that seemed to quell her hysterias.

"What is it about the foods that begin the day, Doctor?" She looked up at me from the chaise lounge, indicating with an aquatically tired gesture a breakfast tray on the terra cotta floor tiles beside her: pancakes and syrup, a half glass of orange juice, a half grapefruit—all of it barely touched, hardly eaten, and quickly lusted after by a slow circle of fat flies. "Too sweet for any dessert, but we expect, crave them for breakfast. Dreams, Doctor, maybe dreams hunger for sugar, for syrups and compote—maybe that's why we can tolerate such sugars only in the mornings."

Gardenias and then, with those words, a child's plaything: a porcelain doll outliving some child, then an adult, then a matron. Life burned away, but her beauty was preserved like a doll still beautiful despite ages on a shelf. In her case, the flame burning up her life wasn't age, but rather some unknown trauma, some daylight nightmare—a cryptic brutality that turned a girl into crisped petals and cracked china.

"You have been good to me, Doctor," she said, looking up at me from under a cream-colored sun hat, flashing at me eyes the color of polished amber. "To everyone else I'm just another monkey in this zoo, but you, Doctor, you look and you see me. For that, kind sir, I am eternally grateful."

She looked again at the breakfast tray, as if seeing the crystallizing syrup, the feeding flies, the thick juice for the first time. Those amber eyes widened, for a moment seeing not discarded food and dirty dishes but something else. She looked up at me. "You deserve kindness, Doctor, gratitude for the humanity in your lovely eyes. I would cure myself of this madness if it were in my power, because that would be the best gift to give you, but I cannot. I would demonstrate myself to you in other ways, but I can tell that would not be a gift you would . . . appreciate, as I will always be patient to your doctor."

My face flushed red, my mouth too full of things to say—so silence was the only thing that made it out.

"Beyond a healthy will, which I cannot give, I know what you want, Doctor. Ha! I know your real desire, Doctor, I know your scientific hungers—so I will, despite my horrors, give you a taste this morning of what occurred, what happened that Thursday last, the beginning that has ended here, with you, and this place.

"But, Doctor, before I begin I must tell you what I have learned. The real lesson. We all have hungers, Doctor, we all crave and pursue. What you hunger for is truth, to solve the puzzle. But with the smallest taste, appetites can grow, Doctor, they can become something large and terrible and . . . consuming."

She paused to brush gently at her faded skirt, smoothing the material: an echo, a memory of how things must have been, before saying, "There's a road . . . "

XXX

THERE'S A ROAD up by the highway—you may have seen it—that rounds a low hill. A perfect place, Sebastian said.

Somewhere I read in a book that just as we all wish to consume something, we also have something to give. Tragedy is when you live your life without discovering what it is you have to give. True cruelty is when you have something to give, but do not give it. Sebastian was neither tragic nor cruel, but something else: a man without definition, a man with appetites, but also with a true gift, greatness to give. Sebastian is my brother, and if you ever had the pleasure or misfortune to make his acquaintance, then you, too, would know that definitions fail to capture him. Sebastian was my brother, and Sebastian was . . . Sebastian.

"That road," he said to me a year ago—maybe a year and some months, "is perfect." Where it curls around the low hill, he did his building. Because Sebastian is the oldest by some years, Mama and Papa left him some money. Not enough for true luxury, but more than enough for a man like Sebastian to begin.

Mama adored Sebastian. She would sit in the drawing room in the afternoons and simply talk about Sebastian like his was a face that decorated the lobby of the Odeon, rather than her own flesh and blood. "That Sebastian," she would say, fanning herself and sipping the sweet drinks that I would make her, "is a man like no other," and I would agree, for I, too, saw his as a face that could possibly flicker and shine in a matinee.

Papa did not hate Sebastian, but he did not love him the way Mama loved him. Papa would talk about Sebastian like he wasn't in the same room or even standing right there before him—right there. "That boy," he'd begin—though Sebastian was not old, he certainly was not a boy—"is too different for this world," and I would agree, for I, too, saw him as I saw no other man I had ever met, or seen. Sebastian was an angel face, but he was also a man with cold marble eyes.

I did not hate him, nor did I adore him with blushing cheeks, as did Mama. Sebastian was the boy who picked wildflowers and sprayed their petals on my bed one morning. Sebastian was the boy who put a dead frog under those same covers. My brother would, for no reason, call me a beauty like no other—singing poetry about Helen of Troy and the names of movie beauties like Elizabeth Taylor for no other reason, he said, than that my face caught an evening light "just so." But he was also the boy who told his friends, my friends, complete strangers, that my legs swung wide and often, sometimes for trinkets, sometimes for coins, mostly just because I liked it.

Later, after many summers of petals and dead frogs, we both traveled to the big school in New Orleans. In a big house dripping with ivy, and a yard pressed under lethargic willows, we moved forward in our lives. I discovered the fabrics, cosmetics, perfumes, and laughter of being a woman. I also learned both the power and the shame of being a woman—how I was what men wanted, but that they also hated me for that wanting.

In high rooms framed by curling iron balconies, and in steaming kitchens, Sebastian discovered something as well: He discovered pans and pots; flour, starch, and sugar; temperatures, coolings; spices and flavors. With first whispers, then with pleas, Sebastian's audience of students and teachers asked for new and better delicacies. Nothing seemed impossible for his teaspoons and tablespoons, his measuring cups and ladles or his . . . yes, his hands, I suppose. Watching people eat what he put in front of them, you would swear, as did I, that there was something beyond simple cooking involved in his recipes. Angel, devil, my brother put all of himself into what he prepared, and as he cooked, and as more and more people sampled his wares, Sebastian asked for and received greater and greater rewards. Sebastian, it seemed, had discovered his gift—as well as the power in not rewarding it to the hungry.

Our parents' death—the result of an interaction between their habit of a Sunday morning drive after services and an early freight train—came, for Sebastian at least, at a fortuitous moment in his education. Between experiments with sautés and bouillabaisse, a teacher, whose own specialty was baked goods and sauces, was discovered bent over a hot stove with Sebastian's own baster between his buttered buns. Much was ignored, much was denied, but too much had been done of both, and so Sebastian and I—my guilt solely by familial association—were politely asked to leave.

But Sebastian's dismissal from the school did nothing to remove the beautiful expression from his perfect face. Leaving me to put our parents' affairs in order, and to make the arrangement for their interment, he spent long days driving in the country, looking for something he wouldn't specify.

The day of the funeral, after the minister praised their goodness and denied their guilts with much better conviction than the school had done for their students and teachers, Sebastian drove me many miles beyond the city into the rolling hills. At a certain point, where the road rounded a low hill, he stopped the car and said, "A perfect place. A perfect place for what I want to do—what I was born to do."

The day was hot, though not as hot as this day, Doctor, and I was still in my black dress from the funeral, but even so I felt a deep chill as Sebastian spoke those words: the feeling of ice, of goosebumps, on a heated day. With his gift, and the pleasure he felt in withholding it, my brother had found the ideal location. I didn't want to go with him, to help him in what he wanted to do, but I did nonetheless. Sebastian was many things, Doctor, but most of all he was my brother.

Then he began to build. From the city he hired teams of big, sweaty men to come up with him to that low hill, that spot along that road, to lay brick, hammer nails, lift great beams, and pound sheets of corrugated steel. That summer was not just hot, it was the hottest. The air was not just humid, but rather the most humid anyone could remember having felt. But still Sebastian was there, helping those brawny men lay, hammer, lift, and pound until piles of bricks, nails, beams, and corrugated steel grew into the architecture of Sebastian's desire.

I helped him as much as I could. At first it wasn't a place for a lady, but I still came up every day with a lunch of potato salad, fried chicken, and beer for him and the workmen. When it was finished, I was there right beside him when he took down that crudely painted OPEN SOON banner to put out an OPEN sandwich board.

The name of the place was Sebastian's idea, of course. If it'd been up to me I would have certainly named it something else, say, French—those lovely, pretty words that would be on the lips and tongue like sweet cakes and lemonade, not something crude like those words Sebastian chose to hang out front. But that was Sebastian, you see: He knew all those pretty French words, but what he wanted to do, what mattered more, was what was on the plates—not that the place settings were guilded, or even that clean.

Like his menu, for instance. Chalk on blackboards in simple block letters: grits, hominy, biscuits, corn on the cob, and most of all, those three letters, Doctor, those three very special letters: BBQ, as in BBQ CHICKEN, BBQ RIBS, BBQ PORK. "If it walks," Sebastian would say, "I'll cook it—and if it talks, I'll serve it."

Serve them he did, Doctor. At first it was long nights there in the cool darkness of the place: Sebastian in the kitchen, slicing, stirring, feeding the ovens, the grills, the air heavy with sweetness, with honey, with butter, with the sound of crackling meat, the sputters of fat and grease on the coals. I would write on those blackboards, trying to improve Sebastian's simple lettering with my own feminine swirls and arcs. In the kitchen, Sebastian was a magician, turning bleeding raw meat into delicacies glowing with spice and glazes, transforming raw vegetables into steaming feasts shimmering with butter. Watching him, through clouds of aromatic steam, I remember feeling the bite of jealousy—that my brother was in his place, performing his talent, when all I could do . . . all I could do was write down what he was doing.

It wasn't long before people started to come in droves. How they heard I don't know, because Sebastian didn't advertise or even talk to many people about what he was doing up there on that road. Maybe the wind shifted one day, and that rich steam from his roasting meat, the alluring scent of his cooking vegetables reached down to the city, into the noses of a lucky few—and maybe those few told their friends, until the smells of Sebastian's magic, or just their rapturous description of them, spread throughout the whole of the state.

People came. Sebastian stayed in his kitchen, doing his magic. People came, and people ate. Soon there were too many for us, and so I hired a pair of colored girls to help with taking orders, cleaning tables, and washing up, while I walked around, dressed in my finest, making sure everyone was happy. I like to think that some of them came up that road to that little brick-and-iron building to see me, but it's a sad little dream, Doctor, because they came and they ate. Their faces never turned away from the BBQ, the grits, the hominy, the biscuits and ears of buttery sweet corn. But I stayed. I stayed because Sebastian needed my help, or I hoped he needed my help, and . . . I didn't have anywhere else to go.

Sebastian didn't want to go anywhere else. Sebastian was where he wanted to be, doing what he wanted to do—and doing even more, because Sebastian's passions were great, but never simple. In the kitchen, he made his magic, turning raw, cold, meat into honey-glazed brilliance. I used to watch him, see the flames in his eyes, both from the charcoal as well as his own deep burning, as he brought his cleaver down on a slab of beef, chopping it hard, neatly separating rib from rib. Or when he broke a chicken with his bare hands, dipping a fat drumstick in his boiling cauldron of sweet mixtures before putting it over the glowing coals—the sauce bubbling and hissing almost in an echo of the sounds our customers made when they took their first bite.

But Sebastian smiled at other times, Doctor. Like when every table was full and our girls were all a fretting and worried so at not being able to handle all those hungry people, and I would bring my hand to my brow and feel myself damp, almost wet, Doctor, from the heat of the kitchen, the warmth of the day, and the demanding stomachs of them all. Days like that, when all of the state, it would seem, was demanding their BBQ, pushing one drumstick, one steak, one pork rib, after another into their sucking, chewing mouths, Sebastian would step out of the kitchen and stand there, watching—just watching them all until first one, then others noticed him. They knew, you see, they knew that there wasn't anyone else in the kitchen, and no one else they'd accept even if there were another available. The magic was Sebastian's and Sebastian's alone. No one else could turn meat into glazed ambrosia—the BBQ of the gods.

He'd stand there, just watching them eat, then he'd walk by them, and their eyes would say what their mouths, so full of tasty meat, could never speak: *Get back to that kitchen, boy. Feed us, boy.* He'd walk by them, his smile growing with each tep, until his face was lit by a glow of pleasure—wicked pleasure, devilish pleasure. Then he'd go to the door, hold it open and call out, as loud as he could, "That's the last, folks. Eat what you got because today we're closing early."

Oh, their faces. Bankers who bankrupted folks with swirls of a pen, priests who offered last rites, schoolteachers who spanked disobedient children, policemen who cracked bones everyday—they'd all just sit and stare at my brother, the meat he'd prepared sometimes even falling from their shocked loose mouths. Looking at them, their appetites still clawing at their fat bellies, you knew what they were thinking, what they all wanted to say: *Get back to that kitchen boy*. But did they? No, Doctor, they knew where they sat, they new their place—high-class rich men with iron balconies, fancy clothes, big cars—they knew their place. They were on the bottom, and Sebastian was high above them. They knew that if they said a word, made one little squeak, then who knew what would happen? Maybe Sebastian wouldn't open tomorrow, or the next day, or maybe something would be missing from my simple blackboard menu, the one thing they didn't realize they couldn't live without until it was gone.

So all of them, they did what Sebastian asked: they stuffed their mouths with the last of his glistening meat and then they shuffled out, not a complaint from one of them—not even from their unfulfilled bellies. Out they went, under the rapturous joy of Sebastian, who was happy when he was in the kitchen with the steam and his raw meat, and ecstatic when he told them they could have no more. Not cruel—Sebastian wasn't that, and neither was he tragic. He was simply my brother, and he had a gift—a gift that consumed him. Yes, that's right—very right. It consumed him in many ways.

Many ways. Not too long ago I learned that Sebastian had appetites beyond his need to work his magic in the kitchen, as well as his need to hold his tangy creations just out of reach of a hungry mouth.

Do you hear it in my voice, Doctor?—the dread, the terror— the memory is still too clear in my mind. There. It's right there, in all it's details. The deep purple of an approaching summer night, the scuffed arcs on the floor from where someone had pushed back a chair, the pale sweep of chalk from a clumsy sleeve against one of the blackboards, a fat crow sitting on the roof, the buzz of the back porch light, the shadows—yes, the shadows. I remember I had gone around to the back, looking for one of our girls—the foolish thing having gone off and forgotten once again to put the lid on one of the pickle barrels.

I never went around back before. I never needed to. Sebastian said I shouldn't have to . . . Doctor, did I know but didn't allow myself to understand? Did I really know what happened back there, when the sun had set behind the thick pines and the shadows bled off into the dark night? Did I understand what was happening but always keep my eyes turned toward the front, toward the buzzing electric lights?

I thought the night was moving. Trees, I remember thinking, the trees are moving—that's why darkness seemed to be slipping over darkness. But there was no breeze. The night was hot and still and simple: the distant pines, the back door, the hard, glaring light in its curled metal shade, and Sebastian, standing there.

Then I saw them. Not shadows. Not trees moving in a nonexistent breeze, but men. Shabby men, dirty men—hobos, tramps, beggars. Their skin wasn't white or black, just dirty. Fall far enough, Doctor, and does everyone become the color of an old dirt road? They had fallen a great distance. They wore old burlap sacs, coats missing sleeves, pants missing legs, belts of rope, shoes that were nothing but bags tied with twine. They shuffled and limped, and held their hands out.

"You know the rules," Sebastian said, wiping his hands on his filthy apron. Hearing his voice, I stepped back, hiding behind a corner of the building. Burs, I remember, scratched at my ankles.

The men—the things that used to be men, I mean—heard what he said and I knew, then and there, that they'd heard it before. This wasn't a new thing I was seeing. This was something Sebastian had done before, something he did often. Maybe it was something he'd discovered about the place, or more terrible still, maybe he'd picked that place on that road because Sebastian knew those things were there.

"A lick for a lick, a bite for a suck," Sebastian said—and, oh, there was such a laugh in his voice—a dark steel, razor-sharp laugh. He'd laughed before in the kitchen, but never, not once, like he did then.

He laughed, and his hands went under his apron. He laughed and pushed his apron aside, and there—in the too clear light from that shaded electric lamp, my brother held himself. It is a bad thing, Doctor, for a sister to see her brother's . . . manhood, but that night I did. Heaven help me, I did, and I didn't just see it, I looked at it. The details locked forever in my mind, and I found myself thinking of him as not my brother but rather a man, a man standing with his member hard, projecting out into the warm night air.

Here was the baster that he'd used too well in school, the portion of his anatomy that so many staff and students had seen, touched, and no doubt sampled as much as they'd sampled his dishes and delicacies.

Big—and was that pride I felt or a woman's hunger? Am I forever damned for thinking such things about my own brother? But I did think such things, and even more: the strength of the shaft, the hardness, the veins, the plushness of the head, the glimmers and gleams of sweat. The heaviness of his testicles, and the way they seemed distant, out-of-focus from his thick tangle of dark hairs.

He repeated himself to them, or maybe it was to me? "A lick for a lick, a bite for a suck," he said, but this time he turned slightly. The back door was ajar, and he put his hand between the door and the jamb—coming back with a thick, heavy turkey leg. Even in that merciless light it glistened with juice, with sauce, and just as my body had responded to Sebastian's erect manhood, I felt my stomach react to the sight of that meat; a new kind of hunger, but equally strong and determined. My stomach rumbled softly, and if my other, womanly, anatomy could have made a sound, it would have in response to its own cravings.

"Who's first?" leered Sebastian, holding out the fat drumstick in one hand and his erection in the other. For a moment, none of the shaggy men moved—then one did, stepping forward on quaking legs, and then, equally shaky, dropped to his knees. He seemed uncertain, his cloudy eyes shifting from penis to meat and back again. "You know the rules," Sebastian said, booming, angry.

The man—or the thing that used to be a man—did, it seemed, because he dropped his filthy, tooth-rotten mouth without hesitation over Sebastian's erect penis and began to loudly, sloppily suck. The sounds . . . there aren't any words to describe the sound of that bum, that hobo's lips around Sebastian's hard flesh. I was no longer hungry, and what food remained in my tight belly threatened to expel into the night air—but still, I watched.

The bum sucked on Sebastian like his erection was the fountain from which all life grew, as if through diligence he could draw into himself Sebastian's talent, wealth, intelligence, and power. Finally, Sebastian put his hand out and pushed the hobo roughly back. "That's enough," Sebastian said as the dirty thing fell back into the dust and dirt. "Bite," he said, holding out the drumstick.

This time his lips did not hesitate. With a hungry lunge, the filthy thing was on the meat, tearing at the tender flesh with his few remaining teeth, swallowing as much as he could before, again, Sebastian shoved him back—this time with a cruel kick to his shoulder. "Okay, who's next?" my brother called out to them, his voice thundering, jeering, mocking them and their pathetic lives. Standing high above them, holding tasty meat and his glistening erection, he laughed at them.

But still they came. The one may have been black or he may have simply become part of the night, like a rat that scurries along a gutter. But he came, toothless mouth gasping for my brother's flesh, my brother's meat. First, though, the flesh—rolling his dirty, scabbed mouth over Sebastian's gleaming erection, pushing himself onto the stiffness of him. Lacking in control of muscle what he had in determination, he impaled his lips onto Sebastian, pushing him deeper and deeper into himself and even clawing at the ground.

Sebastian, his face like a marble angel in the pure light, a halo of moths swirling around his golden hair, tilted his head back and slipped out a low moan, like the sound a cat might make while killing just the perfect moth, or a woman might while giving up her chastity. But Sebastian was not about to finish, not yet. Again, Sebastian's elegant hands fell to the dirty shoulders of what once had been someone's son, maybe even someone's brother or father, and pushed him away, brutally hard, sending him sprawling into the dust.

"A prize earned," Sebastian laughed, throwing the creature a whole drumstick, the plump meat slapping onto his dirty coat and rolling down into the dirt, collecting rocks, sticks, and more foul matter than I could ever imagine. But what to me was foul was to him the world, and before his gasping, clutching brethren could steal it away, he wrapped clutching hands around the meat and eagerly stuffed it into his spasming jaw.

"Who's next?" bellowed Sebastian, my brother, his eyes mad, his body immense—and they came, more of them, dozens of them, with dirty hands pushing at each other for a chance to feast on Sebastian's manhood, to earn his currency, to buy a taste of heaven. I watched, Doctor, I watched and did not turn away. I felt trapped, as condemned to stare from my dark vantage point as they were doomed to be ground even further into the dirt by their desperation for even just the smallest taste of finery.

But I watched for another reason, Doctor, for as I was shocked, revolted, by the spectacle of my brother's game with these wretched creatures, I also watched because I was in awe of my brother's power, his control, and, yes, I must say to my undying shame, to my utter humiliation, my brother's manhood. I've always loved my brother, Doctor, but that night, watching those bums and hobos suck and chew at his member, I wanted more than just a love a sister might feel for her brother, but rather . . . rather, I wanted to be down on my knees, down in the dust and dirt as well, I wanted to taste my brother's magnificence, to consume his meat—both the flesh the Lord above gave him and also, as a reward for my services, the meat Sebastian's divine gift had enriched, made almost holy. I wanted to take communion, Doctor, a communion of a man's—no, not just a man's, but rather my brother's—penis.

I was not the only one. No, even though I knew Sebastian had done this before—many, many time I was certain—I also knew that this time, this one night was special. It was something about his recipe, something about the stars, or the moon, or some other form of cosmic alignment, but that night those wretched creatures wanted their own transubstantiation, wanted Sebastian's complete divinity. They clawed and fought each other, beating and tearing at themselves to get closer, to get their postulant mouths around him, to suck and lick and draw as much of my brother as they could into themselves.

Through it all, from the start to the very end, Sebastian laughed. He laughed—I knew, I understood—because this was the ultimate for him, the pinnacle: Sebastian was everything to these once-men; he was everything they'd ever wanted, and they would do anything, endure any pain, any humiliation, to get to him.

As I would I have, Doctor. Hungry mouths working him, tongues washing his body from his penis and testicles to his booted feet, they worshiped him. He sprayed them, and they arched their gasping mouths to catch as much of the silvery ejection as was possible, fighting again for the tiniest drop, the smallest taste.

Sebastian, his head thrown back, his eyes wide open and glassy, let them pull more and more of himself out through their fingers, mouths, lips, and more, much more. My brother, Sebastian, was at the peak of his life, the crowning glory of all he'd sought his entire life. Then, at that moment, he turned his head and looked straight at me—our eyes meeting for eternity in the staccato beat of my heart. Sebastian, looking at me—and I knew then he'd always known I was there—smiled.

But then, Doctor, it happened—the thing that pushed me too far, that started the screams that only your drugs have dulled. The thing that happened only last Thursday, yet is as present in my mind as if it were just a moment, a second ago.

A flicker of pain, like lightning on a hot summer day, struck across Sebastian's face—but his smile never left his lips, never broke through his joy. The wretched things became even more excited, more fevered in their activities. Their clawlike hands reached up, clutched at Sebastian's apron, his pants, his belt, and with a great surge of starvation they pulled him down into their seething mass, teeth and gums and lips and hands tearing, ripping away at my brother, at Sebastian.

They'd had a taste, you see, Doctor, and their appetites couldn't be satiated with his drumsticks, hog ribs, or beef anymore—no, they hungered for the ultimate flesh, the perfect meat. They hungered for, and consumed before my very eyes, my brother, Sebastian.

I did not stay to see what else occurred. No longer frozen in horror, I turned and ran, screaming into the night, toward the road, the images and sounds of what had occurred, and was still occurring, behind me. I ran until a car stopped—the sheriff, of all people, who drove me to a hospital, thinking my wounds were of the flesh and not in my mind, my spirit. I told them, I tried to tell them what had happened that night, but they did not, would not, believe. Even after the sheriff had gone up that certain road, looked behind that brick-and-iron building, they wouldn't believe. I know what they said, Doctor: an accident, some kind of horrible accident with machinery. Or—and I do know they've whispered this as well—that perhaps Sebastian was murdered by my hands. But I tell you this, Doctor, I saw what I saw. I watched my brother, my beloved Sebastian, as he was consumed, feasted on by those men. I saw the appetite he'd awakened in them bloom forth in a maddening rush. I'd seen Sebastian consumed by his own mad, awful hunger.

You may think me insane—everyone here may think my mind is broken like a cheap china cup—but I tell you the truth. I cannot make myself well, Doctor, but for your kindness, for your caring I can at least give you this truth of what happened to my brother and to me. I just hope this does not stir your own hideous appetites.

xxx

I WENT ABOUT my rounds the rest of that day as a somnambulist—nodding thoughtfully, holding the hands of the patients, listening to their deliriums—but I was not there. My mind was gone, lost in its own dark pathways. I did not know what to make of her story. Her pathology was obvious, her mental disease clear—but something remained, something nagged.

When my shift ended, I climbed into my car and drove. I did not consciously think of where I was headed, my hands guiding me along darkening streets, out of the city, and toward the rolling, distant hills. I did not mean to go there, but perhaps I needed to go there, to add substance to this fading flower's delusions—to see if anything was real about her torturous dreams.

I drove for a long time, much longer than I expected, until it was there in front of me. A low brick structure with a corrugated iron roof. A single sign hung out front, a bold proclamation. I didn't get out of my car—instead I just stared at the building, certain, as I was never certain before, of the horrible truth.

Finally, I turned the car around and headed back, determined with my insight to pull her back from the precipice, the living nightmare that had happened to her.

I left EATS behind, and went back to her.

That Sweet Smell

"**THIS CITY'S A** cesspool, Sidney. It's our own little black hole of Calcutta, our own special swamp of corruption and degradation."

"You're right, JJ—absolutely."

"I am right, Sidney—I'm right because I know every inch of this filthy place, every dive and gin joint, every showgirl and crooked senator, every bent cop and bowery bum. You know something else about this city, Sidney?"

"No, JJ, what?"

"I wouldn't have it any other way." He held out an unlit cigarette, not even looking at me. "Match me, Sidney."

xxx

"**HEY, SIDNEY, WHAT'S** JJ's ass taste like?"

"Just like your wife, Bert." The loading dock was quiet otherwise, heavy evening all around us, too much for even the stars; they hadn't come out all night. Oppressive, it was. Even the city's steam pipes kept their vapors to themselves, kept them underground. The streets were clear and sharp.

Too much for the stars, for steam, too much for Bert. He didn't get down off his stool next to the print shop door. This was good, because I was in a mood to punch someone, anyone, and he was close enough.

I guess he knew that, because he just snapped his morning edition in front of his fat face, mumbling something pissed-off and stupid into the sports section. He could tell that Joltin' Joe's picture was much less easy to piss off tonight. I needed to do something with my hands, so I lit a Lucky. The smoke soothed my nerves.

At least I didn't have to wait long. Ten minutes, maybe twenty, and the door rolled up. Before it even hit the top, the ink monkeys started hauling out bundles of the morning edition.

I cut the first, twine popping like a cheap firecracker, and grabbed a copy. "About Town" was there, JJ's black and white picture flat and cold over the byline. Flat and cold, that was JJ, right there. In print and everywhere else. There was the column, but there wasn't anything about my client, not one damned word about Clifford Lehman.

"Like crap," I said to Bert, stuffing the paper under my arm, and flicking the cigarette out into the quiet night. "He tastes like crap."

xxx

HIS USUAL TABLE, at his usual place. The faces were different, but not the type: the same dogs hoping to catch a few miserable scraps. I was a dog too, but at least I was top dog.

That's what I thought, at least. I'd done my tricks, but I hadn't gotten my bone. Five to Curtis, the maitre d', to let me get back there. No chairs free. So I walked up. Stood.

He was on the phone, a huge black Bakelite beast. The receiver was small in his hand, the base held expectantly by a young waiter. "I heard you the first time, Senator, I just thought it wasn't worth wasting my breath telling you how foolish you sounded. But I can tell, now, that you're one of those poor unfortunates who actually needs to hear it, directly—or are you?"

He listened for a moment, rolling a just-started cigarette between his fingers. "That's right, Senator. You understand me perfectly." The Senator's voice was high and scratchy until it was cut off by the hollow sound of the receiver being replaced on the cradle. "What is it about politics that makes diminished capacity an employment qualification? Take that thing away," he said to a waiter, who bowed once and vanished, reeling up the cord as he left.

Three chairs faced him, the pack of the night. A fat producer type with chins and gold rings; a blousy blonde showgirl type with unfocused eyes; and a little wolf in a double-breasted number at least two years out of style. I knew his species; they nipped at my heels every day. If JJ didn't snap his nose I'd have to.

"Not like a press agent. No; at least with that rather dubious profession intellectual capacity is required, though morality and ethics are definite career hindrances. Right, Sidney?"

"Whatever you say, JJ. You know best."

A cold look from steel blue eyes. I stepped back.

"That's right, Sidney, I do. I absolutely know best—unlike creatures like yourself that know only which way to turn to avoid being kicked." He ground his cigarette out, bending it into flakes of gray ash. Another appeared in his hand from the depths of his beautiful suit. He held it out.

I was still burning deep inside, the smoke obscuring my brains. "Not right now, JJ."

He looked at me again, and my fires died under icy rain. "Right now, Sidney, right this very minute. You see, Sidney, you suffer from a specific ailment, one that you need to be reminded of periodically: the thought that you really matter to me, to the world, and most of all yourself. Match me, Sidney. This instant."

I looked at the end of the cigarette. Paper wrapped around tobacco. His strong fingers crushed the far end, making tiny flakes of brown stick out the front, toward me. My right hand was in my pants pocket, tight around my lighter. I fought the urge to pull it out, to push it toward him, to open it, flick alive a hot flame, and do it for him. I fought hard, trying to concentrate on anything except the cigarette or JJ's eyes.

I knew it, and he knew it: It wasn't just flame to tobacco. It was more than JJ's cigarette that was being pushing into my face. The place was cloudy with smoke; breathing in was like taking a drag. I could imagine the end of it in his mouth, lips around the paper, sucking in deep drags of smoke. The tip of his tongue resting on the warm end, just for a moment. Sometimes the smoke would be as warm as blood, like breathing in the essence of life. I didn't want to light it. I wanted to take it in my own mouth and draw it in deep, mix his warm smoke with my own blood, just for once taste the air that he breathed all the time.

What would it taste like, JJ's smoke? Oil from the presses? Some of the rare, best things in life? Roses? Gardenias? Maybe it just stank, the aroma of the careers he'd killed, the lives he'd ruined with his newspaper column. I didn't know, and maybe I'd never know that sweet smell of success, that taste of power—and that made me want it all the more.

"I'm waiting, Sidney. You know I don't like to be kept waiting."

I shrank like a cheap suit in hot water. My lighter, still tight in my fist, was the only thing that mattered: taking it out, lighting him up—or not. I stared at him, at the cigarette, steady in his hand. In the end I pulled it out, flipped it open, spun the wheel, waited for the flame, and then touched it—slowly, carefully—to the tip. I did it because he asked, because he was JJ and I was not. It was as simple as that.

"That's it, Sidney. That's a good boy," he said, admiring the glowing end for a long second before grinding it out in an ashtray.

XXX

I LINGERED IN the background while the wolf in the cheap suit, the fat money-man, and the plastic doll begged for attention from JJ. The doll was in a show, something glittery and stupid waiting to be born just to die. The show was put up by the producer, something fat, greasy, and idiotic, also nearly dead. The little wolf would pick over their carcasses, like his kind always did.

JJ made them sit up and beg. He made them roll over. Finally, in a dress rehearsal, he made them roll over and play dead, but they were too dumb to know it. All they saw was the great and powerful JJ paying attention to them, mouthing empty promises between acid assassinations of their intelligence and talent. When he'd had enough fun he dismissed them, promising a strategic mention in his next column, and they left wearing uncertain smiles, knowing deep down that they'd performed for nothing.

I knew they were going to their professional graves. I'd seen it too many times before, been there at too many of JJ's slick, clean kills after an evening of cold humiliation. What hurt, what got me in the belly, was the knife JJ had stuck there. After all these years, all the crooked little things I'd done, all the dirt on my hands and not his, to still have to feel the knife go in deep, like the rest of the little people.

"You still here, Sidney?" he said, looking up from his elegant handwriting on a sheaf of notes.

"Where would I go, JJ?" I said, trying to keep the sneer out of my voice.

"Oh, yes, where would you go? There can only be so many people in this fine city of ours who need your admirable services." He turned back to his notes, maybe scratching out "intelligent" and replacing it with "jackanapes."

"People like Clifford Lehman, JJ. Maybe you've heard of him?"

"Who's that, Sidney? Someone else you're sniffing around, looking for scraps?"

"My client, JJ. The one I told you you'd mention in your column tonight."

"Take a look at me, Sidney. Take a good long look." He reached into his coat and produced a cigarette, began turning it in his hands and examining it like it was the only thing in the universe. "Do I look like you, Sidney? I don't think so, at least not the last time I looked in the mirror, and I can see that you are obviously not me. That's important, Sidney. I decide who I put in my column, not you. Do we understand each other?"

He held the cigarette out. I should have reminded him of his promise to mention Lehman in his column. I could have reminded him of the dirt under my nails—his dirt. But I didn't. I looked at that cigarette and felt my knees weaken. "I got it, JJ." I said, my voice so soft I didn't think he heard it.

But he heard it all right. He hears everything. He took his eyes from mine and returned to looking at the cigarette, turning it slowly. "But sometimes, Sidney, I look in my mirror in the morning and . . . see something there. I don't see it often, but I do see it—around the eyes, Sidney. Right around here." He stared at me again, one long middle finger tracing next to his firm nose, down his cheekbone, up around the side of his face, and back the way it came. "I look in the mirror and see you there, Sidney. Like I said, not often. But I see the little fool I used to be."

He held the cigarette out to me. I looked at it, and for me it was the only thing in the entire universe. His gesture was slight, almost hidden, but to me it was obvious: a cant of the wrist, the filter tilted toward me—an offering. I knew what it was, the dance we did with lighter and cigarette. I knew why I got a hard-on for filter tips, for Lucky Strikes; why the pop of sulfur from a match, the whiff of gas from a lighter, reached down deep and tugged at my guts. It wasn't completely a dick thing, but that was part of it. It wasn't that JJ was hot for me, or I for him; it was me, on my knees, lighting him. It had become this thing we did, his way of standing over me, and—god help me—I'd gotten used to it, almost looked forward to it.

This was different. JJ wasn't on his knees, but he hadn't pushed me down, stuck the unlit end in my face, and told me to light it up. This time he was offering me the filter. He was sitting and I was standing, but he offered me one as though we were equals.

I didn't know what to think. Even my guts didn't know what to think. The place seemed to have gone all quiet.

"This is a special arrangement, Sidney. A limited time offer. Take it. You know you want to."

I reached down and pinched it between my fingers. For a heartbeat, JJ didn't let go; then he did, and I brought the cigarette up to my face. I felt the texture of the tobacco through the crinkling paper, the virgin smell subtle—almost imperceptible. I looked over the filtered end at JJ.

"That's it, Sidney, that's it. Feels good, doesn't it? That sense of control, the influence. You can make the world dance for you, Sidney: a waltz, a jig—you call the tune. Or at least you could."

I heard it between the words, and what I was holding was just a cigarette, just some dried weeds wrapped in cheap paper. Just that. "What do you want, JJ?" I said.

"You know me too well, Sidney. There's this . . . annoyance, over at the *Tribune*. Calls himself a columnist, when he's barely capable of writing a shopping list, let alone wield words in an effective, or even competent, manner. You know people, Sidney . . . people who might be able to show him the error of his arrogance. Do that and my thanks will be . . . impressive."

That was it. Back on my knees, my lips open. I wanted to pulverize the cigarette in my fist, throw down the pathetic thing onto his table. Would I? Did I? No. I didn't because I could really smell it, sweet and alluring, for the first time in my life. I could take his demands, his condescension, his games of blood and tears, because I held the first cigarette he'd ever given me.

"Okay, JJ. I'll do it." I hoped he could hear the hidden "last time" between the words and understand that everything had changed when he gave me the cigarette. It wasn't just his. That day, it became ours.

JJ's hearing is excellent. He can hear the tiniest little gossiping bird on the busiest part of Broadway. But he looked at me like I hadn't said anything. In his hand was another cigarette, filter toward him, raw tobacco demanding a light.

XXX

I KNEW PEOPLE. I knew a lot of people, and some of them were even speaking to me. I slipped into my office long enough to grab my little black book, avoid a call from Clifford Lehman, get that special little bag I keep behind the radiator, and get out before anyone saw me. Burt Kello was one of those names in my little black book: a bull-necked cop who wasn't happy unless he was breaking someone in half. Some people had blood in their veins, others—like JJ—had ice water, but Kello had other people's blood. The sight of it, the smell of it, animated him. He smiled when other people screamed, frowned when the city was quiet and behaving itself. I hated Kello, but I needed him, which made me hate him more.

I ducked into a little coffee bar on Broadway and called him. Gave him a name, a time, and what to look for. It wasn't true, of course, but at least it would be in an hour or two.

I also knew a guy named Ernest Odets. I'd read his column a few times on and off ever since he started at the *Tribune*. He wasn't JJ (thank God there was only one JJ) but he was good. I thought about hitting him up for some coverage, getting some of my clients their slice of the limelight. But there was something sickly honest about him, as if he was blessed with a glow while the rest of us burned with guilt. I knew a few other things about him—like where he'd be tonight, and what Kello would find in his pocket an hour from now.

XXX

THE GASLIGHT WAS too well lit for its name. Walking in I felt the bright lights over the bar and had to shade my eyes, as if the dark streets had permanently blinded me in anything other than twilight.

I found him in the back, rubbing his forehead as he struggled with something scrawled in a notebook. Pieces, no doubt, that would be tomorrow's column. He saw me, eyes big and pale blue, and went back to his notebook. I felt my back stiffen. Kiss my ass or kick it, but at least see that it's there.

"Hey, Ernest," I said, sliding up to him, trying to make out the scribbles in the notebook. "No rest for the wicked, eh? Let me buy a hard-working Joe like you something to lubricate the pen a bit."

"Go away, Sidney," he said, still not looking up. "I don't have anything to say to JJ."

"I'd have those eyes checked if I were you, Ernest. I don't see JJ here." I signaled to a waiter. "Two, straight-up, with ice."

He looked up from his book, shook his head at the waiter, and finally turned toward me. "No, Sidney, JJ's not here. But you are, and that's the same thing, isn't it?"

"Give me some credit, Ernest," I said, tapping out a Lucky Strike and making a show of hunting for a lighter or a match. "This is Sidney you're talking to here. Sure, I do things for JJ, and he does things for me—just like I'd like to do something for you."

He looked at the cigarette in my hand. "Those things are bad for you, Sidney. Quit while you can."

I felt a frown crease my face, in spite of myself. I "found" my lighter and lit up, breathing a gray cloud down at the table. The smoke was sweet but faintly bitter. I'd had it too long in my pocket, the tobacco was stale. It wouldn't burn cleanly. "Lots of things are bad for you, Ernest. Lots of things. Doesn't mean you can't enjoy them."

"That's pathetic," he said, closing his notebook with a soft slap. "No, you're pathetic, Sidney—sniffing around, playing JJ's lapdog, his pet, his boy, his punk. Do you like sniffing around the dregs that JJ passes down to you? You've got to; that's the only thing that makes sense. You've got to like getting down on your knees and lighting him up. That's it, isn't it, Sidney? Be honest for once in your life. You like giving it up to him. Say it."

I rose, crushing the hot end of my Lucky into his open notebook. For a moment, stale tobacco mixed with burning paper. "You want honesty, boy scout? You want the Big Truth for the column no one reads? How's this for a scoop: it's not pretty, it tastes like crap, but people like JJ run this town, and run this world. People like you don't see it till someone's boots fall on your face, till you're dead and the dirt's in your mouth. That's the truth, Ernest, and it's about time you figured that out."

I turned and left, not looking back. I stopped at the door just long enough to put my coat on—and put the special little bag I'd taken from my office into Ernest's coat pocket. Outside, the night was just as I'd left it: cold and dark, with only the glow of Broadway to light my way. I stood there for a second, breathing hard. As I was digging into my pocket for another smoke, I saw Kello's car pull up, and he and another beefy flatfoot got out and headed into the place. I stood outside for a second, the unlit cigarette in my mouth, before finally lighting up. As the flame touched the end, as the paper and then the flaked brown leaves caught with a crackle, I inhaled. I was expecting the smoky hit, the warm glow from inside out, but it didn't happen: the smoke was too hot, the smell harsh and old. Still more stale tobacco. A cough reached up and grabbed my chest in a lightning spasm, and the cigarette fell to the sidewalk. I looked at it, still smoldering among the garbage, and thought for a second about picking it up to take another sour hit. Instead I threw the rest of the pack away, planning to get myself a fresh one on the way to JJ's penthouse. A little celebration for a job well done.

xxx

IT TOOK ME awhile to get there, a nice little stroll through the leaden night. The city that never sleeps was nevertheless not quite awake. A cop directed traffic like a slow ballet dancer. A shoeshine boy polished with steady, lethargic grace.

I finished my fresh cigarette as I walked up to JJ's lobby door. The smoke was light and feathery in my lungs, a glowing warmth that made the night seem warm. A smoke had never tasted sweeter. For the first time in my life, I felt the way JJ must feel all the time. I looked at the burning end of my cigarette and felt the world revolve around the hot tip. It wasn't just a Lucky, it was my dick that the whole damned city was revolving around.

I finished it with a flourish and flicked it in a glowing arc. It landed with a tiny shower of bright orange sparks as I went inside, and up.

xxx

THE PLACE WAS dark, almost as black as the night outside. The only light came from a bedside lamp in one of the side bedrooms. I almost missed JJ, who was out on the balcony; his white bathrobe outlined him against the distant gray towers of the city. I only knew that he was facing me, and not the tiny lights of Manhattan, when he said, "Come out here, Sidney."

"Done and done," I said, stepping out into the crisp night sky. I tried to keep my face cool and indifferent, but he heard the smile in my voice.

"So how does the canary taste, Sidney? As sweet as you expected?"

"Just doing what needed to be done, JJ."

He smiled, showing a lot of porcelain. "What I needed done, Sidney. Don't forget that. I asked, and you did."

He stepped back inside and I followed, walking in just as he was opening a small brass box sitting on an elegant marble table. "Kello informs me that Mr. Odets has managed to escape his long arms, but that he should be arrested momentarily."

The thought of Ernest being in Kello's fat, calloused hands made me hesitate, whatever I was about to say vanishing from my mind.

"Not that his arrest is all that important to developments, eh, Sidney? In this town, all it takes is the suggestion of impropriety, the implication of some misbehavior, for the axe to fall. At least, a suggestion that comes from an unimpeachable source." He smiled wryly, knowing that many little birds had whispered many hideous rumors into his ears, all faithfully passed on to his hundreds of thousands of readers. "The fact that Mr. Odets was brought in for questioning by Kello will do the job just fine, and his inevitable booking and sentencing for possession will simply be a satisfying conclusion to my readers: a reminder that, for the wicked, there is no escape from the law."

He stood, holding an unlit cigarette. In the dim apartment it was pale white, almost glowing in the distant lights of the city.

"And a reminder of the power of JJ," I said, the words coming before I could stop them.

He turned toward me, his face lost in shadow. He was the white form of his bathrobe, the slender streak of his cigarette. "Yes, Sidney, that is the lesson to be learned here—for more than the unfortunate Mr. Odets."

The cigarette hovered near his waist. I couldn't see, but I knew his robe was open. He was naked under it. His dick was hard.

"You know what's expected of you, Sidney. Don't disappoint me." The cigarette bobbed slightly, the pale, narrow shaft dipping and rising in the low light.

Without thinking, I dropped my hand to my front pants pocket and my hand closed around the hardness of my lighter. Carefully, slowly, I pulled it out. It gleamed from the distant reflections and light spills of Broadway. I stroked it, once, my mind full of nothing but traffic noise.

"Match me, Sidney," JJ said, his voice low and powerful.

I moved toward him, but he stepped back, pulling the cigarette away. "No, Sidney. Get down on your knees."

I started to say something, but I could feel him staring me down, his cold blue eyes pushing through the front of my head, into my brain.

The carpet was plush, ashen, like I was kneeling in a manicured ashtray. I could feel the heat from his naked body, and I started to sweat—really sweat. In my hand, my lighter was slippery.

"That's it, Sidney. You know what to do."

I flipped it open, the flame bright in the darkness. I turned my head away, trying not to see all that it revealed, but I saw enough to make me swallow hard. Carefully, I touched the blue and yellow flame to the end of his cigarette.

Seeing the paper and tobacco catch, JJ pulled it away from my sight, up to his lips. I could hear, but not see, the faint crackle, the tiny roar, as he took his first drag.

I didn't wait; I climbed right to my feet—took two big steps back, the hard marble of the table hitting me in the calves. "Okay, JJ. I did what you wanted," I started, but then I saw a shadow in the side room. A shadow that moved.

"This is an evil city, Sidney. It's a place full of darkness and corruption. It's my job to tell my readers that, in order to expose the underbelly of this decaying Gotham. But there's something else you seem to forget about this city, Sidney."

Kello stepped out of the side room, his huge, burly body filling the doorway. He looked at me and smiled, showing wide, brown teeth.

"It's mine, Sidney, and I won't share it with anyone." He turned away from Kello and me, neatly closing his robe. "It seems to me, Detective Kello, that Mr. Odets must have had a supplier for his illegal substances. Someone perhaps in the same industry, say, a certain press agent. I do believe you would be doing this fine city a great service if you would bring someone like that in for questioning. I'm sure, too, that Mr. Odets would be more than willing to agree that he was the supplier in question—for a diminished sentence, of course."

I didn't say anything because instantly I knew there wasn't anything I could say. I just ran.

XXX

THE NIGHT WAS still cold, but even more empty. This wasn't my town anymore, if it ever was. Everyone I saw as I ran was connected by newsprint and ink to Kello's big, bruising hands. Every cab only went one place—to the precinct house—an express to a cement cell, a rubber hose. The only thing being served in every diner and café was ashes.

I couldn't go home, I couldn't go to my office. I couldn't get out, and I couldn't stay. I might stay out of Kello's reach for a few hours, maybe a few days, but I'd never escape JJ. I almost laughed because what I wanted, more than anything, was a smoke.

Behind the Gaslight was an alley. Garbage cans and rotting food and broken crates. It could have been anywhere in the city, every alley merging with every other one, making a hobo highway through the dark city. It was that alley, the one behind the Gaslight, that I finally stumbled into, exhausted, struggling for breath.

Did I really hear the voice? I'd been hearing a lot of strange things since I ran from JJ's apartment out into the dark city: sirens racing down the canyons, Kello's footsteps from every doorway, JJ's voice from on high pronouncing my death, celebrating my destruction to a city of faithful readers.

I looked up from where I crouched behind broken boxes to see a shadowed figure, clothes torn, hair a mad disarray. "Sidney?" the figure asked, in a low, conspiratorial voice.

His name burst from my lips. "Odets? My God—Odets! They're after me. You're got to help me. They're everywhere—I have to get away."

He looked as if he were made of stone in the dim light of the alley. His face barely moved as he spoke. "Maybe, Sidney—maybe I'll help you. After all, I know exactly how you feel. Exactly."

"Thank God! Thank you, Ernest—oh, thank you . . . if there's anything, *anything*, you need you just let me know . . . "

I thought I saw a smile slide across his lips. "Oh, you will, Sidney. You will thank me. That I guarantee." There was a cigarette in his hand—a crumbled, almost broken cigarette. "Light it, Sidney. Light me."

Bitch

THERE WAS A used condom in the trash. Just lying there, slightly yellowed, glistening, full at the tip. Next to the rest of the garbage—the bloated white plastic, the dark-stained brown paper bags—it was brilliant and shocking. Envy was a burning bile in Quinn's throat as he looked down at it. Finally, the weight of the trash in his arms broke through his thoughts, and with an unconscious hiss of strain, he lifted it high and slammed it down into the can.

Walking back down the narrow alleyway, retracing his slippered steps to the stairs up to his apartment, he caught sight of one of them up on the balcony, leaning flamboyantly back, a half-full glass in his hand glimmering in the dying sunlight. Looking at him perhaps too long, Quinn summoned him, causing the young man to sip from his glass and look over and down. Eye contact: the lean body, the delicately sculpted hair, the perfect porcelain smile, the wicked mocking grin, directed at Quinn. Then a kiss, not blown but rather thrown—like a stone, mocking. At Quinn, at the garbage. Face burning, heart pounding, Quinn walked with heavy steps up to his own place, each note of the laughter, each bird-chirp sound a cut into his back.

Upstairs (sticky key in gummy lock, stubborn door groaning with age) Mr. Boots was waiting for him. Sometimes, not often, the sight of the skinny little black-and-white cat made Quinn feel that he had, indeed, arrived home. Other times, like evenings discovering the leftovers of someone else's pleasure, the sight of the old mangy cat just reminded him of Billy. The Latino hustler had taken much—his camera, his stereo, the $2,500 in his bank account—but he'd left at least two things behind. One was a note, the condescending words a bitterness he recalled too often, and the other was the sad little kitten they'd picked out together at the shelter.

"Okay, okay," Quinn said, shuffling inside and dead-bolting the back porch door. "I'll feed ya." It was a standard, the closest he came to a religion, part of a litany that held his life together. Again, the dark, smelly kitchen, the piles of magazines and newspapers. The *Tom of Finland* signed print in the dusty frame given to him by Lorenzo—who had left with not as much money, not as much damage, and so more frequently dropped into Quinn's fantasies.

The living room was as dark as the kitchen, with a bouquet of its own—a musty, lethargic smell. A weight of too many days too much the same. Walking in, Quinn thumbed the set on first, and then the machine. The old television crackled menacingly, humming a firm base, then glowing into a newscaster's head and shoulders. The other machine made a much cleaner start, showing the familiar ribbed chest backdrop, the same perfect pectorals, the intimate parade of icons down one side. Normally, when the litany of his days was more comfortable, he might have wandered down to the Shamrock, watched some game or other with the cronies there, or sat at the kitchen table with his latest *Honcho, Inches,* or *Torso,* sipping from an amber bottle until the images seemed to swim in a lazy haze of self-imposed steam.

Condoms in the trash. The anger was too present, too acid. The old desk chair creaked under his ass, the mouse skipped across the screen—a half-conscious reminder to clean it—and with a click Quinn opened a door.

It hadn't always been that way. It was the quicksand of life, a slow descent. He hadn't struggled—at least not at first. His birth had been in a cool house in Virginia, inhabited by a mother who drank, a chief petty officer father, and then Benjamin, their "sensitive" son. His first memories, painfully recalled as a dull ache when he sat at the kitchen table, were of muscle magazines smuggled up into the attic. Thinking of those men, of their strong smiles, their marble muscles, made him long for their innocence: children's desires mixed with ancient dust. One summer, the summer he'd first seen another boy's penis at swim camp, he'd stayed there so long the dust had lodged in his throat. Till the day his mother died, she was troubled by the allergies that had so affected him then.

He used to keep some shutters open, like the one to the left in the bay window, looking across the narrow alley at the neighbor's mirror Victorian. Sometimes, sitting in front of one glowing screen or other, he would catch sight of them—the boys with the golden hair, the magical eyes, the so-smooth skin. A picture book he'd seen as a boy, that same year that the allergies had made his eyes water, the artist long since forgotten—but the images, naiads flitting through carbonated pools under an azure sky with clouds like white satin, had remained: an ideal, an absolute. Mythical sprites, with skin like fresh cream. A favorite fantasy from then on, being something other than the old Quinn, the bowed and balding Quinn. Being one of them, diving through the bubbling waters, hips brushing against theirs, mouths fluttering sweet kisses, eyes full of love and sweet desire.

Once the painting had been across that tiny alley, once he'd looked out the frame of that open window and seen them: blue eyes, wheat-field hair, laughter like the chiming of precious bells, chests like marble carved by swimming, running, fucking. Then one of them had looked, had seen Quinn staring back. The stuff of dreams . . . but he had laughed, producing the cruel biting caw that had since begun living in his disturbing half-sleeps, his hollow and lonely nightmares.

Are you horny tonight? The bluntness of the newbie, flashing up on his screen. The skies were phosphors, microscopic dots arranged in a grid, illuminated by a tight spray of electrons. No clouds. No water. But the boys could be as lithe and alluring as in that painting. All it took was a polite deception, a sensual lie. It wasn't idyllic, wasn't perfection, but maybe someone, somewhere, would think that. For old Quinn, in his threadbare slippers, his old cat, his stacks of yellowing porno magazines, it was still a kind of magic.

Tonight, though, he didn't feel like being Troy, or Lance, or Julian. Tonight, Quinn was too much . . . Quinn. He didn't answer the message, and instead just lurked, watching the scrolls of chatter, feeling the anger chew and gnaw.

Empty-headed peacocks. A simple, bold font.

You're insulting peacocks, Quinn clicked/clacked back, his hands dancing on the faded letters of the keyboard. *At least peacocks produce something.*

It hadn't always been this way, which made it so much worse. When you fall, however slowly, you know what used to be, what is possible, what's being denied, been taken away. He'd never been one of the . . . peacocks, but he hadn't always lurked in the heavy darkness. Some good timing—the death of his father, a heart attack at fifty-five—had left him some real estate. His mother dropping into a sullen old age had cut the ties, severed them quick and clean. He'd had money—enough—and a mission. To put flesh to dreams, to make dusty attic fantasies real.

Disgusting. Just disgusting—

Rude, inconsiderate, Quinn typed back, watching the characters appear on his glowing screen. *Parading around, flouncing it up. Rubbing our faces in it. Yeah, fucking disgusting—*

Many good years, a heavenly parade of memories. Boyfriends, money, glitter balls and beer. Snapshots that flipped through his mind when he didn't want them: the Latin boy, all darkness and smiles, jeans too tight, lips too full. The hot kiss after the parade. Back then the world had been wide, open—full of love and potential for more. The blond treasure, who'd served him coffee one day—beaming grin, flirting eyes. "Call me, hon," slender fingers grazing Quinn's palm. The seven digits on the check.

He'd been too scared to call, too intimidated by perfection. These days, he masturbated in the dark, hating himself for his cowardice.

Hate them. Know how that is. Disgusting peacocks. So pretty, so stupid. Shoving our faces in it.

He felt lied to, the bitterness seeming right, justified. He'd crossed that bridge of knives, lived with the hatred: "Fag! Homo! Fucking Queer!" He'd wanted to be welcomed, embraced, brought into the Muscle Academy, whisked away to the dude ranch where cowboys would use him to his utter enjoyment. He'd wanted . . . to taste it. Now though . . . now he knew it for what it was: a rainbow lie. It was there, but only if you had the money, the looks, the courage. If you didn't have any of that, then it was all out of reach or—soiled condoms in the trash—just a bitter reminder of failure.

Just disgusting. Hate looking at them, he typed, feeling a little strong in his hatred, his bitchiness. The other, Rollin58991, was an illusion—but one he felt a closeness to. An illusion because so much was unknown—or just unnecessary to share. Quinn imagined him as a mirror, somewhere in the city, somewhere like where he was, seeing the beauty, having the hunger, but knowing the smiles were mocking—not inviting.

They chatted for a few minutes more till the anger exhausted Quinn. Slippers on his feet, he shuffled off to bed. He thought about masturbating, but the sourness in his throat made their lithe young bodies hard and cruel, distant and viscous. He let sleep take him.

XXX

A DAY LATER—or it could have been just a bit longer. He did remember the walk back from the bar. Three beers in his pale belly, legs tired from the hill. Disco thumping down the tree-lined street. With the first note he knew it was a party, knew it was next door.

It was. Pretty young things, features cut from tanned stone, brilliant smiles flashing desire. Lithe bodies poised on the balcony, sparkling laughter and gruff desire drifting down, mixing with the sexual base of the music.

Quinn got older, fatter. He hadn't noticed his reek before, but now it hit him—booze and cigarettes, the perfume of the pathetic.

Key in the lock, gate swung wide. Down the alley, upstairs, to the other balcony. Cheap plastic tumblers in thin, strong hands. So easy . . . so easy he did it without thinking: those hands around his cock, those soft lips on his own. He felt himself stir despite the pain of reality.

One of them turned, looked down with a smile that lit up the world, a burst of innocent light. That it could have been pity never entered Quinn's mind—that he had looked and not looked away was enough. It was a kind of touch, a kind of love. Distant, yes; never more than a look, but there was something special in this young statue, this young David's glance. He saw a man like himself. They had something in common—a lust for men's bodies, for men's love.

But then someone took the young man's arm, pulled him back into the tanned and buffed chaos, back into the merciless rhythm of the party. Words, maybe his or maybe someone else's, drifted down, lacerated Quinn, poured alcohol into the cuts . . . "fucking troll . . ."

He didn't feel it at first, not as it slipped past his ears and into his mind. But with the first heavy foot on the old wooden steps, it started: the anger, the shame. Upstairs, the dark, smelly apartment, the cat—and the reminder of the acid in the smile, the promises not kept, and being taken advantage of. "You just ain't got anything I want," the little Latino had said, almost his last words to Quinn.

Nothing was there—the apartment, as always, was empty.

Alone and burning, he walked into the darker front room. He'd left the machine running, a fact that surprised him. A creature of habit, Quinn had rolled his routine around him — a warm blanket, thick armor. The machine had been left on. Unusual.

A screech of mating modems. Chat at first — pleasantries, but feeling forced, wooden. He was a false Quinn, one following the rules he'd set out for himself.

There's something wrong. "Them" again?

Fingers paused above keys. The anger, the shame, were bubbling — making his ears ring, his breath come in ragged gasps.

Fucking hate them, he finally typed, slowly.

I know. I know how they make you feel. I understand.

Disgusting. Stupid, fucking, pretty-boys.

Let it out. All of it. It'll help.

So he did. Fingers, slowly at first, but then faster, spelling out his pain. The hate. Later, looking over his shoulder at that dark room he'd typed in, lit only by bluish technology, he realized just how much hate had dribbled . . . poured out of him. He'd opened a vein and bled on the keys — frustration, bitterness, resentment. The lies of love and happiness. The lies of *Honcho, Torso,* and *Tom of Finland.* The rainbow lie. It could all be yours if you were anyone but Quinn — fat, ugly, and old.

Mostly, he had talked about his anger. The disgust he felt for them — they way they paraded around, showing off their shallowness, their petty, whining voices. Peacocks, empty-headed peacocks. Giggling like girls — nauseating.

Finally, he couldn't see anymore. Going into the bright yellow bathroom, he pulled off a long streamer of toilet tissue, blew his nose, then gagged and threw up — something that always happened when he cried.

When he went back, the machine was still on, the screen still glowing.

Can you sleep?

Smiling, Quinn typed an affirmative.

Then sleep. It will all be better in the morning.

XXX

NO ALARM CLOCK. Sirens, instead. A short, sharp whoop. The sound of tires scraping a curb, breaking a bottle. Quinn rolled over and felt sleep tug at him again.

But then—another sound. It wasn't something he was used to hearing, so it pulled him back out of his doze. A basic kind of sound. Getting up, he threw on his threadbare yellow robe and fumbled to the window, the one that looked out onto the narrow alley. Opening the old window, the sound was louder. For a moment, and just that, he thought that it was, perhaps, the cat—trapped and maybe dying somewhere. But a glance over his shoulder showed him the small animal, asleep, curled into a ball on the kitchen table.

Crying. No—sobbing. No—screaming. No . . . a sound he hadn't quite heard before, but still essentially human. It came from within the house next door, in waves.

Quinn went around to the front, saw blue and red flashes through the thick curtains. Parting them he saw a police car. No, two. And a white panel van.

Quinn watched, not feeling much of anything, as the stretcher was brought out. Long form in a black plastic bag. One of the men, nothing more than a boy, walking alongside, face haunted, drawn.

After awhile, the cars and the van left. The neighborhood became soft and quiet. Quinn didn't think all that morning—at least, he tried not to. He was confused, puzzled, and sad. Instead of thinking, he absently watched television, the sound loud, booming. Finally, as the sun started to set and the night grew cool, he went into his living room, to his computer.

A piece of mail was waiting for him. The words at first didn't make any sense. So he read them again and again.

Disgusting fags, the message said. Then, *I hope that will make you feel better.*

When he did believe it, the tears started again—but not for himself.

The Hard Way

A HALF-DOZEN BLOCKS from the hall, a bum offered to blow him for a dollar.

Stanley'd left the hotel on Flood Street in the afternoon. That morning at two or so he'd stripped down to his BVDs and T-shirt and stretched out on the stiff sheets, the yellow-stained window shade tap-tap-tapping against the sill from a steady breeze. At first he didn't think he'd be able sleep, but despite the humming of his nerves and the sound of the shade on the sill, he closed his eyes once, twice—and opened them again at five.

He'd taken a few minutes to shave, scraping the old safety razor across his cheeks, the raspy strokes echoing in the small bathroom. Despite the butterflies in his stomach, he'd taken his time getting into his last good suit. He'd carefully polished his shoes night before. The Hamburg he'd picked up in Philly. The two-grand roll went into his suit pocket, a few bucks for food and booze went into the pants. Hand on the knob, he noticed a smudge of something white and powdery—probably plaster—on his slim leather case, so he stopped, walked over to the sink, and carefully cleaned the faded leather with the corner of a towel.

He walked. He didn't want to be late, but being early was just as bad. Late would have been rude, but almost expected of a damned good player: it meant he was too good to bother looking at his watch before a game. Early, though . . . early meant he was wet behind the ears, and he'd be admitting to jittery nerves. So he walked, feeling the day cool into night, watching Baltimore's lights hum and flicker to life.

He didn't know where he was, but he knew where the hall was. Tevis's Pool & Billiards was four blocks straight, four to the left.

From the heavy shadows of a narrow alley, the spook's voice was soft, musical. "Hey, hey, hey . . . " until Stanley turned toward him.

"Yeah? What the fuck you want?" Stanley said, tone more bored or distracted than threatening. He'd taken and given more than his fair share since riding out from Oakland. His knee still hurt when it got real cold, a memory of when a couple of crackers in Memphis had got him with a five iron. He didn't need to see the guy to know he could handle him if he needed to.

"Hey, mister! Got a buck, mister?"

He wasn't as old as he sounded. Not a kid, but not gray and hunched either. Maybe as tall as Stanley, but a lot of meals fewer in size. Hair cut real close, probably only a week out of stir. Eyes brown. Skin like the faded leather on Stanley's shoes before last night when he'd sponged on the dark polish. He had a stink, like booze—but also like a lot of spooks Stanley had known, so he knew he might not have been drunk.

"Come on, brother. All I's want is a spot or two for a couple of long-necks and a room."

Stanley's hand was in his pocket, the crackle of the bills making the spook's eyes brighten. Normally, Stanley would have told him to fuck off, but not tonight. Tonight was too bright, too clear: it was a game night. A big game night—probably his biggest—and he was just feeling too good to get pissed off.

Then the guy offered to blow him for a buck. It was so smooth, so quick that at first Stanley didn't pick it up, thought it was just a different melody in his concert of panhandling. Stanley had thought of rounding up a whore the night before, but somehow it hadn't felt right. He'd spent it instead having a good steak and potatoes in the Blue Ewe on Mason, then he'd gone back to his room to try and relax enough to read the paper. Besides, he didn't know Carson well enough to know how he'd react to his imported shooter getting laid the night before the big game.

His cock was hard, surprising Stanley. He'd played it both ways, both before he'd hopped the rails and his few times in stir, but he always preferred cunt to cock. But still, his cock was hard. His nerves were buzzing like too many cups of black coffee, and a bright burst of fear ran up his back and into his brain. In a flash, he saw his fine white hands shake, felt the green felt slide under his unsteady fingers. That's all it would take.

"You're on, brother; just better be damned worth it."

The wino grinned an old picket-fence smile as Stanley walked past him into the alley. "I'm worth it, brother. Oh, yeah, ol' Richie's worth it. An arteest, I am. Got the best fucking lips in Joliet, they say about ol' Richie. Take the white right off your fucking dick I will."

Stanley popped his belt and dropped his fly, metal teeth surprisingly loud in the narrow space. "Just get sucking, okay?" he said, tugging his hard cock out of his BVDs.

Richie slowly lowered himself: one knee, then the other. The rotten, almost fingerless gloves he wore came off carefully, to be stuffed in a pocket. He clapped once, like a shot bouncing off the brickwork, and rubbed his hands together in front of Stanley's hard dick.

Then he stopped, looking up at Stanley past his cock. "Fuck me. I know you, right? Baltimore, right, the shooter that took down Legs Elmwood, right? Eight hours, wasn't it? Eight hours at the table. Stan, right? Fast Stan . . . fuck me, if it isn't you."

And fuck if Stanley didn't smile, looking down at this black punk who he'd usually have kicked the shit out of, told to fuck off and die—and fuck if Stanley didn't blush, the red burning his cheeks. "Got me, bro. Got me clean and neat."

"Fuck me," Richie said staring up at him with his Jesus-seen-in-church look, his one dark hand absently stroking Stanley's hard dick. "You're something man. You're really something."

Stanley didn't know what to say, words not even leaving his

brain, let alone getting caught in his throat.

Richie smiled one more time, showing that weathered fence of cracked porcelain again, then dropped his mouth down to Stanley's never-dipping dick.

Feeling big and important, it took a few minutes longer than normal for the sensation of Richie's mouth on his dick to work its way through Stanley's mind. But when it did, when he actually started to feel those soft lips and that hard-sucking mouth on his cock, Stanley had to actually think: He's fucking good.

His legs felt weak, so he leaned back, absently realizing his last good suit was getting filthy from the grimy alley wall. Stanley was all but uncaring on the high he was riding.

Richie worked his dick, sucking, licking, even kissing the fat head—never had Stanley had such a good job done on him. Gals, guys—no one. It was scary, in a way, how good the little creep was. It wasn't right. Not that he was getting sucked off by him, but that he was too damned good. But Stanley didn't do anything about it, and even the little voice in the back of his skull wasn't loud enough to bring his hand down to his dick, to Richie's face, and push him away.

"My treat, brother. I scored good off a ten-shot I put down in that game. Not that I don't want the five, you know what I mean?" Richie said, smiling up at Stanley, spit and sticky come on his fat lips.

Weak to near collapse, Stanley could do nothing but smile and start to say, "Put another ten down tonight . . . " when the little bum started to work his cock again, swallowing all the way down deep.

That was it. Stanley felt it down deep in his balls—the good ache, the quivering bolt of juice up and out of his so-hard cock and right into Richie's slobbering mouth.

After his heart stopped hammering, and his eyes cleared from the spots that'd flashed in front of them, Stanley pushed himself carefully away from the wall—suddenly self-conscious of how crappy his suit now looked. Then he pushed his still-hard cock into his shorts and hauled up his pants from where they'd fallen to his shoes. He gave the wino a twenty, the biggest bill he had that wasn't on his roll.

With Richie thanking him over and over like a broken record behind him, he walked the four blocks forward, four blocks up to Tevis's Pool & Billiards and the game he was there to play.

xxx

"YOU READY, KID?" Carson said from his seat by the door as Stanley walked up the tall flight of stairs to the hall. Carson was dressed the same as when Stanley had first met him three days before, in a bright white shirt, a thin black tie, and a simple black coat and pants. Stanley thought that he looked like a minister who should be leading his flock rather than making book. He smiled, wide and broad, friendly despite the money he had riding on the game—or at least he looked that way.

"I'm ready," Stanley smiled back, strength in his voice. In his pants, his cock was still semi-hard from Richie's sucking.

The hall was on the second floor above a dark little bar Stanley had never been in. He never drank that close to a hall or a game. The windows were dark from smoke. Against one wall was a narrow caged booth. In it was an elegantly dressed black man, as much the preacher as Carson. He watched Stanley walking across the hall, like a cat casing a mouse.

Along the walls at the base of those heavy-smoked windows were the spectators' seats. They were empty, red plush upholstery looking like a thick red river under the glass, except for three. In one was a kid maybe half Stanley's age, in a white shirt and bright blue tie, sleeves rolled up to show blond hairs like a glow on his arms. His head, too, was bright blond, like polished brass. Next to him was some muscle, a dockyard worker or ex-fighter crammed into a wrinkled and musty suit that looked like something borrowed from a mortician brother. The muscle's eyes were dark, like bricks missing from a wall, and hooded by thick brows and ridges. He was too far away, and his eyes too small, for Stanley to see if he was watching him—but Stanley felt him nonetheless. Just as Stanley had scoped the tables for faded velvet, obvious warps, or any shaking from the bar downstairs, he knew the muscle was sizing him up, deciding which bones he could break if he needed to.

Next to the muscle was the other side of Carson, the dark to his white. While Carson had dressed like a minister about to step in front of his flock, this guy was dressed for a club in a neat, pinstriped, double-breasted number with dark wingtips. Stanley had spent years crouched over a table, knocking the polished balls into black pits, listening to their clicks and clacks as if trying to decipher some secret language of balance and English. This guy had spent twice as long figuring out how to take money from people: sometimes by getting his muscle to break their fingers, sometimes by using people like Stanley. His face was dark. It wasn't dusty black like Richie's, and it wasn't mahogany like the manager's; it was like midnight, pitch, or a starless night. The only thing that shone from his face were his teeth when he smiled— and he was smiling—and his eyes, which were like gleaming scales judging Stanley's worth.

Carson was suddenly next to Stanley, speaking to the hard darkness of his opposite. "Gossod evenin', Portaphoi."

"It is gonna be that, ain't it, Mr. Carson," Portaphoi said, his voice a deep lilt, "fer at least one ah us." It didn't seem possible, but he smiled even more broadly, showing a rear gold tooth in a flash that surpassed the glow from the boy standing next to him. "So dis be ya shooter from da West of the country, Mr. Carson?" He turned the brilliant white and gold to Stanley. "Ah be hearin' good t'ings about you, Mistah. I hear ya can shoot da moon straight inta da pocket."

Stanley smiled, knowing he should be scared, shaking in his

shoes, but he wasn't. He was the shooter. The light was on him. The evening would be good for them if it was good for him, if he shot a good game of pool tonight. The question of him not shooting the moon into a pocket didn't even occur to him. He smiled back at Portaphoi, not caring that his own teeth were piss-yellow from too many cigarettes. "And I can do it straight off the break."

"Haha!" Portaphoi's laugh reminded Stanley of an empty barrel rolling down an alley, the growl of thunder after a big damned stroke of lightning. "The boy does have spunk, he does. You be doin' good, Mr. Carson, if his cue be as big as his dick, no?"

Stanley smiled right back, never dipping his eyes from Portaphoi's deep brown pits.

"Dis here be my gun, and he always be shootin' straight," Portaphoi said, turning toward the golden boy with a nod. "Billie, this be Stanley. He be the man you gonna be beatin' tonight."

The boy didn't move, didn't smile. His face stayed polished bronze, but his hand slowly rose. Stanley took it, shook it coolly, once. The rule was never to shake, it being too easy for a loser to squeeze too hard, try and throw a game. But then, there, Stanley knew he had to—Stanley showing he was going to shoot a straight game of pool, and Billie nodding right back.

"Let's play some pool," Carson said harshly, not being able to keep up with Portaphoi's fancy steps. "Let's make some money."

But Portaphoi had one last word: "For only one ah us, Mr. Carson. Only one ah us."

xxx

THEY ROLLED FOR break, Stanley barely losing. The kid leaned across the table, elbow on the wood, cue sliding neat and clean between his fingers. Watching him moving the pale white cue, Stanley remembered his cock in Richie's hands, his mouth, and he smiled. Give the kid the break, give him a few balls, even a few games—but Stanley knew the night was his.

The eight danced away from the side pocket, spinning just enough to bounce free. Stanley stepped up, dusting the tip of his cue with pink chalk, seeing the movements of the balls even before he bent over the velvet. He'd heard other hustlers talk about that—seeing the game before the first ball even moved— but hadn't really felt it before; yet there it was, like seeing the end of a movie before seeing the start. He knew what was going to happen. The rest was just making the right movements.

The balls obeyed, sliding across the velvet in smooth, perfect tracks, their clacks and deep thunks as they fell into pockets like a lovely tune to Stanley. He called out the shots, his words feeling cool and distant because he was already two, three shots ahead. The table cleared in what felt like a single beat of his heart. Then the next game, and the game after that.

Carson stood next to him as the old black man from the cage racked him. His hand was heavy and shockingly hot on Stanley's shoulder. He passed him a long-necked beer. "Goin' good, Stan," Carson said. "Goin' good."

But Billie wasn't just a kid, and the next two games fell to him. His voice was strong, almost bored as he called out the shots. Every once in a while he'd look up at Stanley, as the cue elegantly tapped the next ball, and give him this look—a warm, smoky kind of look. The first time Stanley barely noticed, the second time he saw it, but the third and then the forth time Stanley looked for it. Then he was waiting for it. There: a slight smile on his pale face, a twitch of muscle, a sparkle in his pale blue eyes. The balls were almost secondary, just an excuse for the boy to look up at Stanley and smile.

Stanley put the bottle to his lips but it was empty, and he couldn't remember taking even the first drink. For a second, he wanted to turn to Carson and demand to know why he'd given him an empty soldier, but then he felt that little pressure in his gut down near his pisser and he knew he'd drained it himself. Nodding his head just a little he gestured to the old black guy for another.

The next two games went to the kid, but then a four banked too hard off a cushion and knocked an eight just short of the pocket. Stanley stepped up feeling good—and even better at not having to keep catching those looks from the kid. The edge was there, and his hands and the cue were magic. Ball after ball obeyed his will, spinning, clicking, sinking into the pockets. One game, two, three.

Then it slipped away for just a breath, giving the kid a chance to run the table. Stanley stepped back, looking for an excuse not to watch the kid shoot, and realized that his gut was aching. He glanced quickly down at his watch: fifteen after one. Catching the eye of the old black guy, he gave him five bucks and sent him to get an egg and cheese sandwich and some chips.

While he waited and ate, the kid ran the table twice more; but then he too must have felt his belly growl, because a three smacked into a pocket too hard, bouncing free.

"Da weather, it is wild tonight. Maybe it rain on me, maybe it rain on you. D' clouds are busy, dey hard to read," Portaphoi said, walking up to stand next to Stanley as he moved to shoot.

Stanley turned to smile up at him, seeing Carson out of the corner of his eye looking angry. "If I were you I'd buy a fuckin' umbrella," he said, breaking near and quick, sinking a four and a six neat and thick, the sounds of the balls in the pockets like belly-punches.

That game was Stanley's, and the one after that. Somewhere along the way Stanley had tossed his coat onto one of the spectator seats, loosened his tie, and undone a couple of buttons. His belly was full, but now his eyes were starting to get tired. A quick look at his watch: 3:00 A.M. They were almost even, with Stanley just two games ahead. The night was young, but Stanley was feeling his age.

Then a ball betrayed him, touching the bumper before the pocket, spinning out into the middle of the table. The kid stepped up and cleared it—hard and neat, the fall of balls into pockets becoming punches into Stanley's gut.

The looks continued, too. After every shot, Billie would stop and look up at him—his eyes gleaming ice, his lips hot and full. Despite his nerves, Stanley felt his cock start to get hard. Yeah, after all this, he'd get himself a whore—some babe with easy hips and hungry lips, or he'd walk that way again and see what Richie would do for a ten-spot.

Billie sank a seven, quick and sharp. Looking up at Stanley he smiled and licked his lips. The next ball missed the pocket.

Stanley stepped up, walking stiff to hide his stiffening cock. But he felt the edge nonetheless. Even though his mind was foggy with dicks, assholes, cunts, and tits, he still felt it—there—the game spelled out before him. The balls still respected him and they did what he wanted. One game, two, then it slipped away. He felt like he woke up, and the dream wasn't real life. The balls laughed at him, slipping and sliding away from each other and the pockets.

Angry at himself and his throbbing dick, he walked back to the seats. He called over the black guy and asked for some Daniels. As Billie cleared the table and won the game, he finished the bottle. As Billie cleared the next, putting them in a tie, Stanley put the bottle on the linoleum floor—and saw that his hands were shaking.

That was it. The kid was ahead by two and they only had three more games to play. He looked up at Carson and saw the anger in his eyes, the fury that comes when you realize that your sure thing isn't going to deliver. Another glance, this time at Portaphoi, gave Stanley nothing but a cool shiver as the black-on-black fancy-dan was smiling again—a little too wide, showing yet another gold tooth.

Stanley looked at Billie, and there was that smile. That hot, inviting smile. In a moment, Stanley hated that smile. Hated the fact that the kid was going to smoke him, that he was going to run the game, take home his cut, put another gold tooth in Portaphoi's head, and make Stanley a loser.

Then it happened. Portaphoi couldn't have seen it, but Carson certainly did, just as he certainly placed a fat roll in the kid's pocket—but that was something that Stanley didn't figure till later, laying in his still hotel room bed and staring up at the fly-specked ceiling. Stanley only saw it because he knew what it was: a shift of balance, too much spin, too little strength in the hit: the kid was playing the game several moves ahead too, but not to win. The kid had thrown the game, he'd tossed it away. For Stanley, probably just a little bit; but mostly for the game that Carson had played with him—the game they'd played on Portaphoi: and won.

The eight skipped too far to the left, bounced against a hovering three. Billie swore—a short, sharp "fuck!"—and moved away.

Stanley sat there in the spectator's seat, more aware that the sun was rising behind him—slowly heating the pool room—than he was that he was up. It took Carson walking toward him to make him blink, stand, and grab his cue. The rest of the games were easy, and he could have shot them even if he wasn't somewhere else, lost in that last game of the kid's.

It was over, the last ball sank neat and clean. He stared at the velvet for a long moment, at the empty table and at the pale, narrow shaft of his cue—which didn't look anything like his dick, just a cheap stick of wood. He didn't see Portaphoi leave, didn't see the muscle go. He only looked up when Carson put a wad of bills in his shirt pocket, saying "Fucking great, Stanley." When he did look up, he saw the kid standing there in the doorway, an inviting look in his eyes. But Stanley didn't agree or disagree; he just looked down at the velvet and shook his head.

XXX

THE WALK BACK to the hotel was longer than the walk there.

His steps were shorter, the blocks were longer, and the air—even though the sun was up—was much cooler. But he must have walked the same way back as he had going to the hall, because as he passed an alley he heard a voice, gruff and thick with phlegm, say "Hey, hey, hey . . . "

But Stanley didn't reply, even as the voice changed. "Mister! Got a buck, mister? Hey, you—I'm talkin' to you."

One foot in front of the other. Small steps. "Fucking loser asshole," the voice in the alley said as Stanley walked past. Realizing suddenly that he'd been recognized—again—Stanley just kept on walking.

Utter West

PONY USED TO come into my room, naked and immaterial.

As my Mitsubishi player had deteriorated, so had the hologram – until Pony was just a pink streamer of two-dimensional amateur porn, twisting and wrinkling in an unfelt breeze. A few days after Pony told me he was leaving, Pony had offered a brand new player and a disc. It was a kind of tech I'd only seen in the entertainment centers of rich friends. The disc's label had been faint, torn and ripped. Had Pony really reached into my bedroom that many times, to curl and crisp that label? Now nothing but nylon curtains rippled and fluttered in my room. Now it seemed like Pony had never stepped through the glass and smiled like honey on toast—it was all too long ago.

Pony had only talked once during one of his visitations—only once adding his voice to the display. It had given Pony's normally mute ghost a slightly time-lagged voice. At the time it was odd, both of us whispering conspiratorially, one real, one hologram, in case Mom or Dad (either set) were listening. "I want to suck your cock." "I want to suck yours, too." I had found it hard to focus, too easy to see Pony as a bad curse, whispering the words to his own haunting.

Now I wished I had taken that disc, the player: to have something, no matter how scratchy and low-res, to see, to remind me, to recall, to sort-of-second-hand *see* him—now that Pony had gone West.

XXX

Truck called himself that, he said, because everywhere he went he hauled ass.

I always wanted to catch him on vid, snoozing in his shit-box car, and play it all over the town, to hi-jack into the local FunNet distributor and just flood it. Especially when he was being all empty and posing: "I'm the scene here, man. Just check it out—" hands fluttering in the hot night air, thick logic-display shades, Scrapin' Jesus shirt from the wastes of L.A., synthetic leather jacket, black jeans. The smile, can't forget that: the nasty, I stole it and ate it, grin—"I'm the one, ain't I? I got it all, don't I? I crack, I freak, I rip, I strum, I got it all." But since Truck had his machine (and I didn't know anyone else in WW with wheels), always had some good score and a willingness to share ("Take, take, got plenty more, Jaz, got enough to share—"), and had the cheapest hot gear and software, I just couldn't do it. He wasn't much of a friend, but he was an okay connection. Instead of torching in macho image, I always ended up just nodding along, saying something hollow but agreeable like: "Right, man. Sure you are."

Pony had hated WW. Hated the flatness of the New Mexico plain. Hated the artificial, the synthetic, the plastic, the dead brush, the hot summers, the freezing winters, the factory town and all its factory homes, the bright red shingles on all the commercial buildings, the regulated Kid Strip and its watered down "let them have a little so they won't hunger for more" drugs, VR, flesh-pools, viterias, and shops. Back when he was . . . when he was with me, we used to sit on Truck's cruddy car and glare at the regulated rebellion of the Strip. Truck had always seemed to be somewhere else: inching his hand into someone's pants, or hustling Lew at the Discus chain for not selling the new, banned Scrapin' Jesus CD.

But Pony was gone. Alone, I sat in the open door, waiting for an over-the-counter roach to burn my fingers, my brain barely tingling with the watered-down THC. Truck was doin' what Truck did when nothing was coming his way and he felt anyone within earshot was better than he was. I nodded at another wave of brag and said, again, again, again: "Right, man. Sure you are."

My folks, Lester and Mary, had tried to be good, tried to find us a safe place when Chicago had turned out to be a place dripping blood and bad drugs. Sometimes, when we wrapped Spandexed and leathered legs together in one of our bedrooms, or in the backseat of Truck's car, and (really high on legal grass or some of the designer shit that managed to leak into WW) I would say to Pony: "Where do you go after you've gone?"

I said it all again, this time to Truck, looking across the asphalt of the parking lot, past the dinged and banged hood of Truck's shit-box monster: "The only place left: out, out, out."

Pony had hated WW: the software factory town with its tracts and mini-malls. He'd hated his own parents, had hated all the petty shit he used to pull—and hated always getting caught, hated the nodding understanding of the rehab folks, and hated the blame-game they pulled when they couldn't fix him.

Pony was fire. Pony was anger. Pony, trapped, had rattled the cage of WW with fights, drugs, rehab, and fucking me. Then, when it had gotten too bad, so bad that not even I could have kept him, he had gone . . . out . . . taking the special way he'd discovered: "I've seen the numbers," he'd say to me, rubbing his rough hands on my soft cock after we'd fucked. " I know the secret of this place. I'm going to go west. West. I'm going all the way west."

"I wanna score," Truck grumbled to me, to the beating lights of the Kid Strip. Chicks, boys, drugs—he didn't say, didn't need to. Or maybe we'd just run as fast as Truck's shit-box would allow on crappy back roads, past empty Indian reservations, and the ghostly squares of foundations from some never-finished housing tract. Truck said it, and I found myself forgetting Pony for a split second, saying, "Sure, man, sure."

And then I remembered that it wouldn't be Spandex and leather in the back seat tonight as Truck cruised for chicks or drugs or just trouble. Staring up at the hard black sky, I wished again that I'd taken that ghost, wishing I knew how Pony had gone—or that I was brave enough to follow.

xxx

"IT'S ALL A waste, man." Truck, driving too fast, again.

"Yeah," I said, not caring—again.

Then there was a flash of light—a pulse of glare as we passed one of the huge billboards that overlooked the main highway. We were on a barely paved access road, one that dipped down every few miles, just low enough to bathe us in the light from one of the signs.

"It's all a damned waste, man," Truck said, intentionally nailing the ruts and potholes just to feel something.

I didn't care—again—I just floated and crashed in the back seat with each successful hit, trying to sip weak Kid Strip Waste beer from an accordion can. I knew, in my body, in my mind, everywhere, that Truck was going to lose it again. All it would take would be the right set of words to push him just enough: add another deep dent in the car, shoot out more lights with Truck's shit-box repro revolver, get us busted one more time. One word and he'd do it.

Truck stood on the brakes, giving me a few moments of zero-G before smacking the back of the front seat. Instantly, my cheek, right arm, and left leg started to throb. I, at least, was feeling something.

When I got out, dropping the can and looking down at the lights streaking into and out of WW on the highway, I saw that Truck was standing against the support of one of the huge flickering billboards – also watching the lights of people like his own folks racing somewhere below. I knew the car was adobe brown, that Truck's face was pale white, that his pants were industrial caution yellow and black diagonal stripes—but that was just memory. The appeals to buy Coke, Pepsi, this fast car, that feminine hygiene product, that pill, this tissue, that home, vote this, and watch that made the road, the car, me, Truck, and his pants nothing but violent, flickering television colors.

In the back seat was one of Pony's old players. I'd seen it back there the day after Pony left and hadn't touched it since. "I've Gone West" had been the only words on my telephone system that night. "I've Gone West." Gone. No details: nothing but the act and the direction.

Pony's parents had hung around for a month or two before finally moving away. They'd never talked to me, which was fine.

Pony had told me about the trick, the way he was going to go, but I'd never believed it. I didn't want to believe it. "Gone West." Utter West. It was like magic — maybe math magic, but still magic — and I knew there wasn't any magic in the world. Not unless you counted Pony and me.

I had my chance. I could have gone with him, but I didn't. I was scared. I chickened out. You know what it fucking feels like? It feels like a burning, a burning down deep in the belly – you drink, you stuff shit in your veins, but all it does is get hotter and hotter. The worst is you never burn up from it. Shame just gets hotter and hotter.

I'm in WW for life, now: maybe school, maybe college, a nowhere job, becoming Lester — of Lester and Mary, my folks — brain-dead corporate gears. Life without Pony, because Pony had balls, Pony had done what he could to get the fuck out — gone into numbers and into legend.

I was too scared to follow.

Truck was still leaning against the metal legs of the sign, hypnotized by the lives racing by below us. The sign was old, as was most of WW's cheap municipal equipment. Its access box popped easily. Inside, a flickering laser, tiny disc. Pony could have done it quicker – but he was gone. Utter West.

I really didn't know what was on that player, just one of those weird things that Pony had been working on. One of the many players he was always leaving behind.

I tapped PLAY. The batteries were low, Pony being gone several months now.

Pony naked, cock very hard, shimmering bead of pre-come at the tip—looking stuttery and warped through the billboard's old equipment. I stood and looked for a very long time, at the image of my naked lover fifty feet high above me, and at the cars and all of their invisible faces burning by far below.

xxx

PONY WILL NEVER get "sent to center again." He went West. Utter West. That changed, but the center hasn't: same Indian gibberish on the same fake adobe walls, same monitor with the same flicker, same videos telling you to love West Way Estates, same cops, same doctors, same treatments. "It's okay to like boys a little when you're young," they say. "It's all right—we understand. You'll grow out of it. We know that."

They know, they say. They know why you do the things you do. They understand the Up!, the vids, Twister, Boil, the damage to shareholder property, the nights sucking and getting sucked, the tentative pressure of cock against asshole, and the rest of it. They understand the kisses, the leather and the spandex, the screaming around West Way in Truck's car and scaring people. "We understand—" and they try and help us. No—they try to help me; now just me. They try to help me, and they never really do. When they're tired of trying they bill my folks, smile, and let me go.

Not Pony, not anymore, but it's also not just me—we got others now, Pony, got some others now: some kids who've seen us yelling and screaming high, and using inappropriate language. They're the ones who saw us hack into billboards and throw you naked, hard, and ghostly at their folks. They're the ones who ache as we used to ache, Pony, till you went—the way you went.

Truck's still here, but now there's Wave: always a hissing laugh, always clicking her chrome fingers, and waving her chrome arm in the air. Kids, too, and others—watching and cheering with frozen faces at our daring, our raging boredom.

Got so bad without you, man, I had to do something. I screamed like we never screamed, man. I cried like we never cried. I think I know your anger now, man. I think I know it.

I wish I could kiss you. I wish I could fuck you. I wish you could fuck me—but you're not here, are you, man?

You went West, man. You did it, and that scares the fucking hell out of me.

"What're you reading?" Truck said from where he was leaning against his front fender, looking down at the streaking lights that could have been cars or comets. Hard to say.

"Just my own mind, man," I said, closing the little computer.

xxx

THE MUNINET'S RUNNING a special tonight, something they've been teasing on the WW cable feeds as Vital Information to Parents of Teenage Children for the last week. Wave leaked us the news a month before, patching the flash-commercial into our emailboxes.

The Strip had never been so full of gaudy colors and yet so basically gray. You couldn't look at the Strip, at its plastic and chrome and Lucite and holos and wrap-around sound, at its vending machines, discomats, groove-a-ramas, make-out booths, and arcades without seeing the gray. Lots of light, but nothing real, nothing that wasn't approved by a committee of psychologists. It was an explosion of screaming brilliance, of eye-burning intensity that pulled your eyes with flash and boom and an alluring subsonic come on—but then made sure under penalty of not being able to afford coming back, that you got up in the morning and got to work on time. The machines in the arcade all warned about the dangers of hard drugs, played only sanctioned songs, dispensed only low-intensity joints that wouldn't get the family dog high, legitimized near-sex while watching for the dangers of losing any virginity (mirrors hiding monitors).

The night before, Truck had coaxed a couple of kids into sitting on the hood of his car. After a few sniffs of Up! they'd sat frozen, naked and entranced into matching pale female/male ornaments by the gray lights of the Strip. I'd manned the feed that night, booting their glossy, unmoving smiles into the munigrid and all over West Way Inc.'s domestic housing telecom links. No voice, no nothing, just the two fleshy statues frozen by illegal highs into blissful immobility against the gray chaotic background of parentally approved recreation. Truck had reported his car stolen just a few minutes before.

Wave had stripped once, leather motorcycle pants down to latex panties, Chinese combat vest opened to show a black bra sprinkled with blinking LEDs. She'd done it slow, taking her time to clanky Mexican jazz combo blasting out of Truck's machine — dancing on the roof, showing all that mom and pop's genes had given her to the nearby off-ramp into downtown. They counted four accidents during the whole of the six-minute strip. The only descriptions Securitech got were of Wave's tits.

I sat, watching the Kid Strip, looking at my own reflection in Truck's side window, trying to see Pony in there somewhere. Pony had said as much, once, running a smooth white finger under my jaw, under the sandpaper of beard that the sleek and almost hairless Pony had always liked. I couldn't see the blue-eyed Pony in his own brown pupils. I couldn't see the rail-thin, ghostly Pony in my own thick, brown arms. No sandy blond hair somehow hidden in my close-cropped black curls: just me, staring at my own face in the car window — the Strip's pulsing amusement, distractions beyond.

"I'm in there." Pony had said that one night, staring into my face. "You know that. I'm in there—with you."

I had never felt like crying before. But I did just then, my tears adding their reflective shine to the flickering lights of the Strip. At my feet, one of Pony's little black boxes chirped merrily, telling anyone who knew the tune that it had completed the upload of a file. Moving as though underwater I leaned down, unjacked the box from the line we'd run down to the road and into a muni access plate. Even though I really didn't have a reason to, I started to coil the cable up around the box. Just something to keep my hands busy, I guess.

Truck, next to me, snorted a ten-ninety mix of Up! and sneezed violently. "Number one with a bullet, man." This was funny to him and he started to giggle, high pitched like Wave. "Number one and counting."

All I could do was shrug and keep reeling up the cable. Vital Information to Parents of Teenage Children was gone, erased with that little musical beep—replaced by the growing, ever-growing complexities of a Mandelbrot set. Locked, loaded, and rolling through the muninet mainframe, it would reach new heights of complexity before finally knocking down the pillars of the net software and greet the Parents of Teenage Children with nothing but static.

XXX

HE DID IT. I know he did it, and I'm scared.

Pony went West, Utter West, because he couldn't deal with it anymore. Any of it. He showed me once, the way, in one of his designs.

Jill and Dave had passed out in their room with their own ill-gotten Up! and a Dick & Jane porno tape. Up in his room, Pony put a finger to my lips (taste of his own come lingering) and pulled a black box out from under his bed. Big. Lots of power—its on-light like a little green star, showing under the bed even before he pulled it out – and jacked it into a flatplate.

Colors, colors, colors. High res. Scared me, man, scared me so I couldn't look away. The colors radiated off the plate, hovered there. Ghosts. Dreams. Mist. Sun. I touched a part of it to make it go away, to make the eye-sucking detail cease for just a few seconds, but it bloomed up at me with more detail, more designs on designs, patterns that were there before but too small to really see. I couldn't look away—especially couldn't look at Pony, because I was scared of what kind of person could make this.

He was talking. The words were just words against the brilliance and the colors. I caught some of what he was saying, captured some of it, like a rope tossed down a brilliant pit to me, drowning. "—everywhere, man, they're everywhere. Even things that we think aren't, are really. Patterns in everything, man. Hidden till you know where exactly where to look." Hang on, man, hang on, just listen, I remember thinking. "Special patterns, like right here, all around us. Everywhere—if you know where to look. Listen—"

And then I did look up, and into his blue eyes—got lost again. Pony's eyes. "Look, it's math. But this kind of math is everywhere. The way a leaf, ice, storms grow. Crystals. It's all fractals. It's all numbers.

"There's this one. This one, right here. It's called a Mandelbrot set. It's big. You play with it, and it just gets bigger. Bigger than the whole damned universe. And there's this special way you go on it. You head towards where it gets thin, real thin, and it goes on forever. Forever. You're going West, man. Utter West.

"It's math, though, right? It ain't real—" he'd said, tapping the flatplate in my hand, jiggling the awful colors "—but it is. You just gotta know where the biggest damned Mandelbrot set is, then you walk it, drive it, and think it. People are on it all the time, walk it all the time, even drive it, but they don't go anywhere 'cause they don't know it's there. But I know, man. So I can do it. I'm gonna do it. I'm gonna walk West, man. I'm going Utter West."

I didn't realize I'd miss Pony's eyes so much.

But he's gone. Gone into math. Into pure colors.
He did it. I just wish I was brave enough to follow.

xxx

THE PLACE WAS wrong—all wrong, for them that is. It was right, just right, for the rest of us. From the outside, it was invisible among its industrial knock-off kin, just another corrugated face— maybe a little more rust/acne scared than most. The door was just a sheet of diamond plate with a knob spot welded on.

The ground outside vibrated with a steady 4–4 beat. You could take the bus (coming packed full as the sun went down, going packed full at dawn), or catch a ride (if you knew wheels), or just walk the mile and a half from downtown WW (look for those with mud or dust on their boots)—then you'd stand outside, letting the ground ease the tension from your feet (and the dust or mud if you walked), and wait for the clap of wailing Scrapin' Jesus as two more were let in.

The neighbors never complained. Small business assembly workshops, storage sheds, truck garages, paint shacks didn't care how much noise you made when everyone else—decent, hard-working folks—were home sleeping the sleep of the shareholder.

If you were lucky maybe Wave herself would be out front cooling off from the heat inside, or maybe the legendary Truck would come screeching up in his monster and skid to a banging stop. Maybe one of the Mesa brothers would sell you half a cap of Heavy, a baggie of Red Dust, an inhaler of Up!, or just a poor, sad old joint of bad Mexican, which was still better than the official stuff.

When you got inside, it was all flashing lights, clips and fragments and pieces and bits and chunks of blitzing media thrown against the walls. If you were really in the groove, and the Mesa brothers had been selling, then the walls weren't there—you sat at one of the cable-spool tables in the middle of a hurricane of colors and shapes and people and numbers and fractals and Mandelbrot sets, sets, sets.

It was new, so new that West Way hadn't caught it yet, hadn't made it go away. Four others had come and gone quickly before it, and a lot more probably would go after someone opened their damned mouth and let them know about it. Until then, it was Scrapin' Jesus, hardcore, blasting, blasting, blasting, nothing controlled, nothing official and (important) nothing, nothing, nothing approved.

I was feeling old. Truck was in his element, playing the big bad biker he never was to some of the kids in one corner, trying to pick one to take home that night. Some kid, rusty with acne, was mixing the visuals somewhere in one corner of the big room. I sipped cheap Mexican beer and watched the walls dance with the underground transmissions. There: a U.S. flag waving over a mountain of dead soldiers. There: het porn. There: a Mandelbrot set—and, reflexively, I tried to follow the route that Pony must've taken but then the image flickered away. There: a broadcast from the battles still ranging in Northern China. There: Queer porn, cocks sliding into puckered assholes (and I raised his glass to the kid). There: a series of autopsy images. There: a cop beating up someone. There: a family photo. There: a distorted announcement from the muninet. There: Pony's face, an elongated digital ghost.

I sipped my beer and smiled. The beer was heavy, and the air was crisp with half a dozen smells of half a dozen very illegal drugs. Things had changed, and it was good – if not great. Now we had places, if only for a few days, a week at best, where things could happen without parental control, without the muni knowing. Pony would have loved it. His absence was still a deep, hot, ache in my belly. Wherever he was, I think he would have been proud of the changes we'd made.

There: another fractal bloom. There: a nuclear explosion. There: a children's show. There: a crazy dance of untuned lasers.

There: a beach and pounding surf. There: Pony, looking very solid.

"Hello," Pony said, very solid and very real, sitting down at the table and reaching for a sip of my beer.

xxx

TRUCK'S CAR HIT another chuck in the road and, again, I left the Mexican-upholstered back seat: zero-G for a second and then a crash back to gravity. Somewhere under the old car springs and struts complained shrilly. My legs were in Wave's lap. She was neurotically lacing and unlacing my battered boots while I stared up at the roof of the car, fascinated by the torn roof liner and the guts of the smashed dome light.

Wave leaned down to my ear, brushing my hair aside. She didn't say anything for a very long-time, just sort of leaned there, over my body so that her lips hovered an inch above my ear, her chrome arm heavy on my leg. I was just meat, not thinking thoughts, really, just watching and being. I felt like I was locked up tight, but not with anything I could really feel. Numb. Listening to the bouncing race of the car, feeling the springs and the cheap upholstery, feeling the heat of Wave next to me.

We'd just come back from screaming around the Kid Strip, endless circles around and around the glitz in maniac celebration of Pony's return, Truck yelling at the top of his lungs while gunning his monster's engine to its max, trying to keep us from rolling over. Wave had been scared, after the things I'd told her, and was treating Pony like some kind of ghost, refusing to touch or even get near him. To Truck he was a bad biker god, the man who'd lived a legend and come back for a beer—just a good excuse for Truck to get wasted, drive fast, and yell out the window.

Before we'd peeled off, a few of the kids that had taken to following us—enraptured with the legend of the man who'd gone . . . well, the way Pony had gone—eyeing Pony with the x-ray vision of a con for a narc: snickering in a broken chorus at his clean shirt, new pants, buffed shoes, diamond earring. "Bet that must've cost some," one said, before vanishing into the gaudiness of the Strip.

"Run them ragged!" Truck yelled out the window at the darkness of a side road. "Peel them raw! White-knuckled all the way!"

In the front seat, Pony was bug-eyed scared. From the back, I could see his pale bones through his thin white skin. "Oh my God!" Pony said, holding tight to the seatbelt across his chest.

When Truck had popped his Up! one-handed and knocked it back, Pony had leaned over to me and said in a quavering whisper: "Should he be doing that here? Suppose a cop sees?"

When Wave had appeared that night, walking across the parking lot in just her jeans and denim coat, silver arm flashing reflections from the yellow sodium lights, bare breasts swaying back and forth under her coat, Pony had said, "She can't be dressed like that—"

When Truck had peeled out for nowhere at high speed, Pony had grabbed the dash and whined ultrasonic. I had caught just a fraction of what he'd said, because the words were mangled in the racing engine, "—Jesus, please slow down!"

"Aren't you glad he's back?" Wave said in a questioning tone.

I didn't say anything—I just stared up and through a tiny slit of window at the starry night sky.

XXX

PONY WAS IN my room, solid and real.

My parents were out that night, as usual. They wouldn't be back until Mary had completed her company exercise routine and Lester his drug abuse therapy group. Two or three hours alone.

I hadn't bothered to change much about my room, and it was

one of the first things Pony commented on when we came in. I had all sorts of questions – too many – so all that came out was a shrug.

"It's good to be back," Pony said, sitting on the edge of my black futon and staring at the Domina poster on the ceiling. "Things don't look as dull as they were."

I shrugged again, angry at myself for not just grabbing Pony to feel his smooth skin again, smell his smell again, grab the hardness of his cock, taste his sweet come, feel him enter my ass. I wanted him back so bad that I didn't know what do to with him. "Couldn't take it anymore—"

"That's why I got out."

I tried to keep the fear out of my voice. "Where did you go?" *Are you a ghost from the Utter West? Are you something else? Are you a memory? Mist? Dream?* I hoped for an answer that would make me feel anything but the disquiet that filled me, make me keep my eyes from looking directly at him, into his eyes.

Pony just laughed. Even that had changed. No more strumming wires and hissing through teeth: Pony's laugh was now an explosive hiccup. "Just walked to the Main, hitched to San Jose. Got a place there," he smiled and sipped his beer.

I lay down on the black-carpeted floor and stared at the glowing little tell-tale under the bed, another of Pony's old devices—now mine. "Is that the only way you went?" I tried to keep the awe and fear out of my voice. I knew I failed.

"Just caught a ride, that's all," Pony said, shy and uncomfortable.

"I know the way. The secret's that you have to know what you're looking for. There are folks living right there—right on the way out—but they don't go 'cause they don't know, right? But, I do. I know the route, I know about the numbers. It's there: I'm going."

"Things have been okay here," I finally said, killing the silence with stupidity.

"Is everything okay? You don't look so good. Have you been in trouble?"

"Spent the summer at rehab. Folks bailed me out when I wouldn't eat for a week."

"What are your plans?"

"Don't know really. Not getting bored."

"I'm dead here. You're dead here. Everything's dead here. But things are alive, I know they are. I've seen them. You look at these things, these fractals, and know they're living, man. They have this fire: they grow, they change, they die or they go on forever. This one, Mandelbrot, you follow this one line and it goes on forever. Dig it, man, a road map to forever. It just goes on and on. No stopping it. Just head out Utter West and you're on your way—"

"I'm working at this software lab. Great job. You should check it out. You still like computers, right? It's really fun, and, God, they pay me close to six figures. And benefits. And my own office. And all the great stuff I get to use." Pause. "Your parents okay?"

"They're fine." I picked at a piece of white lint on the black carpeting.

"Come here," Pony liked to say, usually when he'd gotten juiced on his thoughts and talks of numbers and patterns and the West that was a simple place on the compass. I loved it when he said that, when he reached in and stirred me, made me smile (and I hate to smile) and we started to touch. Pony was someone easy to fall into, someone to hold and be held (where one of us stopped and the other one started wasn't important, not at all—just skin and touch and lips and hands and dick). "Come here," with that smile and dancing eyes, lips opening to kiss, to suck.

"I finally hooked up with mine. They're in Phoenix, working on that big reclamation project. Had a big get-together, even saw my sister who I haven't seen in years." He looked around the room, slowly. "Good to be back, Jaz. Things have changed and yet they haven't. I feel like I'm home, but this isn't my real home anymore." Quiet for a beat. Nothing to say. "So what are you planning? Gonna go back to school? Still want to write music, do reactives, that kind of stuff?"

"Maybe," I said. "I haven't decided."

Pony liked to get his cock sucked—but it wasn't a passive thing with him. He liked his cock, and liked it touched, looked at, kissed, licked. He used to stand by the window and look at his hardness, this sweet, little-boy smile on his face—as if for his roughness, his tension-singeing frustration for WW and everything, he was just a little boy who had discovered this hard, pleasurable part of his body. Having it sucked was like an exploration of it, just as fucking me was another way of discovering what could be done with it, what more could be felt.

"That's the way to go—for the dollars, man. Reactives. I mean, the guys I work with, even the guys who just do the rote work, make some serious bucks—and the guys who write or score make the really big ones."

"Sounds like a good gig."

Pony had been shy about his asshole, but it, too, was a part of his body that was new—and everything new to him was potential. One day . . . a hot, miserable day outside but in his room it was a sweet, special day, he'd come in my mouth then sat quiet, finally saying, softly, almost a whisper, "Play with my asshole." I didn't fuck him—not that I didn't want to, but it had somehow felt wrong, as if I'd be fucking the little shy voice and not the calloused toughness that usually fucked me. It was a gift to me, a special thing. We didn't do it again—and I'm glad, because that way nothing else diluted it, made it seem less unique. It was something between the two of us, on that so-hot day.

"It's great. One of the best things I did was get out of here. You know, you should, too. Get some college—maybe one of those interactive courses in assembly, structure, that kinda thing. Get out and go to Austin. Plenty of opportunities down there. Good benefits. You've just got to decide where you want to go—and, frankly, Joffrey, I don't see you going anywhere right now. What with the people you're with, the things I've seen you doing. You've got to get it together."

I smiled. "Good to have you back." I looked up at Pony's blue eyes, his clothes, his hair, and then back down to the softly pulsing tell-tale under the bed.

"Gotta see where you're coming from, to know where you're going, right?"

After a long series of heavy heartbeats: "I missed you."

"So did I, but I had to go somewhere, Joffrey. You'd like it there."

"Maybe—"

After Pony had left, with a firm handshake, I stood and stared out the window, imagining the pale holographic ghost, remembering dry lips and a tight chest. "Gone West." I remembered the talks and the images Pony had shown me of those absolute colors and the math hidden behind everything. Mandelbrot Sets. I stared out the window till the sensor on room lights squealed for me to move, then clicked off the lights when I didn't.

Just after hearing the door and muffled chatter of my folks coming home, I bent down to the recorder hidden under my bed and switched it off. Then I took the holographic recording I been making of Pony, broke the microdisc in two, and dropped it in the trash.

xxx

THE HOUSES, PAINTED a soft series of Indian pastels, throbbed by. The tires made a mournful hum on the warm asphalt, and fine grains of sand began to build up on the windshield. The engine was running hot, but then it always did. The civic readout on the dash blinked an incriminating seven, the number of violations I'd rung up since starting out. Truck wouldn't care—it had read three before I'd even pulled out of the Strip.

Muniregs dictated where everyone's house numbers were located: they beat by the passenger window in dull sodium-lit streaks, climbing as the tires moaned and squealed. 3001, 3002, 3003. Every once in a while, like some kind unknown marker a party would flicker by—bright house lights, a throb of music (a single dull bass then gone)—or maybe a moving van and boxes, or a house in the process of repair, being born, or growing larger (there a sudden flash of bare, exposed yellow wood).

The air was hot when I started, but was now cooling as the sun began to set. 3345, 3346, 3347, 3348. On certain numbers, maybe the square root of something, maybe a fraction, a prime, the sunset would suddenly slide into my eyes.

I drove through the suburbs of my life, following the numbers.

8898, 8899, 8900. Night brought a change: the house numbers going from dim, hard to make out, to bright, glowing numerals as they automatically compensated for the sun setting, stars appearing.

The numbers flowed through my head, making a map.

I was following the route, the directions that had lain under West Way and its streets since its conception in the mind of some social scientist, some engineer, some publicist.

A brightly glowing signal. I slowed but didn't stop, only glancing down at the gas gauge. Half-full. Half-empty. I hoped it would be enough—enough to take me to where I was going.

The streets were almost deserted, like West Way had put the rest of humanity aside just for me, so I could see the way, follow Pony's route—the route he hadn't taken.

Two human silhouettes blurred by, walking hand-in-hand just as a line of streetlights switched on, receding into the distance. I desperately tried not to look at them.

9921, 9922, 9923.

The road curved in on itself—a series of cul-de-sacs that seemed to go on and on, one sprouting from one to another.

I knew the road, I'd seen it before: on the muninet, on a flickering monitor, on an endless parade of maps in bus kiosks, in school, in directions to anywhere in WW.

I'd seen it before, too, in Pony's bedroom—in colors so vivid they pulled at my eyes: vivid colors that were made of numbers, expositions on a progression of counting. Fractals.

West Way was laid out in a fractal, as a Mandelbrot set.

9988, 9989, 9990.

I didn't really know where the knowledge came from—that this was the trip that Pony hadn't taken. I'd been in my room, thinking about Pony in a half-sleep, thinking about where Pony—my Pony, the old Pony—had gone, had really gone, never ever to return. Then I thought about where he had wanted to go.

"The colors, man, the colors mean a depth that we can't realize. There's more here than there are stars in the universe. This is a picture, a pattern of numbers that can contain more than anything, anywhere. And this one, the Mandelbrot, with this one you go can go Utter West—"

—go in a direction that never ended.

The house numbers started to waver, to vibrate—to become something else. At first I didn't believe it, didn't believe what I was seeing but then they were too much to ignore: a faint wash of color, the road slowly becoming a vanishing point of misted bronze, the windshield fading into ghostly cobalt, the hood of Truck's monster sliding into nothing but a form of living emerald, the dash glowing painful azure.

The road, the homes, the night, my hands on the wheel—it was all color, color, color until there was no substance, no texture, no feeling. In my mind I drove, but in my mind I wasn't driving on a road anymore. I knew I was following that special route, I knew the map. I knew where I was going. I knew Pony would be waiting for me there.

Pure indigo, then absolute gold, then mad crimson, then painfully deep jade. Everything was color—pure, absolute, painful colors. It hurt to look at them. So bright. Then my arms started to tingle, like my body falling asleep. My eyes ached. West,

West, West. Wherever that was.
    Then no sounds: just blue, red, yellow, green—
    Just the colors—
    Just the absolute, pure colors—

Imago

SUSPENDED BY A ceiling beam in the middle of a room redolent with Crisco, echoing with the disco beat of strap on flesh, flesh propelling into flesh, the moaning anvil chorus of impact and impacted, he hung.

Not seeing, burly, slapping, lithe, the arc of cat and cane in the cool shadowy dungeon, the grins, grimaces, growls, or gasps of pleasure, of pain, of both combined, he dangled from sturdy block and tackle, secured by hefty bolts, many ties of strong cord. Not smelling the salt sea of come splattered here, there, everywhere, or the musky rut of beefy beasts, he swayed gently, tapped into motion by the occasionally errant hand, leg, dick, or swept-back arm. Not hearing the music of impact, the opera of fuck, the libretto of suck, the opening bars of teeth-to-nipple, the crescendo of come, he hovered above and beyond it all.

Mummified, he floated. Enwrapped by leather, buckled with brass, head swaddled in opaqued gas mask, pendulum encased in darkness, he drifted.

Breathing a cavernous roar in his ears, his heartbeat the trot of steaming horses, vision nothing but soft black, taste of his own sweat trickling down from his upper lip, touching nothing but steaming self, reflected back by his insular cocoon, he was between floor and ceiling, self and other, here and there.

Suspended there, above the middle of the playfloor, he felt it begin: a pushing, an expanding, a mushrooming (from the mushrooms?), a surging, and the thought, *Am I emerging from a dream?*

XXX

SECURE IN THE womb. Wrapped up. Surrounded by comfort, nurtured and protected. Held close, held safe. Good. Nice. But— a fleck of light in the dark—all good things must come to an end, if only to make room for better things.

Birth: brilliance, luminosity, clarity where before there was only possibility, knowledge supplanting suspicion. Before his newborn eyes, the light grew—fleck to point, point to dot, dot to squiggly line, squiggly line to . . . ah, that's what it is.

Knitted together, his wings unfolded, brilliance showing around the rounded tips, then—fully extended in a lovely, liberating surge of air—brilliance.

Downbeat, upbeat, downbeat, upbeat, he flapped, and by flapping, he flew, and by flying, he soared. Swimming through atmosphere, passing pale streaks of cloud, rolling and climbing and plunging. Flying free.

But even freedom can get dull, and after tearing apart wisps of stratocumulus, spinning in mad corkscrews, roaring as high as he could go, then dropping like a stone, he looked. And looking, he saw. Rounded tips of wings? Flap up, he noticed pinions had spirals and twirls of prints; flap down, he gazed upon pale jewels of unpainted nails. Handy, his wings were. Very handy indeed.

Propelled through the sky, applause with each stroke of his fleshy fingers and thumbed wings, he did more than see. Body feel, the movement of muscles tied to bone with sinew, made a picture his pupils and corneas could not reveal. Tight muscles, strong bones, hefty sinew: a broad self, a strong self, a pumped-up self, a studly self, a fucking hot self he'd become.

Hot, heat, and a new muscle. Long? Of course, natural, realistic, a fleshy tail joined at his pelvis, front rather than back. Like a circumcised streamer trailing behind as he rowed across the too-blue ceiling of sky, tipped by a pale bulb of head.

Wind buffeted the shaft, wrapping invisible currents around it, pillow-fight impacts on tightening, firming skin and muscle.

Turn and bank, glide and dive, hands up, hands down, cupping air, winging his way through it, following—always following—the actions and sensations that worked his kite-string-long (though far thicker) phallus, which the wind had wrapped unseen hands around, sensual contact on tighter, ever-firmer tissue and capillaries.

Kite string once, now an udder, the endless extension of himself pointed to the unseen, unfelt ground, its firmness a fist rooted in his groin, a reaction to the action of his flight: a swing through, a perpetual changing of course.

Spinning, sky above and sky below, rotating, twirling, his body the center, his reborn cock the end, inertia, centrifugal force pulling evermore, exerting a further concentration to his rising erection, a tremendous tug filled him, stronger and stronger.

Pleasure once—the simple abstraction of the way it all felt, the play of skin and tissue, swelling blood and dancing senses—then intent. Cock hard, wanting to come.

Following once—trailing behind, snapping and twisting in his swim through crystal and cloud skies. Rudder once—pole ninety degrees from groin, a mast tipped by a finial bead of pearly pre-release—now leader, unbent with determination, a spear jutting forward, out past his eyes toward the direction of his flight. Atmosphere streaking past the quivering head, that creamy drop flattened, then streaked back, glistening it.

The head leading, he followed where it pointed, went where the atmosphere was restrictive, thicker, denser, in pursuit of elusive sensations to punch through.

Flying, he fucked the sky. Dick through cumulus, white vapor hazing from the tip of his cock, contrails of determined weather buggery. Dick through nimbus, dark smudges pregnant with rain tearing aside smeared remnants of heaven, which flecked his face with the cool spray of aerospace intercourse.

Blasting with speed, ripping open the tight security gates of the sound barrier, he flew. His cock a missile, a horned warhead, he broke the limits of a screaming come, a jism jet firing away from him, sticky threads flying faster than even he.

Not enough. No rules, not a one. Physics only memory, aerodynamics a scant suggestion, biology forgotten. One come (usually enough, here and then, high and fast), merely the beginning.

Up beginning to dull, however, down he went, cock seeking the surface, dick diving for the ground.

Found. Curtains of gauzy clouds, pulled aside and behind in a beat of hands, his wings, and there was the tropical sea: a rippling expanse, crests and waves, frothy tips flattening to glassy dark water. A wet dream, an oceanic fantasy.

Moisture, the aroma of strenuous pleasure—warm salty spray and crusty aftermath. Skimming, a hand-winged seabird, he glided, beating slowly, rowing leisurely across the surface, cock trailing behind.

There! And there again!—a touch of sea to his masthead, a dip in flight and impact, a water kiss to his roping stimulation, the salivary oceanic embrace charging around its apex.

Swelling, changing angle of the degrees from following behind to jutting ahead, cock at the ready, excited from kisses and wet washes, from lick after lick of wave crests, then plunging into the sea-sucking troughs between. Dick-fleshy extension rigid before his eyes, stabbing into the surging depths with each spearing dive, he is fucking the sea: in and out, down and up, then intensely up.

High above once again, looking down at the cresting white, at the dark blue glassy expanse, he remained very, very hard. The sea was good, the ocean pleasurable, but what he now desired, what exactly he needed, was . . . manifestation, culmination into white-tipped waves, into pale rises of saline lips.

A seabird dive? No, not precisely, but the animal mimicked was not as relevant as the action performed. Dropping, inserting his penis into the mouth of the sea, fluttering, hovering, the wet mouth blew him, worked his member like a merman luring treasures from his depths. Then, with a bellow of pleasure, he combined his own salty spray with that of the ocean and fluttered up and away undiminished, only to find himself poised and ready again. So down, to another drenching pair of lips, for another dip and relish in the sea, another coming into a warm watery mouth. Up and back, not a bird but something else with wings, dipping into semen-perfumed lips, to take pleasure and give come. Fluttering from one to another, one to another, in and jet, up and away, in and orgasm, up and away, in and out of ecstasy.

His wings, he now understood, were less fleshy fingers and more panoramas of color, a brilliant display, showy bursts of color exploding from his back. The sea became less a vast moist expanse and more a sprawling pink and blue forever of dewy petals, the air less a tangy perfume of salt and more a bouquet of earthy fragrances, his cock less a totem jutting before him than an exploratory probe, dipping into and sampling each delicious set of petal lips.

From one to yet another he hovered on chromatic wings, his every insertion into a blossom-mouth an ascension, a progression up a humming scale of delight. One more, one more, one more, from rose to orchid to violet to chrysanthemum, from snapdragon to buttercup, and so on through every family and strain, from blossom to blossom, sampling and depositing his essence into each and every dewy mouth—one after another into infinity plus one, until the day after eternity, until he had taken enough pleasure, given enough of his sweet, aromatic spray.

There was nowhere left to go but . . .

XXX

SUSPENDED BY A glue of his own making beneath a branch in the middle of a forest redolent with green life, echoing with the soft hushes of leaf on leaf and live wood creaking, he hung, enwrapped in chrysalis. Buckled with veins, head swaddled in nutritious fluids, pendulum-encased in metamorphosing darkness, he drifted.

Many hearts, a rapid tapping roar in his simple insect ears, vision nothing but soft black, the taste of his own transformation on his antennae, touching nothing but steaming self, reflected back by his insular cocoon, he hung between branch and forest floor, self and other, here and there.

Suspended there, in the middle of the glade, he felt it begin: a pushing, an expanding, a surging, and the thought, *Am I emerging from a dream?*

xxx

HIS NAME WAS Mel Lewis. He was suspended from the ceiling in the middle of a playroom. He was wearing leather chaps and a wife beater. His dick was hard and out, jutting from his crotch in muscular determination — another man, standing before him, just as determinedly sucking it, feeling the many inches of Mel Lewis down his throat.

It was so good, so perfect a blowjob that Mel felt the surging begin without having to exert the least bit of effort. The pleasure peaking and exploding in his mind, and bodily into the other man's hot wet mouth, it was a wondrous, dreamlike orgasm that filled his spirit with light and his being with joy, until there was nowhere left to go but up and away.

Nowhere left to go but . . .

Friday Night at the Calvary Hotel

"EXCUSE ME FOR saying this, but you're a freak."

He smiled, almost shyly, but didn't say anything. He didn't need to. It was a given, the reason we were both there. Don't ask me why, I just had to say it—maybe to make sure he didn't really think he was in any way normal, or maybe because I just needed to say out loud what I'd been thinking all week.

He certainly didn't look like a freak. He was actually kind of handsome: tanned, lean, with curly dark hair, and skin that was nearing, but not quite, leathery. He works outside, I thought, no button-pushing and fluorescent lights for him. Construction, maybe. Nothing heavy, though—he didn't have any serious heavy-lifting muscles.

Arabic? Swarthy Italian? A touch of the Hebrew brush? Hard to say. Definitely not from a place with snow-covered peaks. Hot sand, sweet wine, dates—that kind of place.

"Did Judith get the money to you?" he asked, the smile staying on his face. His voice, though, was musical, a choir voice if ever there was one. If small talk was on the menu—and it wasn't—I would have asked if he was a singer. That kind of voice.

I nodded, slipping on the security chain. The door probably couldn't hold up against a good sneeze, but I needed something to do with my hands. My heart was hammering in my chest like it wanted out. "Spoke to the bank this morning," I said. "The wire transfer went through yesterday. Thirty thousand dollars. A lot of money." I almost thanked him, but didn't; it was a lot of money, money I'd definitely earn tonight.

"It's just money," he said, with a dismissive wave of an elegant hand. "Don't have much use for it myself. Root of evil and all. I like to indulge in a different sort of sin, if you know what I mean."

I certainly did, but I didn't say anything. I didn't need—or want—to hear anything more. Not that I wasn't curious. God knows I was dying of curiosity, but I was already in pretty damned deep. Sure, I'd gotten some fairly good assurances from the mysterious "Judith" that it was a straightforward, simple job—no responsibility, no liability, and all that—but, hell, it was just too damned freaky. Too freaky for me to want to find out if there was anything else. This guy and his trip were bad enough.

It started out simple enough, with an ad in the miscellaneous section of the local paper. Innocent enough. "High Pay No Risk," and then something about an assistant needed for a gentleman with "special recreational needs." I don't have it anymore; after I called and spoke to Judith, I burned it to fluffy ash in my kitchen sink. And then I took a long, hot shower.

But I called back. Freaky was freaky, but I was flat, busted broke. Out-on-the-street-at-the-end-of-the-week kind of broke. Watching-panhandlers-to-pick-up-moneymaking-tips kind of broke. Shoplifting-to-eat kind of broke.

I called back and I listened, trying not to fuck it all up by showing how much the whole thing freaked me out. The first thing was a shopping list, pretty specific—more than I would have expected for someone with "special recreational needs," but then what do I know? Before that all I could do to get off was watch TV and think about Ginger and Mary Ann doing each other.

"Is that it?" he asked, nodding at my sheet-draped handiwork.

"That's it," I said, and damned if I didn't feel proud. I'd started out nervous as fuck, but then I'd started to really get into it. Kept thinking about my dad, about all the stuff we built when I was a boy. "Measure twice, cut once, kid." "Always go with the grain, son." "Accidents and screw-ups happen in a hurry, lad." Yeah, but there's a big difference between banging together a tree house or a bookshelf and what this guy wanted. Still, I couldn't help but think about dear old Dad as I hauled the lumber home and got to work.

"I made it in sections, held together with a couple of bolts. Strong as fuck but easy to haul around. The whole thing fits right into a big gym bag; no one noticed a thing."

He stepped up close to it but didn't touch the sheet. He was breathing real slow and deep, like he was going to run in a marathon. Psyching himself up, I thought—either that, or trying real hard to keep his excitement bottled up.

"Not that anyone in this place would have cared," I added, prattling stupidly through my nervousness. The Calvary Hotel made other shitholes look like the Ritz. The morgue's body buggy could probably find its way there on its own, just out of habit. The atmosphere was hazy with pot and crack smoke, decades of BO, and toilets never flushed. Hauling the stuff up the back stairs, I counted at least a dozen pitched sets of works and one—possibly two, but I couldn't see if one guy was breathing—dead junkies. The bed was as soft as a boiled marshmallow, the walls looked like they'd been used for target practice, the TV was busted, the wood floor was hazy white from too many chalk-outlined bodies, and the windows were nailed shut from the inside. It was perfect. Beg, scream, fire off a whole clip, the worst that could happen would . . . fuck that, nothing would happen; that's what made it great.

It even had a couple of bonuses. The "bridal suite" I'd rented had a spare, windowless room, perfect for stowing my stuff, and the main room had a retaining wall, the studs almost too easy to find—and no one would mind my quarter-inch bolt holes.

He was still standing there, still breathing slow and deep. My nerves were jangling so loud I was surprised he didn't hear them.

"Want to see it?" I finally croaked out.

In a real soft voice, he said, "Please."

So I pulled off the sheet, and there it was in all its glory. Freaky? Damned straight, but I'd done a good job, and a little burst of pride slowed my heart down a bit, just enough for a question to leak out: "So, tell me, you Catholic or something?"

XXX

THERE WAS A long—very long—minute, as he stared at what I'd made. "Something like that," he said, finally, turning his head slowly to look back over his shoulder at me, that wry little smile back on his lips.

"Ah," was all I could say, struck more stupid than usual.

"This is wonderful," he said, stepping up and running his hands over the smooth wood. "A perfect job."

I wanted to say "aw shucks" and start in about the hours of sanding, the three coats of lacquer, the buffing. But then I remembered why he'd had me build it, and what he wanted to use it for.

He rubbed it a long time, like he was communing with it. Watching him stroke it, I noticed something about his hands. I asked, "Is this your, ahem, first time? I mean . . . doing this kind of thing?"

It took him a long minute to pull himself away. "Oh, no, not at all. It's just something I developed—well, I guess you could say 'a taste for'—a long time ago. Every once in a while I like to indulge myself, you know, when I can get away from the family business."

"Hummm . . . okay," I said, not wanting to know more. He'd done this before, he knew what he was getting into, he wanted it: that was all that mattered. I was absolved of responsibility. Still, it didn't keep a sudden deep wave of nausea from surging up my throat.

"Can I see the rest?" he said, one hand still on the wood. "Good,

I see you thought of the pegs—something to hold on to. Makes it much easier," he added, smiling. Smiling, dammit. He was actually smiling—an honest-to-goodness, God's-in-His-Heaven-and-All's-Right-with-the-World kind of grin. The nausea bubbled in my throat.

I went into the side room, breathing deep in the dark quiet. Dust, mildew, old wine, piss, butane. Still, I was away from him, so the air felt damned good wheezing in and out of my lungs.

Anyway, I'd been paid, and he wanted it, so I grabbed my toolbox. On the way out I remembered the stepladder, so I caught it with my free hand and pulled it behind me, the metal legs scraping thin lines in the wood floor.

He was almost dancing with excitement. I put down the toolbox, flipped open the latches, and handed him the stiff brown bag, then turned to open up the ladder.

"They're perfect," he said, his voice breaking with pleasure. I turned, catching sight of his deep brown eyes. Good eyes, kind and knowing eyes—but they were also junkie eyes seeing a fix. "Just perfect."

It took me a while to find the perfect ones. Not too thick, but long and very sharp. He held the first nail, then the other three, up to the dim yellow ceiling fixture, turning them slowly, entranced by the reflections coming off the steel.

He lowered them, a junkie gazing at my face, finally seeing me. "I want to do it. Now," he said, starting to unbuckle his belt.

"You're the man," I said, a serious quaver in my voice. "If you're ready, I'm ready."

"I've been waiting to do this for ages," he said, sitting on the bed, kicking off his running shoes. "Again, I mean," he added. The pants followed. Then the denim shirt. He had on a pair of faded yellow . . . well, it almost looked like a diaper, something wrapped around his waist and crotch. It didn't look comfortable, but then nothing about that Friday afternoon was even remotely comfortable—to either him or me.

There was something else. Something I noticed even though I didn't want to. He was hard. Very hard. I couldn't help but look, even stare. Hard as a fucking rock, his wrap-thing tented out by his cock. When he stepped toward me, I watched it, a big, stiff finger waving back and forth in his weird, loose underwear.

Before, what I'd made had been just a big wooden . . . thing, like something Dad and I would build in the garage. But watching him step up to it, climb up on it, I couldn't lie to myself. I'd built a cross. He'd paid me to build a real, honest-to-goodness cross. Life-sized. Anchored to the wall of the Calvary Hotel with big fucking bolts. And that's not all he'd paid me to do.

"I know what you're thinking," he said. I'd phased out, realizing that I was minutes, maybe just seconds away from doing it. "I really do know, and it's all right. I want this. More than anything, I want it. It's going to be okay. Trust in me."

I was scared. No, fuck that, I was terrified. I wanted to puke, I wanted to run, I wanted to scream "No fucking way!" but I didn't. Yeah, part of it was the thirty grand in my bank account, but a lot more was . . . well, it was him. He wanted it. He wanted it bad, so it was all right to do it. He wanted it. He really did. Don't ask me how, but it was, really, all right.

After carefully, gingerly climbing the stepladder, he slowly turned around, balancing himself with one very tanned hand on the wood. When his back was up against it, he reached up, grabbed the right-hand peg, and pulled himself up onto the little step I'd attached, as per instructions, to the vertical beam. Then he was up there, hands spread wide, legs calmly crossed. He was up there, on the cross. He was on the cross. His eyes were closed and his breathing was slow and regular. And his cock . . . his cock was still very hard.

I needed to get away from the sight of him for just a moment, so I stepped into the side room. My own breathing was quick and shallow, and spots swam before my eyes. I wanted to pass out—just close my eyes and wake up someplace else.

"Are you okay?" His voice was calm, collected, with just a tiny vibration of excitement. Even though it came from the other room, it felt, sounded like he was standing right next to me.

"I'm . . . I'm fine," I said, taking a slow, deep breath. A bundle in one corner caught my eye. The tarp. Right, the tarp. "Just getting a few things."

"No problem. Take your time."

I grabbed the tarp and stepped back into the main room. The room was still dirty, broken, smelly. He was still on the cross, a beatific smile on his face. Stupidly, I showed him the tarp. "Just in case . . . you know . . . spillage."

"Sensible," he said. "I like that. You think ahead. Thank you." He closed his eyes for a moment. "The right one. Always start with my right wrist. If you please."

"Right . . . " I said, carefully—overly carefully—laying the tarp on the already stained floor. After I spent way too long getting the tarp positioned just right, I knew it was time. The moment of truth. Do it or not. Walk or stay.

"It's okay," he said in that perfectly melodious voice again. "I want you to. The right one. Start with my right wrist, please."

Small sledgehammer from the toolbox. Nail from where he'd left it on the bed. Up the stepladder, slowly, carefully, bracing myself against the dirty wall. Absently, I noticed little piles of plaster dust on the floor from where I'd drilled the anchor bolts. Another step, then two, his groin at eye level, then below, his cock still very hard, very obvious. A little stain, too—fresh. The smell of sweat and salty come in the air.

I put one hand on his arm, to balance. He was hot; the skin was slick with sweat, though not dripping. Just a light sheen. I felt his pulse, distantly, as I put the tip of the nail against his wrist, between two bones. What are they named again? Radius and something else? I'd have to look it up when I got home; got a copy of *Gray's Anatomy* around somewhere.

Then he said, "Please, do it now," and so I did.

The nail was sharp, very sharp, and the sledge was heavy, very heavy, and I put a lot of muscle into that first swing. I don't know what I was expecting—the nail not to go in at all, or the nail to go all the way through, biting into the wood with the first swing—but I didn't get either. The nail dented his flesh, breaking his skin, sinking deep into his wrist—but not all the way through.

He clenched his teeth, but didn't scream. His breathing became fast, but still deep, and his eyes were squeezed tight shut. "Again," he hissed between his straight whites, "do it again." He groaned, deep and heavy—the kind of groan I thought only came from sex.

Again. This time the nail went through, but this time I'd swung at it with everything I had, trying to hit the dull gray head even though it gently rose and fell with his steady pulse. There was the bass sound of steel hitting wood, and for an instant it was Dad and I again, building a soap box racer, a bookcase, a birdhouse, a tree house—anything but driving a nail through a man's wrist.

Blood welled up quickly around the nail, then started to slowly drip down onto the floor in heavy, steady drops. It was very thick, I remember that. Drip. Drip. Drip. It smelled of copper.

"The other one," he said. "Do the other one."

I walked down the ladder, surprisingly calm inside, and moved it. Back up, new nail in my hand. I knew how to do it now. I knew what it felt like to drive the nail. The surprise and shock was gone. Why does the murderer shoot back at the police? Because they can only execute him once. What's one more murder? What's one more swing of the hammer?

Still, it didn't go through with the first blow—again, it stopped halfway through the muscle, the tendons, the veins, the arteries. Before he could ask, I swung again, this time driving the nail straight through, wrist to bone in one clean swing. I felt a flash of pride in a job well done—right before the bile rose in my throat and I had to swallow it down.

"Thank you, thank you, thank you . . . " he said, his voice

distant, lost, but also joyous, ecstatic. His blood was a steady metronomic drip, but not in time to his pulse—that was shown by the hard, throbbing lift and sink of his cock. "Thank you . . . now, please, do the rest. My feet. Do my feet."

Planning. No one ever accused me of not being good at thinking things through. I might not be able to hold a job, keep a girlfriend, or do anything else worth a damn, but I do know how to look at something and know what's required. A cross that comes apart so you can haul it around easily. Big fucking bolts so you can attach it to the wall. A stud finder, to find where to attach it. A tarp, to catch some of the blood. A stepladder. Two long nails for the hands or wrists. A real long one for . . . for both feet.

I didn't have to climb the ladder. I did have to kneel down, though, get down on my hands and knees to be able to reach his feet. I almost giggled, thinking of what I was doing, the position I was in.

He was mumbling, his words gone soft, lost in his perverted indulgence. Happy, so happy. I had to really listen to make out the words. Actually, it was only two of them, over and over again: "Thank you, thank you, thank you . . . "

I had the hammer in my right hand, the nail in my left. I could have put them both down on the bright blue tarp, turned and walked out. Craftsmanship, planning, maybe that was it. Maybe I just wanted to give him what he wanted—everything he wanted.

The skin over his ankle didn't dent as much as the wrists had. Stronger. More muscle. Bone. I pulled my arm back, putting everything I had into the first swing.

I'd never heard a bone break before. A wet snap, a gristly, moist kind of break—like a piece of fresh bamboo. My fingers were gripping the nail, so I felt it tear into his skin, hit the bone, and splinter under my sledge. I didn't let go fast enough, so I also felt the torn muscle jerk, spasm. Blood oozed around the metal, slid down the top of his foot, slipped between two toes, and dripped, dripped, dripped to the floor.

His breathing accelerated and a down-deep groan vibrated out of his narrow chest. His head was lifted back and his body arched out, pulling at the nails in his wrists and I feared, for a second, that he'd tear himself free.

Something wet dropped onto my forehead. I reached up, smeared it, then looked at my fingers. No red, so it wasn't blood. It smelled salty. Then I noticed the large, growing stain on the front of his diaper.

The words came again, a little more forced, heavy with panting ecstasy. "Thank you," but "more" was also there. Over and over again: "Thank you" and "more."

More. I swung the hammer again, as hard as I could, as hard as I ever could. I hit the nail right on the head, and with another crackle and pop of bone and cartilage—all the great red, wet stuff in our ankles—the nail went straight in and through.

He screamed. He screamed loud and long and hard. Not a frightened or pained scream; he screamed like it was the best time of them all, the best time ever had by anyone. I was scared. Not because I thought anyone would come a-knockin'—after all, this was the Calvary Hotel, and a scream was just part of the general ambiance—but because for a beat, a single moment, I was jealous. I wanted to feel what he was feeling, know the bang, pop, wow of the best time you could ever feel.

I watched him for what seemed like hours. His breathing slowed; his body sagged like it was melting from stone, or he was falling asleep, emptied through that roaring voice, that soaking come. His eyes fluttered, then stilled, and his head gently fell onto his shoulder.

Then his breathing, without any kind of warning, just stopped. I stared for a second, maybe two, then my own heart started to race. A burning sweat covered me, and my brain slammed into *ohfuck ohfuck ohfuck ohfuck ohfuck ohfuck ohfuck* mode. Do something! But what? I didn't know CPR, it would take too long to get him down, and he'd already lost blood . . . Call for an ambulance?

Explain to them, then the cops, then the DA, then an attorney, then a jury, why I nailed him to a cross in a sleazy hotel?

So I watched him for another couple of hours, frozen. I watched him till the sun went down and the place got really dark. Finally, I got up and switched on the lights, knowing what I had to do.

It took me a long time; luckily, I'd booked the room for two days and nights. Getting him down was a bitch, but I managed. I wrapped him in a sheet, being careful what I touched, and locked him in the side room. I didn't think they'd be able to lift prints from the plastic tarp, but just to be safe I bundled it up. Toolbox, tarp, and everything else I could think of went out the window and down the fire escape. And the cross. I'd burn it, I decided, when I got home, feed its carefully built pieces into my fireplace. Ashes to ashes.

Just to be safe, I took some regular nails and pounded a couple into the spare room's door, then I dragged the bed against it. No maid service in the Calvary Hotel, but I still wanted to keep any itchy fingers away from him, at least until I could think straight and figure out how to get rid of all the evidence.

Then I left. Went back out into the world, fear riding my back, thundering in my heart. I went out via the lobby, paying the pockmarked night clerk for another week, paying in cash.

I didn't think I'd ever go back. Funny how you sometimes do something you'd never, ever dream of doing. Like nailing a complete stranger to a cross. Or going back to check on his body.

Yeah. I did. Both of those things. It took three days before I decided to do it. Three days of feeding pieces of my carefully built cross into the fire, three days of trying to erase myself from what had happened. But then, on the third day, I started to think about him. Had it happened? Really? Maybe desperation had cooked my brain, maybe he wasn't dead, maybe he was in a coma or something—paralyzed, slowly dying of thirst and hunger, nailed into that dark windowless room. I didn't know the guy. Sure I'd crucified him, and I thought—no, knew—he was a real sick freak. But he still didn't deserve to just be left behind like that, tossed away like the wrapping from a cheap burger.

So, three days later, I climbed the fire escape and slipped inside. The bed was still pushed against the door, the door was still nailed shut, the room was still dark and windowless, and the sheet was there, in the middle of the floor. But he was gone.

No body. No crime. I left, hoping to leave that Friday night at the Calvary Hotel behind me. I tried to forget all about the guy, the cross, the nails, the hammer in my hand, the body. But sometimes I remember, everything coming back to me in one trembling recall.

Especially at Easter.

About the Author

THE WEATHER WASN'T sympathetic.

It should have been pounding down—not just rain, not just a shower, but rather a biblical storm, a fury of wind, a frenzy of sleet, blasts of lightning. His mood, writ on the backdrop of the atmosphere.

Instead, the sky was clear and blue, the air was warm—but not too warm, rare along the flat yellow expanse of hard-packed desert.

The climatic betrayal continued throughout that first day, idyllic weather mocking him through the fly-specked and pitted windshield of the Buick.

A sign said PHOENIX and three digits, the first a two—and he knew he was running behind. Too late a start from Chicago, taking too long to haul his twin scuffed duffel bags down the stairs and put them in the car, spending too much time cleaning out and packing the stained and leaky Coleman cooler he'd borrowed from his sister. This, that, some other things—delays, but less a difficulty getting his act together and more a syrupy hesitation. Two weeks ago, though, he would have stuffed the cooler into the trunk, crammed the bags into the backseat, and hit the road before the sun rose over the brick monoliths of the city. But that was two weeks ago—fourteen days and one obscure article found in a magazine.

Three digits, highway vernacular for *too far*, so when the sun sat on the horizon, hours before the truckers could turn on their brights, he turned off into a gleaming constellation on the flat expanse, an island of gas pumps among pyramids of radials, and above it all, the proclamation of eats.

The sign he was looking for. Parking his late-model American machine into a narrow space between two chrome and grease-blackened trucks (PETERBUILT said one, Mack said the other) he stepped in.

Despite the trucks outside, the place was calm and quiet. Grease sizzled behind a huge metal hood, the cook working it invisibly behind the thin, gleaming steel. At a bend in the looping countertop, a waitress in red-and-white stripes smoked with one hand, held a book in the other.

It took her a long minute to notice him. Snuffing out one in an ashtray, folding a page of the other over to mark her spot, she said "Hi, darlin'," and walked over, grabbing a pseudo-leather menu on the way.

Seated in a plush horseshoe, he cracked it open and picked a chicken fried steak. Something he'd never eat back home, but out on the road it seemed to be the perfect fuel.

After "Anything to drink, hon?" and his "Soda," the next thing was a question from her: "You much into reading? Just picked up this new one the other day. Darned good read, if you know what I'm saying."

He did, and a thunderclap echoed between his ears, fractured bolts of pure white lightning behind his eyes. "No," he said, trying to keep the pain and anger out of his voice. "I'm not one for reading." *Not anymore*, he thought, but didn't say.

✕✕✕

BURNT COW ON a bun, grease slippery between his fingers. A basic thing, part of the firmament of the universe—at least the universe of truck-stop diners. A burger doesn't pretend to be something other than a fatty and cholesterol-laden booby trap. A hamburger is a hamburger is a hamburger. Nothing else, nothing more than a bite to eat between here and there.

Between bites, and sips of soda from a condensation-teared gold plastic glass, he looked up. It was still a quiet night, sunset painting the desert red outside the thick windows, headlights flaring on against the coming night—glare washing into his eyes. His waitress, since he obviously wasn't going to talk to her, had retreated back to the counter with her book.

Beyond the steel range hood, coming into focus through twisting steam and sticky smoke, a face, then a body—but first the face: strong and solid, bright eyes, just enough shadow on a firm jaw, hair shorn back into a stern—and as functional as a steel range hood—buzz cut.

In faces, cocks—that's the way it is. You see one, you think of the other. What it's all about, being gay I mean. The line from the story came right to mind, unbidden/unwanted. He remembered reading it for the first time, a dusty book on a dusty shelf in a dusty bookstore near the university. *Bad Stories for Bad Boys*—that was the title of that book. "Cocksure"—that was the title of the story he'd read in that book. After, whenever he looked into a guy's face, that line was there: *In faces, cocks—that's the way it is. You see one, you think of the other. What it's all about, being gay I mean.*

Cut, uncut? Long, short? Uncoiling hose or stubby fireplug? Hairy thicket or gleaming with reflections like a steel range hood? Hot like steam or sultry like smoke? Red like raw meat or done to a turn?

And, of course, when you think about what he has, you have to think about what to do with what he has—same book, same story, different line. Ever since he'd read that first story, when he saw a face, he thought about a dick.

Back alley, after the cook's shift. Bottles, a Dumpster, the too-sweet perfume of garbage: eau de rough trade. Sprays of reflected light cast by passing chrome on the highway.

More questions: giving or getting? All this between bites, between sips of cold soda. The words he'd read ringing in his ears, a background narration to his fantasy: on his knees—yes, giving—

on the cold hard ground, taking a thick warm cock down his throat. Swallow, swallow, past the trouble-maker gate of his gag reflex, keeping the wolves of teeth at bay, tongue and lips working their soft, flexible way with the muscle of the cook's dick. If done well, a salty surprise, and a treat jetting into his mouth.

Not a job, not an adventure, not an art—a life. The same book, the same story, the same author.

Yeah, that book, that story, but most important the author— and, remembering him, he felt the storm in his mind return.

Killing his fantasy, his tainted dream, he paid his bill, climbed into his car, and got back on the highway.

XXX

ROADS—WHY DID he always use roads, why were his stories always about traveling? The same book, almost every story, had something about someone going somewhere.

The sun, red and tired for the past hour, finally set. Driving into it, he heard a line from one of those stories: *bloodshot as his eyes from too many miles, too many miles passing too quickly.*

That was something else. Sunrises and sunsets, dawns and dusks. Lots of those as well. Way too many scenes opening and closing with the sun either coming up or going down. The weather, too—way too many clouds and too much rain and the hot sun. Simple, he thought, squinting against the stabbing glare of a passing semi. A cheap literary trick. Almost pathetic.

How could I have let myself be tricked by him? But his eyes were bloodshot—he could feel him—and the sun was setting, and he knew he'd never make it to Phoenix without stopping for the night.

Damn. Taking his eyes off the horizon, he searched for the other sign, the companion of eats.

It wasn't a long search. Lodging came out of the purple dusk, and he turned off. Parking, this time alone in the dark geometry in front of the motel, he got out.

Pop, crackle, snap—the breakfast cereal of age. Had he written that too? Was that one of his damned overly clever lines? Frown deepening the topography of his face, he put a hand on the handle and stepped from hot night air into too-cool air conditioning.

Laminated counter top, distorted state map barely visible through the chipped glass top; gumball dispenser left by the Shriners; a rack of brochures for ghost towns, indian casinos, Wild West shows, caverns, The World's Largest Toffee Apple, amusement parks, and outlet malls; a sticker with AAA on it; a poster of Lake Mead, faded from too many lingering sunrises or sunsets.

"Can I help you?" And a smile in front of the poster, behind the counter, to the left of the brochures, and to the right of the gumball machine. Many teeth—good straight teeth. A face delightfully browned by too many of those slow sunrises and sunsets.

"Just need a room," he said, volleying back the smile with one of his own. "On the road a bit too long."

"Good thing you stopped. Sometimes folks'll push themselves too far, and before you know it they're asleep at the wheel."

"Wouldn't want that to happen," he said. "I'll just need one night."

"No problem. Not exactly the busy season. Got plenty of rooms to spare. Take your pick if you want." Was there something else, lingering there in that smile—an invitation for more than a room?

Hard to say—maybe yes, or maybe he'd get the shit kicked out of him if he acted like it was a yes—and he was tired, so he smiled back his own smile, but that was all he did.

Grin slipping, just a bit, the night man quoted a price, trying to ease the shock with free coffee and donuts in the morning.

He didn't have a choice, so plastic was slid across the glass, machines spoke to one another in angry, strident tones, a signature was exchanged for a key, and he turned to leave.

"If you need anything, you don't hesitate to call, 'kay?"

"The Cock Not Taken"—that was the story. Different book this time, one he'd looked up after reading the first. Hand on the cool metal of the door's pushbar, he remembered how it went: Guy walks into a bar and starts to flirt with the bartender, getting them both hot and bothered, twin cocks roaring for mouth, ass, or hand. Soon they're both thinking of nothing but sucking, fucking, or jerking off. Then, all of a sudden, the guy walks out, but before he does he turns to the bartender and says, "Sure, we could do it. But this way it'll always be the best time you never had." Later the bartender jerks off, practically goes blind coming so damned hard—and goes to sleep knowing the guy was right, and that sometimes the best cock is the one not taken.

"Yeah, thanks," he says, walking into the night. A lie. All of it a lie—and like an idiot he fell for all of it.

XXX

TIRED. LETHARGY, A blurring of the eyesight, a weight in the limbs, but not the feeling of being underwater, not the sagging lids and hazy—almost hallucinating—thoughts. Not *that* tired.

Lying on the bedspread, nude, threads itching his back, he stared at a farm report on the only clear channel. Normally, he'd jerk off, push himself up and over into real exhaustion, and get a few blinks from a good night's sleep.

Normally, as of two weeks ago. Back then it would have been so easy to pull up a fantasy, a reinterpretation of one of those stories. Maybe even reread one or two, book cracked open with one hand, the other working his cock.

Then there were his favorites, one or two that rolled through his mind, fantasies living beyond the pages in the books. "Hard at Work," was one: smoke and ash, sweat and high pressure water, muscles digging fire breaks, muscles cracking axes into timber, muscles clearing brush, muscles hauling ropes and cables, muscles wrapped around muscles. Not deep, not really all that meaningful, but there was something in the telling, the visceral, evocative word following word to paint a picture so clear, so crisp, so hot in his mind. He could almost see the two men, heat waving, blurring the air between them, trees exploding behind like pitch and pine fireworks. Tears of perspiration shimmering at the ends of nipples, then hanging, then falling drops to sizzle on the steaming, smoking ground.

In the end, though, it was just two guys fucking and sucking in the middle of a forest fire. It was good—one of the best—but in the end that's all that it was.

Not like "The Golden Rivet." Despite himself, he was there again, that first time. He'd been riding the Loop, tracks clicking out a dull metal tune. He'd found the book in a dusty little shop near the campus, smile on his face at realizing there was a second volume of stories, and bought it instantly.

Two men—but then what else could it have been? Two men during the war. In the Pacific. On a battleship. A torpedo, an explosion (shrapnel ringing the steel hull like a thousand too-loud, too-sharp bells), and they were trapped—just the two of them—in a compartment filling with water.

Desperation, terror, anger—and knowing that at least they weren't going to die alone. A touch, contact between two scared men. A need to love, if just for a last moment of pleasure before the water rose too high.

Off the train, hoping his hard cock wasn't obvious. Home as fast as he could, pants around his ankles in the tiny bathroom. A come like a shot, hard and quick. But that wasn't why the story was a favorite. The come had gone, but the story lingered, hovering in the back of his mind. Two men, that one moment of contact before the end. Not love, not even really *sex*—just a last embrace of life before the end.

Thinking about it, and what the story meant, his cock had risen. Lying on the bed and looking at his feet, he saw his erection as an outline against an earnestly talking head on the washed out set.

It had seemed like a great idea—at least it had two weeks ago. A few sick and vacation days stowed away, no commitments, no relationships, no parents close enough to see. A road trip. A fanciful expedition, a pilgrimage to Phoenix, Arizona, to track the author down.

That was the plan. The world had been wonderful, full of stories and hope and love and dreams and crazy road trips—and ignorance had been bliss. Then he had picked up that magazine, seen the name on the cover—the author of those stories—and inside a rare interview. Never should have bought it, and absolutely never should have read it.

All of it. Every single word. Every story, in each and every book. He'd read the interview, again and again, shame and fury flushing his face, his breath short and hot. He'd read that one line in the interview, over and over, praying the words weren't really saying that—but they were: *How does a straight guy write gay porn?*

It got worse. A girlfriend—not companion, not partner, not significant other—but a woman, for years and years, that he absolutely adored. He was straight, always was, always has been, always would be.

He went from shock and denial to shame and depression. From humiliation and sadness to anger and bitterness. A lover had cheated on him, a lover who'd been in his fantasies, his dreams, his hopes, was pointing and laughing at him.

His cock wasn't hard anymore. The talking head wasn't eclipsed by any kind of an erection, his too-red, too-blue, too-green, too-yellow face was completely there in its cheap television colors.

Suddenly, he was tired—more than tired enough to sleep. No jerking off tonight. Too embarrassed, too many of a straight man's word games in his mind.

It'd been too late to change his plans, so he'd still gone on his trip, was still looking for the author. Sleep tugged at his eyes, pulling his lids shut. Fumbling to the side, his fingers grazed the greasy buttons on the remote, pushed down and silenced the weather report.

Yes—*yawn*—he was still looking for the author, but now for a very different reason.

xxx

MORNING LIGHT WAS a yellow and fat and warm sun rising over the desert. Morning traffic was also light—few cars on the highway into, through, then out of Phoenix.

After a few hours of navigating, he turned the wheel toward his destination. In the end, he didn't need to be much of a detective. After reading that interview, a bit more research had told him what he needed to know.

Another turn and he was staring through the windshield at black metal gates and, beyond them, inexplicable emerald. He was well outside the city, yet also at the gates of a manicured oasis. Looking over his shoulder, back out across and beyond a half-finished subdivision, he could see the distant stone outcroppings and shimmering, sifting sands of the hot, wild desert.

His favorite landscape, he thought, remembering a bit of his digging, a morsel of trivia. Turning back, foot gently down, he cruised through the gates and down a narrow lane. Well-irrigated green to the right, well-irrigated green to the left, he drove slowly along, following a gentle ribbon of asphalt.

Then, a low rise of lawn, and rows of neat squares of marble and cement, gleaming in the overhead sun. Parking, he climbed the rise, eyes scanning back and forth for that one name.

There it was, the same as on the spines and covers of those books: a name, and two dates—one starting with a *b*, the other with a *d*.

So small. He'd expected bigger, something gothic and overwhelming, cherubs or angels with broad, well-chiseled chests.

Instead, there was just a slab of marble and the author's name.

But he was there, and he had something to do. Hot sun above, green grass and cut stone below, he looked around, checking for sad-faced witnesses, but found himself alone in the cemetery.

Alone except for what remained of the author, the man who'd dribbled dreams into his ears, made him, laugh, smile, cry, and come—come hard—so many times. The man who'd put descriptions, streams of musical words, to what he saw ("the glow of excited skin"), felt ("the warm, wet, slickness of sweat"), tasted ("the sharp, ringing tingle of salt"), heard ("a solo of ecstasy and release"), and smelled ("the nose-bite of fresh come")—and who'd lied, every single time. The man who'd never been sincere, never really understood what love, or even just good sex, could be between two men.

Now dead and buried. But that wasn't enough. Checking again that he was alone—and seeing that he was—he zipped down his fly and fished out his cock.

It had been a long, odd journey from that bookstore to the highway to Phoenix to the cemetery to standing there in the hot sun. Originally, before he'd metaphorically caught this literary idol in bed with a woman, he'd wanted to bring flowers, place them on the stone with a simple, sincere, honest—and possibly tearful—"thank you."

But he had read that interview, and he knew without a doubt that somewhere, under the stone or wherever pornographers go when they die, the author was laughing at him.

No flowers, not anymore. Instead he'd salute him the best way he knew how, treat him the way he, the reader, had been treated.

Hot sun above, cold marble below, and a bladder full enough to piss on his grave.

xxx

IN "THAT LONG Night," a garage mechanic fantasizes about one of his clients, begins to see him as everything he's ever wanted. Thinks he's every fantasy on two strong legs. Dreams of them living together, in a clean, elegant house full of fine furniture, both of them sitting down to refined meals of excellent food. Wine, truffles, French things. The sex, too, is clean, elegant, refined, and excellent—as the mechanic imagined opera could be, if you knew what you were missing. Then, after a hard day of balancing wheels, installing shocks, and greasing points, he goes to his local porno palace for a good whack.

In the dark, a hand on his thigh, a hushed offer for a blow. Then, lips around his cock, a good, sloppy, crude suck that gets him off in only three dozen fast heartbeats.

Not dark enough though, and in the flickering cinema he looks down to see the clean, elegant, refined, and excellent client with come dribbling down his chin.

In "Autumn Leaves Falling Down," a college student walks in on his boyfriend getting fucked by the star quarterback. Tears on his cheeks, he gets in his car and drives all over the city, finally stopping at a dim nightclub. There he meets a dark-haired Bohemian type and they start to chat, then they kiss.

The student knows he shouldn't, but his wound is too deep, the betrayal too raw. Then they're at the Bohemian's apartment, and then they're sucking, then fucking. In the morning, the student leaves, seeing a punky artist type in a doorway, cheeks reflective from crying, eyes glaring recrimination—the student knows exactly how it feels, but still he walks away.

In his hand, his dick is warm. His bladder full, but not that full. Two weeks ago he would have brought flowers; today his dick is in his hand, preparing to piss on a grave.

Two weeks, reading one interview—from flowers to piss. The stories were still in his mind, the words superimposed on his landscape. They were still good—that hadn't changed. He still dreamed of firemen loving amid ashes and smoke, sailors holding each other as waters rose.

His dreams—maybe some of the author's but mostly his own. Yes, the writer wasn't who he wanted him to be, but he hadn't turned flowers to piss. The author wasn't doing anything wrong at all. He'd just told stories—stories that some people liked. It didn't matter if they liked him, just the stories.

The stories. He had liked the stories.

His cock was in his hand, but he didn't want to piss—and he hadn't brought any flowers.

"Whispers," was about a bulk of a man, a shithouse built not of bricks but of muscles. A hard man, a rough man. Reading it, his own cock had been stiff and red and hard—he remembered stroking himself between each paragraph. This was a man he wanted, this was a man he wanted to suck, get fucked by.

In the story, he had a boyfriend. A little nothing, just blond and sinew. No one could see the attraction, what held them together. Reading it, he couldn't understand it either.

Until the end of the story, when—in the middle of hot, wild, brutal sex—the bulk, the fortress of a man leaned down to his tiny lover and so gently said: "I love you."

Tears and come, when he finished that one.

Thinking about that story, he felt his cock swell and stiffen in his hand. Soon it was hard. Looking down, he saw the white and pink shaft emerging from his fly, topped by a rose-petal crimson cap. It could have been the fact that he was standing outside, warm air blowing him, or that he was stroking his cock in a graveyard—or it could have been remembering that story.

And there were more: "Hollywood Hustlers," "Following the Rails," "I Love the Big Life," "Waving Goodbye," "On Screen/Off Screen," "The Aroma of Lost Loves," "A Fast Fuck on a Slow Train," "Sweet as Chocolate," "Box Lunch," "Sailors at Sea," and so many others.

More than hard. Stroking himself, he could feel his skin burn, just a little, but he didn't spit in his hand for lubrication. He was too far gone for that—he could feel it as a tightness, a heaviness in his balls.

The idea of piss was gone, shuttled off to make way for come. He smiled, standing there on the grass, looking down at carved stone, as the reason for piss was gone, pushed aside for a deep orgasm.

He came — hard and fast, jetting out into hot desert air, a sticky trail arcing out and down onto the marble, his juice shimmering as it oozed into the name cut into the marble.

Done, happy, glad he had come, he carefully folded away his still-hard cock and left the gravestone and the name — M. CHRISTIAN — gleaming with come, and with thanks.

Author Bio

M. Christian is the author of the critically acclaimed and best-selling collections *Dirty Words*, *Speaking Parts*, and *The Bachelor Machine*. He is the editor of twenty anthologies, including (most recently) *Amazons*, *Confessions*, and *Garden of Perverse* (all with Sage Vivant), and *Blood Lust* (with Todd Gregory). His short fiction has appeared in more than two hundred publications, including *Best American Erotica*, *Best Gay Erotica*, *Best Lesbian Erotica*, *Best Transgendered Erotica*, *Best Fetish Erotica*, *Best Bondage Erotica*. and ... well, you get the idea. His first novel, *Running Dry: A Novel with Bite*, is available now from Alyson Books, and his second, *Very Bloody Marys*, will be out from Haworth Books in 2007.

Acknowledgments

"The Greener Grasses," by M. Christian, © 2003 by M. Christian. First appeared in *Sex Buddies*, edited by Paul J. Willis (Alyson Books). Used by permission of the author.

"Hollywood Blvd.," by M. Christian, © 2003 by M. Christian. First appeared on Velvet Mafia (www.velvetmafia.com). Used by permission of the author.

"Flyboy," by M. Christian, © 2005 by M. Christian. Used by permission of the author.

"Oroborous," by M. Christian, © 2005 by M. Christian. First appeared in *Men & Ink*, edited by Jim Gladstone (Alyson Books). Used by permission of the author.

"2+1," by M. Christian, © 2005 by M. Christian. Used by permission of the author.

"Happy Feet," by M. Christian, © 2004 by M. Christian. First appeared in *Love Under Foot*, edited by M. Christian and Greg Wharton (The Haworth Press). Used by permission of the author.

"Love," by M. Christian, © 2004 by M. Christian. First appeared in *Ultimate Gay Erotica*, edited by Jesse Grant (Alyson Books). Used by permission of the author.

"Six Inches of Separation," by M. Christian, © 2003 by M. Christian. First appeared in *Bad Boys*, edited by Paul J. Willis and M. Christian (Alyson Books). Used by permission of the author.

"Moby," by M. Christian, © 2005 by M. Christian. Used by permission of the author.

"Heart in Your Hand," by M. Christian, © 2005 by M. Christian. Used by permission of the author.

"The Hope of Cinnamon," by M. Christian, © 2003 by M. Christian. First appeared in *Sextopia*, edited by Cecilia Tan (Circlet Press). Used by permission of the author.

"Heads and Tails," by M. Christian, © 2003 by M. Christian. First appeared in *Best Gay Erotica*, edited by Jesse Grant (Alyson Books). Used by permission of the author.

"Suddenly, Last Thursday," by M. Christian, © 2003 by M. Christian. First appeared in *Best of the Best Meat Erotica*, edited by Greg Wharton (Suspect Thoughts Press). Used by permission of the author.

"That Sweet Smell," by M. Christian, © 2003 by M. Christian. First appeared on Velvet Mafia (www.velvetmafia.com). Used by permission of the author.

"Bitch," by M. Christian, © 2003 by M. Christian. First appeared in *Shadows of the Night*, edited by Greg Herren (Haworth Press). Used by permission of the author.

"The Hard Way," by M. Christian, © 2005 by M. Christian. Used by permission of the author.

"Utter West," by M. Christian, © 2001 by M. Christian. First appeared in *Of the Flesh*, edited by Greg Wharton (Suspect Thoughts Press). Used by permission of the author.

"Imago," by M. Christian, © 2005 by M. Christian. Used by permission of the author.

"Friday Night at the Calvary Hotel," by M. Christian, © 2004 by M. Christian. First appeared in *Roughed Up*, edited by Simon Sheppard and M. Christian (Alyson Books). Used by permission of the author.

"About the Author," by M. Christian, © 2005 by M. Christian. Used by permission of the author.